"ALL HANDS, BATTLE STATIONS!"

Lights blink in confusion, fade out abruptly with just as much puzzlement, fade in again, then switch to battle-alert orange. Hurried footsteps, muffled curses, confused mutterings—men pad-pad quickly down corridors. "What the—?" followed by others, swearing, "Come on! That's an alarm! They've found something!"

Korie is sliding through the tumult and confusion like an eel. Unruffled, he hurries surely down the narrow corridors to the bridge, still buttoning his tunic. Other men shoulder past him, some in various stages of undress, rushing to their battle stations. Korie starts to bark an order, then checks himself.

If they don't know what to do by now, it's too late to teach them.

STARHUNT

David Gerrold

BANTAM BOOKS
NEW YORK • TORONTO • LONDON • SYDNEY • AUCKLAND

STARHUNT
A Bantam Book/published by
arrangement with the author

PUBLISHING HISTORY
First published in Great Britain by Hamlyn Paperbacks 1985
Legend edition 1987
First published in U.S. as Yesterday's Children
Bantam Spectra edition/April 1995

ISBN 0-553-56824-8

Published simultaneously in the United States and Canada

Bantam Books are published by Bantam Books, a division of Bantam Doubleday
Dell Publishing Group, Inc. Its trademark, consisting of the words "Bantam Books"
and the portrayal of a rooster, is Registered in U.S. Patent and Trademark Office
and in other countries. Marca Registrada. Bantam Books, 1540 Broadway, New
York, New York 10036.

PRINTED IN THE UNITED STATES OF AMERICA
RAD   0 9 8 7 6 5 4 3 2 1

The Three Laws of Infernal Dynamics

An object in motion will always be headed in the wrong direction.

An object at rest will always be in the wrong place.

The energy required to change either of these states will always be more than you wish to expend, but never so much as to make the task prospectively impossible.

SOLOMON SHORT

Before the *Star Wolf* . . .

The history of this novel is actually a history of my whole career.

The whole thing began with *Star Trek*. The original series premiered on the NBC television network on Thursday, September 8, 1966. I was twenty-two years old and still in college. I had a ream of paper, an IBM Selectric Typewriter, and a delusion of grandeur. I spent the weekend typing, and on Monday morning, I gave my agent[1] a sixty-page outline called *Tomorrow Was Yesterday*.

This outline was my first submission to *Star Trek*. In this proposed two-part episode, the *Enterprise* encountered a lost "generation ship," a gigantic vessel carrying thousands of colonists to a new star system. Designed before the invention of faster-than-light travel, the ship could only travel at sublight speeds, so generations of colonists would have to live and die aboard the vessel before their descendants arrived to settle their new world.

On this particular ship, however, the colonists had forgotten their original mission, and no longer believed that there was anything outside the hull of their own ship. Tales of other worlds and other ships were regarded as blasphemous insanity. So of course, when the *Enterprise* catches up with this lost vessel, Kirk's real dilemma lies in

---

[1] "Agent? You had an agent in college?"
"It was California. Everyone had an agent."

convincing the colonists that he, Spock, and McCoy are not demons. Complicating this even further, the colonists had split into two factions and were warring with each other for control of the vessel, so neither side will trust our heroes; both sides think they're spies for the other side. And just to make the problem even more interesting, the giant generation ship is headed straight for a black hole. Kirk has only a few short days to convince these people to start up their engines again and change the course of their vessel for a safe harbor.

Gene L. Coon, the producer of *Star Trek,* read the outline, and even though he felt it was too expensive to produce even as a two-part episode, he invited me to the lot. He gave me a copy of the *Star Trek* Writers'/ Directors' Guide and suggested that I submit story ideas for the show's second season. One of the outlines I turned in was about little furry creatures that breed like crazy until they overrun the starship. Gene L. Coon bought that one, and it turned into *Star Trek*'s most popular episode, *The Trouble with Tribbles.*

Later, after *Star Trek* went off the air, I began to think about turning the original *Tomorrow Was Yesterday* outline into a novel.

At that time there were no *Star Trek* novels; Paramount had not yet realized the licensing possibilities; so if I were going to adapt the outline to a novel, I would have to create a ship and characters of my own, and let them discover the lost generation ship.

Remember William Golding's *Lord of the Flies?* At the end of the book, the warring boys are rescued by a passing ship. A warship. The implications are obvious. Who is going to rescue the adults from *their* folly? I wanted to make the same point, so the starship I created was a military cruiser, too. I called it the *Roger Burlingame* after the author of *Machines That Built America.* The book was sitting on a shelf directly above my typewriter. I needed a military-sounding name for my starship and there it was, so I grabbed it.

The more I thought about it, though, the more I realized that it was too convenient a coincidence for an FTL cruiser to find a slower-than-light vessel in the dark between the stars. So I began the story with my starship doggedly pursuing an unnamed enemy vessel. When the vessel suddenly drops out of hyperspace, they have to search for it in the dark of normal space, but instead of finding it, they find the lost colony vessel. From there I could step into the original outline.

I hoped that this framing device would give my heroes an even greater dilemma. Now they not only had to save the colonists from their own ignorance, they also had to do it before the lurking enemy detected them and attacked first. This, I hoped, would provide additional suspense. Then, after saving the generation ship from the folly of its own war, our heroes would resume their unresolved hunt, leaving the reader to wonder what godlike deity will intercede and save them from their warlike selves.

It might have worked, except for one small detail. I hadn't yet learned the pacing of a novel. I wrote eighty pages—four full chapters—and never got the *Burlingame* close to the generation ship at all. Instead, I found I'd become much more engrossed in the mechanics of intersteller search-and-destroy operations. Despite my initial intention to novelize *Tomorrow Was Yesterday*, I was telling a totally different story, one that was darker in character and tone. This realization gave me an even greater problem. I didn't know how it ended.

I kept writing anyway, putting down one scene after another and waiting to see how the characters would resolve their separate problems. I admit that this is not the best way to write a novel, but it is the most challenging way.

During much of 1971, I lived in New York. I had a tiny room in the Albert, a residence hotel in Greenwich Village.[2] I had a bed, a desk, a closet. And my typewriter.

I had one window in my room. If I opened it, I could hear New York talking to me. What it said was, "If you don't sit down and write today, I'm going to crush you. You'll be tossed out on the street. You'll wander around

---

[2]For a while Samuel R. Delaney also lived in the same hotel, a fact of no literary significance whatsoever.

with your life in a shopping cart. You'll be a bum. If you don't write today, you'll starve to death next month." New York was a very good motivator then. It still is today.

Very quickly I made a rule for myself. I had to write a chapter a day. I could not go out to a movie or anywhere else until I fulfilled my basic writing commitment. After I did my chapter, I was free to go out and play anywhere in New York that I wanted to.

In the mornings, I took the dog over to Washington Square Park and let him terrorize the squirrels for a half hour. He happily chased every squirrel he saw, and I worked as his spotter, pointing them out to him.[3] Then we'd return to the room, and I would sit and write until the day's chapter was finished. Sometimes I was done in three or four hours; sometimes I worked as long as eight or ten if I was tackling a particularly knotty problem. Then the dog and I would go out to the park and annoy the squirrels again. Then, with the day's work completed, I could go out for dinner and sometimes a movie; occasionally I'd even seek out the company of other people. But I don't think I was very good company while I was in the middle of a story. I don't know how it is for other writers, but I find it hard to decompress. Writing involves immersion. Coming back to Earth can often be a long journey.

At night, while I'd lie in bed waiting to fall asleep, I'd think about the next day's chapter. What had to happen next? How would I resolve the issues I'd raised? How would I advance the plot? What were my characters up to? Sometimes I came to a resolution before I fell asleep, sometimes I didn't; but almost always when I woke up the following morning, the day's work was clear in my mind.

I assumed that one of two things was happening: either my subconscious was solving all the problems while I was asleep, or little elves were sneaking into the room in the middle of the night and whispering in my ear.[4]

---

[3]This explains why there were no fat squirrels in Washington Square Park that year.
[4]I never found any mangled elf bodies near the dog, but this doesn't really prove anything. That dog ate *everything*.

Afterward, I would see that I had created a very powerful discipline, one that would serve me well for many years to come; so the time spent in New York proved to be an important turning point in my writing. It was one of the most productive times of my life, and it was the year I graduated from short stories to novels. During that period I wrote *When Harlie Was One*, *The Man Who Folded Himself*, the first fourteen chapters of *A Matter for Men*, and the rest of the novel that grew out of that first attempt to novelize *Tomorrow Was Yesterday*. The final title was *Yesterday's Children*.

Yesterday's Children was published by Dell Books in 1972. It was twenty-eight chapters long and it detailed a near-fanatical interstellar search-and-destroy operation. It had intentional overtones of *Moby Dick* and *The Enemy Below*, and it was accurately described by some readers as a submarine novel set in space. Well yes, sort of. But there was more to it than that.

It was my theory then (and even more so today) that if and when a war in space does occur, the only appropriate metaphor will be two submarines dodging in the darkness. When you consider the vastness in space, as well as the speeds involved, the dogfight metaphor just doesn't work; neither does the interstellar aircraft carrier; it's too vulnerable.

The physics of interstellar battles involves time, speed, distance—and detection. The hunter is equally as vulnerable as the prey. Indeed, the roles of hunter and prey will be interchangeable depending on the skill of the respective captains.

Because both sides will have intelligence engines running multiple simulations of the outcome of any course of action, the battles will be fought not with weapons but with probabilities, with each side jockeying for tactical advantage. Space battles will not be about strength and position; they will about *strategy*. Not just physical advantage, but psychological advantage as well. Space war will be fought with mind games. It will be about feints and decoys and nasty surprises.

In such a game, the enemy will always be an unknown quantity. He'll be no more than a blip on the display, a pattern of movements in our simulations. We'll never see him face-to-face, we won't know him as a living being, capable of anger, hate, sorrow, or fear. We'll have to hate him as an idea, not a person. And because we'll have no target for our anger, we'll most likely turn our frustrations on those who are closest to us. Our shipmates. Played against the external battles, there will always be the internal ones as well.

It was this line of thinking that gave the novel its final shape. And its first disturbing conclusion. Stop reading at the end of Chapter 28 and you'll see what I mean. That was where I stopped writing in 1972, and that was all the novel that Dell Books published. It got generally good reviews, sold well, and even made the Locus Poll of best novels at the end of the year.

But frankly, I don't like unhappy endings. I liked Jon Korie. I thought he deserved better. In 1977 I sat down with the novel again and started writing new chapters. I wrote twelve new chapters that continued the story and resolved the adventure in a way that I found much more satisfying. Korie finally got to be as heroic as I had always intended him to be, and the new material demonstrated again what I believed would be the nature of psychological warfare in space. Popular Library published that edition. Later, for the English editions, I retitled the book *Starhunt*.

In 1979, a would-be movie producer optioned the novel, and I wrote two drafts of a script for a proposed feature film version of *Starhunt*. The deal fell through, however, and the film was never made. I concentrated on other things for a while, including the first two books of *The War Against the Chtorr*.[5]

A few years later I found myself working on *Star Trek: The Next Generation*. During the first seven months of that show's history, I wrote over a hundred thousand words of memos on every aspect of the show's

---

[5] *A Matter for Men* and *A Day for Damnation*. After *ST:TNG* I wrote two more books in the series, *A Rage for Revenge* and *A Season for Slaughter*. By the time you read this, the fifth book, *A Method for Madness*, should be finished and in the publication pipeline.

development, including the first full Writers'/Directors' Guide for the series. (Despite what has been written elsewhere by those who were not in the room at the time, my participation in the initial development of *Star Trek: The Next Generation* was significant, a point that the Writers Guild of America proved in a subsequent arbitration over back wages.)

While working on *Star Trek,* I was offered the chance to produce two other shows. One was *Return to the Land of the Lost;* the other was a development project called *Trackers,* for Columbia. It was to be a miniseries that would also serve as the pilot for a series about two interstellar bounty hunters.

I left *Star Trek: The Next Generation* to work on *Trackers.* Unfortunately, both Columbia and CBS went through upper-echelon management changes while I was working on *Trackers* and the people who had originally commissioned the series were not the same people to whom we turned in the final draft, so the project was ultimately set aside.[6]

Not too long after that, I was hired to develop still another science-fiction television series for the Arthur Company and Universal Studios. They already had a title, *Millennium.* They wanted a space-going series with lots of action. I suggested two possibilities: 1) interstellar traders, going from planet to planet buying and selling merchandise, occasionally fighting pirates. 2) World War II in space.

Not surprisingly, they liked the second choice.

So did I, because I thought I might be able to recycle *Starhunt* one more time.[7] I even suggested that the *Starhunt* script might work as a pilot, but after some discussion we realized that if we were going to use World War II as our metaphor, the attack on Pearl Harbor had to be the beginning of our story. But there was no reason

---

[6]After Columbia relinquished their interest, I took the *Trackers* outline and turned it into two novels: *Under the Eye of God* and *A Covenant of Justice,* both published by Bantam Books. Nothing goes to waste. And yes, I am obsessive-compulsive. Why do you ask?

[7]I really do like this story.

why I couldn't use many of the same characters, was there? Indeed not. Coming back to Jon Korie, I had a hero I already knew well and liked for his intelligence.[8]

In the weeks of development that followed, we had many discussions about the shape of the series. What kind of ship were we flying? Who were our people? Who were our enemies? Why was the war being fought? In every case, the World War II metaphor served as an anchor to keep us grounded in believability. Eventually, we had a 120-page Writers'/Directors' Guide, even more detailed than the one I had written for *Star Trek: The Next Generation*.

Our ship was a liberty ship, rolled off an assembly line that produced a new ship every twelve days. Our people were ordinary individuals caught in an extraordinary crisis; they had families and careers that they had left behind. Our enemy was the Morthan Solidarity—a self-proclaimed master race who intended domination of all lesser species. And the war was being fought to determine the future of human evolution. Ultimately, we realized that the underlying question here was very simple: *What does it mean to be a human being?*

The more I worked on it, the more I fell in love with the people aboard the ship: Korie, Cygnus Tor, Chief Leen, Molly Williger, Mikhail Hodel, Hardesty, and of course, Brik. These were characters I enjoyed spending time with. I liked writing about them.

The first-draft script for *Millennium* was too dark in tone to be a successful pilot. In it, a Morthan assassin gets loose aboard our starship and eats the captain's lawyer (voluntarily). The second draft was more successful and was generally regarded as a very good pilot script. Unfortunately, the Writers Guild strike of 1988 put all the studios out of production for over six months, and when the strike ended, so had the possibilities for *Millennium* as a TV series.

So I turned the pilot script into a novel, expanding it and developing it in even greater depth than before.[9] Ban-

---

[8]And then I could adapt the *Starhunt* script as an episode later on.
[9]Thou shalt not waste.

tam Books published *Voyage of the Star Wolf* in 1990, and it sold a surprisingly large number of copies; enough copies that my editor began making noises about sequels.[10] I said I'd think about it. I didn't have any stories in mind, but if an idea occurred to me I'd be in touch. . . .

Not too long after that, Mike Resnick[11] mailed a copy of the novel to a producer friend of his who called me shortly thereafter. "You know," he said, "this would make one helluva good TV series."

Right.

After several weeks of discussion and jockeying for position, Dorothy Fontana and I began developing stories for a possible *Star Wolf* TV series. And suddenly I had a whole bunch of story ideas for new *Star Wolf* adventures. *The Middle of Nowhere,* the second *Star Wolf* novel, is based on two of those story ideas. When Bantam put it into their 1995 schedule, they also chose to reprint *Starhunt* at the same time. Hence this introduction. So you'll understand why there are two novels that share some of the same characters and situations, but have major inconsistencies if you try to see them as parts of a larger whole.

This novel, *Starhunt,* might almost be a later adventure of the *Star Wolf.* Even though the enemy is unidentified here, the circumstances of the war are generally the same. If the book were to be rewritten to fit into the *Star Wolf* chronology, it would occur at least a year or two after the first *Star Wolf* adventure.

I could have rewritten *Starhunt* to fit it into the chronology, and at one point I even considered it; but my editors at Bantam Books argued that this novel was fine just the way it was, and my time would be better spent writing a new *Star Wolf* novel than rehashing an old one. It

---

[10]An editor whines like a seven-year-old. It can be really nerve-racking.

[11]Notorious liar and cyberspace terrorist, odious behavior that is excused only by his being a marvelous anthologist and an even better novelist.

He also keeps calling me up at odd hours of the day and night to remind me that he is my "number-one fan." I've tried moving and changing my phone number three times, but it doesn't help. (He is also the author of *Santiago,* soon to be a major motion picture. If he doesn't send me tickets to the premiere, I'm not going to let him be my fan any longer.)

did not take long for them to convince me. If all goes well, you may expect a new *Star Wolf* novel sometime in the next year or three. (Right after the next book in the Chtorran cycle . . .) Please do not hold me to a timetable.

Oh, yes. One more thing. What happened to the original *Tomorrow Was Yesterday* outline? Did I ever turn that into a novel? Yes, I finally did write it as a *Star Trek* novel. It was called *The Galactic Whirlpool*; it was published by Bantam Books nearly two decades ago and it's still in print today.

Waste not, want not.

STARHUNT

One

=====================================

If anythign can go wrong, it will.

MURPHY

The operations of a destroyer-class starship consist of more than seven hundred thousand separate and distinct functions. All of them can be monitored from its Command and Control Seat.

The seat is a harsh throne on a raised dais. It is the center of the bridge and the man in it controls the ship. Right now, Jonathan Korie is that man. Thin, pale, and motionless, he is the first officer of the United Systems Starship *Roger Burlingame.*

The ship has been on battle alert for twelve days, and for ten of those days, Jon Korie has been the highest ranking officer on the bridge. Ten days ago the captain retired to his cabin, and he has not been seen since. So Korie sits in the Command and Control Seat and is bored.

Lean and angular, he sprawls loose across it; his colorless eyes gaze disinterestedly at the giant rectangle of red dominating the front of the bridge. On it is a single shimmer of white, the stress-field projection of the enemy ship. Superimposed below that is a number, 170; the enemy's speed is 170 times the speed of light. The speed of the *Burlingame* is 174 lights.

They are gaining, but only slowly. It will take at least twelve more days to close the remaining gap—and even then, when they do catch up to the enemy, they may not be able to destroy him. As long as the quarry stays in warp, he has the advantage; he is easy to pursue, but difficult to catch. Either he must be outmaneuvered or he must be hounded until his power is exhausted. Both procedures are difficult and wearying.

Korie stares without seeing. The huge screen bathes the room with a blood-colored glow; the image burns into the retina. His nose no longer notices the familiar odors of old plastic and stale sweat. His ears no longer hear the muted whisper of activity, the ever-present, almost silent humming of the computers.

A speaker in his headrest beeps. He touches a button on the chair arm. "Korie here. Go ahead."

A laconic voice. "Mr. Korie, this is the engine room. We're picking up some kind of wobbly on the number three generator."

"What's wrong with it?"

"I don't know, sir. The damn thing's been throwing off sparks for a week."

Korie grunts. And swivels his chair sixty degrees to the left. Above the warp control console is a medium large screen, one of many that line the upper walls of the bridge. On it, the power consumption levels of the ship's six warp generators are shown. The red bar of number three is hazy at its tip with a shallow but extremely rapid oscillation.

"It looks mild enough," Korie says to the waiting communicator. "Could one of the secondaries be out of phase?"

"Negative. If it were, we wouldn't be able to hold a course. It was one of the first things we checked."

"Well, how bad is it? Can you manage?"

"Oh, sure. Just thought you ought to know. That's all."

"Right. See what you can do about it. Let me know if it gets worse."

"Yes, sir." The communicator bleeps out.

Forgetting the wobbly, Korie swivels forward again. He pushes his hair—light, almost colorless—back off his forehead. Stretching out his long legs, he shifts to a less uncomfortable position.

Idly, he smoothes out a wrinkle in his dark tights,

scratches vainly at a spot on his grey and blue tunic. He wets a pale forefinger against his tongue and rubs at the persistent stain until it fades. Satisfied, he reclines again in the chair.

A chime sounds, a bell-like tone. Korie's gaze strays automatically to the clock—abruptly he checks himself. (It isn't my relief that's coming.) The thought echoes rudely in his mind.

The bridge of the starcruiser is a bowl-shaped room. The wide door at the rear of it slides open to admit four low-voiced crewmen. They cut off their talk, move quickly into the room, and separate.

Two rows of gray-blue consoles circle the bridge, the outer row surrounding the room on a wide raised ledge, the other just inside and below. Despite the spaciousness of the room's original measurements, the additional consoles and equipment that have since been added force a cramped feeling within.

Brushing past their shipmates, two of the men move around to the front of the ledge, called the horseshoe. They tap two others and step into their places at the controls. The other relief crewmen step down into the circle of consoles in the center, a lowered area called the pit. They too tap two men. Dropping easily into the quickly vacated couches, the new men settle into the routine with a familiarity bred of experience.

The men going off watch exit just as quickly, and once more the bridge is still. The crew are sullen figures in the darkened room, sometimes silhouetted against the glare of a screen.

One man—a small man on the left side of the horseshoe—is not still at his post. He glances around the bridge nervously, looks to the Command and Control Seat just above the rear of the pit.

Working up his courage, the man steps forward. "Sir?"

Korie peers into the darkness. "Yes?"

"Uh, sir . . . my relief—he hasn't shown up yet."

"Who's your relief, Harris?"

"Wolfe, sir."

"Wolfe?" Korie frowns. He rubs absentmindedly at his nose.

Harris nods. "Yes, sir."

Korie sighs to himself, a sound of quiet exasperation, directed as much at Harris as at the absent Wolfe. "Well . . . stay at your post until he gets here."

"Yes, sir." Resignedly, Harris turns back to his waiting board.

At the same time, the door at the rear of the bridge slides open with a *whoosh*. Red-faced and panting heavily, a short, straw-colored crewman rushes in, still buttoning the flap of his tunic.

Korie swivels to face him. "Wolfe?" he demands. He touches the chair arm, throwing a splash of light at the man.

Wolfe hesitates, caught in the sudden glare. "Yes, sir . . . ? Uh, I'm sorry I'm late coming on watch, sir."

"You're sorry . . . ?"

"Yes, sir."

"Oh." The first officer pauses. "Well, then I guess that makes everything all right."

Wolfe smiles nervously, but the sweat is beaded on his forehead. He starts to move to his post.

"Did you hear that, Harris?" Korie calls abruptly. "Wolfe said he was sorry. . . ."

Again Wolfe hesitates. He looked nervously from one to the other.

"Harris?" Korie calls again. "Did you hear that?"

"Uh, yes, sir." The answer is mumbled; the man is hidden in shadow.

"And that makes everything all right, doesn't it, Harris?" Korie's eyes remain fixed on Wolfe.

"Uh, yes, sir," Harris answers, "I guess it does—if you say so—"

The first officer smiles thinly. "I guess it does then." His voice goes suddenly hard. "In fact, Mr. Harris, Mr. Wolfe is so sorry that he says he's going to take over your next five watches for you. In addition to his own. Isn't that good of him?"

"Sir!"

"Shut up, Wolfe!"

"Uh, sir—" insists Harris. "You don't have to do that—"

"You're right, Harris. I don't have to—*Wolfe* does."

"Sir!" Wolfe protests again.

"I don't want to hear it."

"But, sir, I—"

"Wolfe . . . !" says Korie warningly. "You are now ten minutes late in getting to your post. Are you trying for twenty?" He cuts off the spotlight, darkening the bridge back to Condition Red, and swivels forward.

Wolfe stares at the first officer's back for a moment, then mutters a nearly inaudible, "Yes, *sir* . . . !" He steps across the horseshoe and ritually taps Harris' shoulder.

In the Command and Control Seat, Korie exhales angrily through even white teeth. Ignoring the sound of Harris's quick exit, he forces himself to gaze forward at the screen. (There, that's the only thing to be concerned with—the enemy.) That pale shimmer of white remains tauntingly near, maddeningly far.

Somewhere a computer hums as it measures the gap between the two ships. Murmuring to itself, it notes the ever-narrowing distance, notes by how much it has narrowed since the last measurement, and records the difference. The gain is imperceptible to all but the most sophisticated of electronic eyes. On the screen, the image remains frustratingly unchanged.

Eyes narrowed, Korie stares—seeing and yet not seeing. He ticks nervously at the chair arm.

"Mr. Korie?"

He glances up. A crewman on the right side of the horseshoe, near the front, waits expectantly. In the dim light, Korie can barely make out his face. Thin and lanky, barely postadolescent, the man is Rogers, crewman third class and assigned to duty on the gravity control board.

"Yes?" Korie grunts. "What is it?"

"Ship's gravity is down to 0.94 again—and still slipping."

Korie nods. "You might try checking your available power. That's what it was last time."

"Oh—yes, sir." The youngster turns back to his console and Korie turns back to his thoughts. The problem of the fluctuating gravity is relegated to the same dark corner of his mind as the persistent wobbly of the number three generator.

Idly, he swivels his chair to the right. On that side is Barak, the astrogator. A big, raw-boned black man, he is hunched over his console at the edge of the pit. Jonesy, the assistant astrogator—small, wiry and curly haired—is standing next to him.

"There," says Barak, tapping at a monitor. "There's the error—0.00012 degrees." He drops back into his couch. "We'll just have to watch it for now. It's too small to correct. Give it a couple of days to grow."

Jonesy nods. "I wonder where it came from."

"Engine room, probably," Barak murmurs. "One of the generators must be picking up a bit of heat." He touches a button and the projection on the monitor dissolves.

"It figures," Jonesy snorts. "Can't those field jockeys do anything without screwing up?"

"That's funny." Barak's broad face splits into a grin. "They were just asking the same thing about you."

Jonesy snorts again, pulls his headset back down over his ears, and turns back to his board.

Watching, Korie is troubled. He doesn't like errors. Even the slightest one could add days to the chase. But Barak knows his business; this one won't have a chance.

A sound from the horseshoe attracts his attention. Rogers is standing at his gravity control board crying into a microphone, "Now it's down to 0.89 and still falling. Who's taking all my power?"

A laconic voice answers from the speaker, "The engine room. They've picked up a wobbly, so they're overcompensating—"

"Yeah, but I need power too! I'm supposed to keep the gravity within 2 per cent Earth normal, and I can't do it if I don't have power."

"Power . . ." sighs the speaker. "Everybody wants power. . . . All right, let me know when it hits critical and I'll cut in the auxiliaries."

Korie frowns. That damned wobbly is making its

presence known all over the bridge. He swivels left to look at the warp control console.

There, an engineer is yammering into a mike, "Listen, there's nothing wrong on this end! All of *our* settings are correct. Are you sure your fields are—"

A tinny voice from the communicator cuts him off. "We just finished checking them for the third time. It's definitely a reflex phase wobbly."

The engineer pauses, scratches his chest. "I'm not so sure. The curve doesn't feel right."

"I don't care what your curve feels like. I know what it feels like down here, and we've got static up the *wazoo!*"

Korie's gaze flickers to the screen. The number three generator is shimmering dangerously, a red piston vibrating faster than the eye can follow. A wide hazy area indicates the depth of the wobbly.

He stabs a button. "Engine room! This is Korie. You're wobbling too much. Can you correct?"

The answer is immediate. "Sir, we've got our hands full just trying to stay on top of it. It won't respond."

"What's causing it?"

"We don't know yet. Mr. Leen is down in the well now."

Korie grunts. "Well, damn it—try to hold it within limits. I'm not going to lose that bogie!"

"Yes, sir." The communicator winks out.

Korie shifts his attention forward to the pilot console. "What's our warp velocity?" he demands.

One of the officers straightens in his couch, leaning forward to read his monitor. "Uh . . . holding a 174, plus a fraction; but it's not firm . . ." Questioningly, he looks back at Korie, his face a dim blur in the dark.

Korie frowns. "Damn. If it starts to drop, let me know immediately."

"Yes, sir." The other turns forward again.

Korie glances back to the left, to the warp control console. Angrily, he glares at the flickering red bar on the screen—*that damn number three generator!* Able to do nothing but watch, he beats intensely at the chair arm with a clenched right fist.

"Fix it already . . ." he mutters, "I don't want to lose that kill . . . !"

The screen flickers redly. Somewhere a warning bell starts to chime. Eyes flicker toward the screen as the oscillation increases, widening past the danger levels.

Sudden red flashes on all the boards—the insistent chiming becomes a strident alarm, its shrill clanging shatters across the bridge. Crewmen turn hurriedly to their controls.

A voice: "We're losing speed! One hundred and sixty and still falling!"

Simultaneously a communicator bleeps. The first officer hits it with the butt of his fist. "Yes?"

"Engine room, sir." In the background another shrill alarm can be heard. "Mr. Leen requests permission to shut down."

"Can't do it," Korie snaps. "Is it absolutely necessary?"

"Uh—just a moment. . . ." There is a bit of off-mike mumbling, then the voice returns. "Mr. Leen says no, it isn't *absolutely* necessary, but, uh, if he had another set of engines, he'd junk these."

Korie taps indecisively at the chair arm. He stares ahead with pale eyes. The bogie shimmers and flickers across the screen; the wobbly is affecting the sensors too. Agonized, he hesitates—

"Sir?" asks the speaker.

"Just a moment." He takes his hand off the button, snaps at the officer ahead of him. "What's our speed now?"

"One hundred and forty-three and dropping steadily. It's—"

"Never mind." He stabs at a button on the chair arm. "Radec!"

"Yes, sir?" A new voice on the intercom.

"That bogie—you still have him." It is as much a statement as a question.

"Yes, sir, of course—but he's flickering pretty badly—"

"If I have to shut down, can you pick him up again?"

"After we unwarp, sure, I should be able to."

"How long will you be able to keep him on your screens?"

"Uh—five, maybe six hours ... We can't scan more than a hundred light days, no matter how big his warp is. After that—well, the whole thing gets pretty fuzzy."

Korie sucks in his lower lip, bites it hard. *Damn!* "Do you have anything else on your screens? Anything suspicious? I don't want to be caught by surprise."

"Uh—no, sir. Nothing. No major field disturbances at all—and nothing faster than light."

"All right." Korie disconnects him. Hardly seeing it, he stares at the empty red screen ahead. The enemy shimmer coruscates wildly and uncontrollably across the crimson grid.

"One hundred twelve and still dropping," calls a dark voice.

Damn!

Every eye in the bridge is on him, but he sees only the screen.

"Ninety-six lights."

The first officer is torn with pain—that flickering blur—

"Eighty-seven lights—sir ... !"

"I heard you."

"Sir! The engines are overheating—"

"I know it!"

Suddenly, Barak is standing beside him. "Damn it, Korie! Admit it! We've lost him! Now let go! Shut down those engines before they burn out—"

Korie looks at him, his pale eyes suddenly hard. "We'll shut down when *I* say we'll shut down!"

"Yes, sir!" Barak spits out the words. "But you'd better do it while you *still have* engines to shutdown."

Korie stares at the other. They lock eyes for a clanging moment—

—And then the moment is over. Korie reaches for the button. "Engine room."

The answer is immediate; the crewman has been waiting at the mike. "Sir."

"Stand by to shut down."

"Yes, sir."

Korie disconnects. There is nothing more to say. He looks at Barak, but the astrogator is silent.

Korie turns away then, calls to the warp control console, "Prepare to collapse warp. Neutralize the secondaries."

The routine takes hold. Crewmen move to obey and orders rattle down through the ranks.

"Remove the interlocks. Stand by to neutralize."

"Interlocks removed. Standing by."

"Cycle set at zero. Begin phasing."

"Cycle set at zero. Beginning phasing."

Around the horseshoe, crewmen exchange wary glances. The smell of defeat hangs heavy across the bridge. The chase has been abandoned.

Korie sinks lower into his seat; he stares grimly ahead.

(So near . . . so near and yet so goddamned far!)

Confirming lights begin to appear on the boards. Red warning lights blink out, are replaced by yellow standbys. The strident clanging of the alarm dies away, leaving only a slow fading echo and a hollow ringing in the ears.

(So this is how it ends . . . with a whimper. With just a futile petering out of momentum. . . .)

The ringing fades into a persistent beeping, a sound that has been continuous for some time. Korie looks at the chair arm. A yellow communicator light flashes insistently.

He flicks it. "Bridge. Korie here."

"This is Brandt." The captain's thick voice comes filtered through the speaker.

"Yes, sir."

"What's the trouble? What was the alarm?"

"We've lost it, sir. We've lost the bogie."

There is a muffled curse, then a pause. "I'll be right up." The lighted panel winks out.

Korie stares at it. (Damn it all anyway!) He bites angrily at his lip, a nervous habit. (Damn! It all happened too fast!)

"Sir." It's one of the warp engineers. "The secondary fields are neutralized."

"Good," Korie says dourly. It is not good. "Go ahead. Collapse the warp."

The man turns back to his console. On the screen over his head the third red bar drops to zero. Numbers one and five follow suit; a second later, the rest.

Imperceptibly—on a submolecular level—the ship shudders throughout its length. Its protective cocoon of warped space unfolds, dissolves; the ship mutters back into normal unstressed space. The bright flickering screens that circle the upper walls of the bridge go dark. They become sudden windows of hollow blackness. Space, deep and vast, repeated a dozen empty times, stares hungrily into the bridge.

Simultaneously, the crew reels under the sudden surge of added weight as the excess power flows back into the gravitors. One of the men stumbles in front of Korie while crossing the pit.

"Watch your step," Korie mutters automatically, hardly noticing.

The man catches himself, cursing softly. He looks up to the horseshoe. "Damn it, Rogers! Pay attention to what you're supposed to be doing."

The object of his wrath turns to apologize, embarrassed. He stammers something to the bridge in general.

"Forget it," the man growls in annoyance, swinging himself up onto the horseshoe. "Answer your board."

Rogers turns back to his console, flicks glumly at a blinking light. "Gravity control here. Go ahead."

"This is the galley . . ." says a gruff, sarcastic voice. "I don't suppose you would be so kind as to warn me the next time you're planning to up the G's like that, would you?"

"I'm sorry, Cookie," he says. "It was an accident. I didn't mean to—"

"Well, 'sorry' isn't going to bring back a dozen cakes that you ruined. Just watch it, dammit!"

Rogers stammers, "I'll try—" But the light winks out abruptly, cutting him off. The other crewmen on the horseshoe snort contemptuously at his discomfort.

"Hey, Rogers," growls one of them, "don't give

Cookie any complaints, huh? You got it rough enough as it is."

Rogers ignores him, stares glumly at his control board. Thin and round-shouldered, he toys with one of his safety switches, pretends to adjust it.

The man steps in closer and lowers his voice. "For your own good, huh? Nobody likes having his meals ruined just because some wobblehead isn't watching his board, so pay attention, huh?" He scowls heavily. "Otherwise, you're going to be eating your meals alone, boy—"

A sudden motion at the back of the bridge—a panel in the rear wall slides open. The men on the horseshoe turn quickly back to their boards.

Haloed by the orange light of the corridor behind, Captain Georj Brandt of the United Systems Command strides heavily into the room.

Two

A starship is concerned with two kinds of velocity. There is the realized velocity of the ship in warp, and there is the inherent velocity of that same ship in normal space.

A ship's inherent velocity remains the same, no matter what it does while in warp. If a ship is traveling at 5,000 kilometers per second when it goes into warp, no matter how fast or how far it goes, when it comes out of warp, it will still be traveling at that same 5,000 kilometers per second (plus or minus a fractional gain, but that's another story).

Even if the warp is motionless, the ship may still be moving within it; or vice versa, if the warp is moving, it is possible for the ship to be at rest within.

from DR. HANS UNDERMEYER's
address to the Bridgeport
Opportunities League,
"Understanding Our Cosmos"

Brandt is a big man, heavy-boned and husky. He glances quickly around the bridge, then steps down off the rear ledge to the Command and Control Seat.

Korie glances up, slips out of the chair at his approach. Almost distastefully, the captain drops his wide frame into it and rasps, "All right, what seems to be the problem?"

"We've had to shut down the warp. Number three generator is acting up again."

"Why? What is it this time?"

"Engine room doesn't know yet—probably this damned ship is getting old." Brandt doesn't react; Korie continues, "We're stuck here until they find the trouble." He glances forward, but the screen is empty. "And all we can do is watch our bogie escape. Every minute we sit here, he puts another three light hours between us."

Brandt grunts darkly, but he hasn't time to sympathize with Korie's problem. With a thick finger he taps the chair arm. "Engine room, this is Brandt."

The speaker crackles, "Leen here, sir."

"Chief, how soon can you have us going again?"

". . . Mmm, I wish I could tell you, but I don't know—I don't even know what's wrong yet. I've got six men up in the webs—and they can't find anything. Systems analysis doesn't show anything wrong with the generator. I just climbed out of the well myself. I don't know what it is, and it's driving me out of my mind."

"All right, keep on it. I want to know what it is and how long it'll take to fix."

"As soon as I know myself, Captain."

Brandt switches him off. His iron-gray eyes are troubled. He swivels right to face the astrogation console. "Mr. Barak."

Barak spins to face the captain. "Yes, sir?" With his dark skin he is almost invisible in the dim light of the bridge.

"How near are we to the enemy sphere of influence?"

Barak thinks a moment. "About nine light years."

"Any of their ships around?"

"Not this far out, there shouldn't be—but we're running a probability check through EDNA to make sure."

"Good." The captain's granite features relax a bit. "What about the bogie? Can you catch him?"

Barak grins—a broad, good-natured grin. "I may be good, Captain, but not that good."

"I take it, then, you can't."

Barak shrugs his heavy shoulders. "That's essentially

t. In just about nineteen days he'll be home free. Oh, we might be able to catch him if we could take after him right now at top speed—he hasn't gained that much distance yet—but we'd still have to pace him and that'd take us into enemy territory."

"No good," says Brandt. "On his home ground, he won't come out of warp anywhere but near a war base, and I can't fight him there. All right," he exhales loudly. "Start plotting a course for home." Behind him, Korie scowls in frustration. Barak nods and turns back to his console. Jonesy moves up beside him and the two confer softly.

Brandt taps the button again, swivels farther to the right. He makes a complete circuit of the bridge, glancing at each screen and console in turn, quickly scanning them for the information he wants.

The ship is becalmed one-half light year out from the nearest star. Actually, becalmed isn't the right word—the ship still has an inherent velocity of .07 ^{4}C; C representing the speed of light. But when one is used to figuring in multiples of C . . . well, for astrogational purposes, the ship is becalmed.

The chair slides to a halt, once more facing forward. Korie stands dourly waiting.

Ignoring him, Brandt leans back in the seat, pulling speculatively at his thick lower lip. His gray eyes focus on the empty screen ahead. Apparently, radec still hasn't resighted the bogie.

After a moment, he turns away; he glances around the dimly lit bridge. "Why is it so dark in here?" he mutters, then checks himself; he calls out, "Go to Condition Yellow—standby alert."

Slowly the lights come up, revealing the green-blue control room, revealing the age-stained walls and the use-worn equipment. Men are standing sullenly by their consoles, tunic flaps unbuttoned in the cramped heat. The air circulators whisper incessantly; the sound is an ever-present subliminal pressure, a steady hum just below the threshold of consciousness; but they cannot clear away the heavy smell of defeat that has added itself to the other stale odors of the ship.

The captain shifts his big frame into a more comfortable position. "Hmph, that's better."

Up on the horseshoe, a yellow light begins beeping on the gravity control board. Rogers answers it.

"How's your gravity now?" asks an acid voice. "Have you got enough power?"

The crewman mumbles a hesitant reply.

"What was that?" the intercom demands. "What did you say?"

Rogers repeats it. "Gravity is holding steady at one zero zero."

"Yeah!" growls the other. "We noticed it when it snapped back up."

"Sorry," Rogers apologizes.

The other replies with a loud contemptuous sound.

At this, both Korie and Brandt look up to the horseshoe. They exchange a glance.

"There," whispers Brandt. "That's what we're going to have to watch out for. Everybody's a bit touchy now—especially since we've lost the kill."

"You want me to pull Rogers off the bridge? He's only a kid."

"Uh uh. Give him a chance to work his problems out for himself. I don't want to start interfering in the crew's affairs unless I have to."

Korie nods in grudging agreement; for once the captain is correct in his assessment of a situation. He straightens, running a hand through his light-colored hair, then moves back to the center of the pit, eyeing the men on the horseshoe.

Brandt shifts his attention left to the warp control board. There, one of the engineers is hunched over it, arguing into a microphone, continuing a previous discussion with a counterpart in the engine room.

"Did you check the secondaries again?"

"Again and again and again," answers the intercom. "I tell you the secondaries are all right."

"Well, everything checks out on this end. That means it's got to be something down there—something with your machines."

"Listen, wobblehead, if it were the goddamn machines, don't you think we'd tell you?!!"

The engineer exhales slowly, "All right, if the trouble isn't down there, *then just where in the hell is it?!!*"

The voice from the communicator is filtered, but its tone is recognizable. "I'll come up there and show you if—*hey!* I just thought of something . . . !" He bleeps out, leaving the other in open-mouthed frustration.

Watching, Brandt rubs the thick bridge of his nose between his thumb and forefinger. His eyes narrow thoughtfully. Something will have to be done about morale.

A panel at his elbow blinks. He answers it with a quick jab. "Brandt here. What is it?"

"Captain, this is Leen. We just had a thought down here. Suppose the trouble is in one of the grids . . . ?"

"Go on. . . ."

"Systems analysis shows a dead area in the second phase circuitry—that could be it. I'd like to send two men outside to check it."

Brandt lifts a meaty hand as if to ward off a fly. It is a tradition that only the captain may order a man into his suit. "Permission granted."

"Thank you." Leen bleeps out.

The captain glances at the screens—nothing but dark, shining starfields. He slaps the chair arm and swivels 180 degrees. "You, what's your name?" The question is directed up to the man on the autolog, a thick fellow with sharp uneven features and small darting eyes.

The man drops his feet off the edge of his console, straightens in his seat. "Willis, sir. Ike Willis; crewman second class."

"Right. You're on the log?"

"Yes, sir."

"I want a visual on the main screens. Can you handle it?"

"Yes, sir." A puzzled expression crosses his face. "A visual of what, sir?"

Brandt says slowly, "Of the external maintenance operation."

"Oh."

"Can you handle that?"

"Huh? Oh, sure, I can handle it."

"Good. I want it complete." He taps the swivel button.

"Yes, sir." But he is talking to the captain's broad back. Willis shrugs, then turns back to his console and bends to a mike. "Air lock. This is the bridge. Give me some camera, please." He waits for a confirming light, then touches appropriate buttons on his board.

On the big screen forward, two men—clad only in T-shirts and tights—are shown in the cramped air lock, struggling with their bright-colored leotard-like space suits, one red and one yellow.

The material of the suits is lightweight, strong, flexible—but not very elastic. Of necessity, it must be tight fitting; it is a second skin. Two sour-looking crewmen are helping them with the sleeves and leggings.

A fifth man is cramped against one wall, adjusting the helmets. He snaps a camera onto the left side of one—whatever the man is looking at will be relayed back to the bridge.

When the men are at last secure in their suits, their helmets are lowered over their heads. The "valets" complete the connections to the mobility and life-support backpack units and check them out. That done, and the units activated, the men snap their face-plates shut, check the helmet seals for security, and lower the appropriate filters into place. They are now bright-colored golems, each with a great dark eye for a face.

"Radio working?" asks one.

The other touches his device-studded "chastity belt," a plastic frame around his waist and genitals. "Right."

A wall panel flashes red—the other crewmen disappear through a hatch which slides impatiently shut after them. A hiss signals that the air is rapidly being drained from the chamber.

The suits do not puff out; only an occasional bubble of air, trapped under their second skins, reveals that the pressure is quickly decreasing. And then even these too evaporate away. "Bridge, we're ready to go."

"Hold on," answers a technician. "I still have some

red lights." He watches as one by one they wink out. "All right, I'm green now." He thumbs a switch and the outer hatch of the air lock slides away. On the big screen, a shaft of black widens above the two men.

"Gravity . . . ?" prompts one of them.

Watching from the pit, Korie calls, "Rogers, cut the gravity in the air lock."

"Right," answers Rogers. He peers curiously at his board, "Now where in the . . . ?" He pauses, momentarily puzzled.

Quickly, Korie steps up onto the horseshoe. He reached past the younger man and flicks a button. "There, that's it."

"Oh," Rogers puts his finger on the control.

"It's not necessary to hold it. It's an automatic fade."

"Oh." He takes his hand away.

Korie looks at him curiously, then drops the thought. Rogers is young, yes—but he must know the board or he wouldn't be on it. He drops down into the pit, again turns his attention to the main screen.

The screen flickers and picks up the view from an externally mounted hull camera: a foreshortened square of yellow light against a dark bulge—the open hatch of the air lock. Two dark shapes move up and out of it.

At the rear of the bridge, Willis stabs a button on his console, bends his acne-scarred face to a mike. "Can I have some light for those hull cameras?"

"Right," answers his communicator.

"Thanks." He checks his monitors, then glances forward again, where two space-suited men float dark against the night, blotting out the stars. A bright blaze of light suddenly washes across them, turning them back into gay-colored figures. They shine with harsh fluorescence, one a garish red, the other intense yellow. Caught in the beam of the single remote spotlight, they glare flat and shadowless. Their shadows are hidden by their own bright bodies and they appear as two hard cutouts hung against the void.

One of them drops an auxiliary filter across his faceplate. It glints brightly in the harsh glare of the spotlight. In the background, the dim latticework of the warp grids

can be seen. Light reflecting off the hull gives them a soft,
ghostly glow, turning them into great cobwebs in the
night.

"More light, please," asks Willis. "Farther down—
toward the stern."

"I'm working on it, I'm working on it," growls the
communicator.

"Well, hurry it."

"I will, I will. When was the last time the damn
things were checked, anyway? They seem to be frozen."

"I don't know. Why don't you ask Beagle to check
them while he's out there?"

"I'll do that." The communicator bleeps out.

The screen shows two graceful one-eyed gods floating curiously above a metallic landscape, their movements
taken from a *ballet mysterieux*. The surface beneath them
is curved and the single harsh light gives the whole a sur-
realistic appearance of blazing whites and intense darks.
Here and there the hull is studded with round-edged
metal and plastic devices: cameras and spotlights, glisten-
ing sensor domes, disc-shaped scanners, innocent-looking
laser and phaser mountings, and stress-field antennae
looking like miniature warp grids. Many of the devices
have plastic covers across their muzzles, shielding them
until they are needed.

Willis glances away from the screen, stabs a button
on his board. Another hull camera slides out of its protective blister and an auxiliary screen blinks to pick up its
image. Because of the camera angle, the two cyclopian
figures are now in stark relief; this camera sees them lit
from one side. A second spotlight swings around toward
them and lights, throwing another bright cone of white
against the hull.

Other cameras and spotlights swing into place. Other
screens light to follow the space-suited men. Now they no
longer look as flat; they are illuminated from several
sides. Slowly they drift down the curvature of the hull toward the stern.

One of the men pauses, as if listening to his suit radio. He swims over to a nearby spotlight; the plastic
cover of it is still across the lens.

The man braces his feet against the hull and tries to move it with his hands. It's no good; the cover is stuck. He lets go, drifting backward as he does. Unclipping a small cylinder from his belt, he moves toward the spotlight again.

Holding the cylinder at arm's length, he aims its stubby nozzle at the recalcitrant cover and sprays a pale mist across it. Almost immediately it slides open and the light within glares suddenly into his face.

A short, sharp expletive is heard over the all-talk channel. "Goddamn it! What are you trying to do—blind me?" He lowers another filter across his eyes.

There is amusement on the bridge. Here and there a contemptuous snort is heard. Korie, fidgeting impatiently in the pit, mutters softly, "Come on, you two. . . ."

Brandt, talking with Barak, glances up, notices the screen, hesitates, then touches his chair arm. "This is the captain. Why aren't you men using gravitors? You know my orders about outside duty."

The speaker crackles. "Yes, sir. Sorry, sir."

Reflected on many of the screens lining the bridge, each from a different angle, a faint, almost unnoticeable aura envelops each space-suited figure. They drop to the hull of the ship; first one, then the other.

Satisfied that his orders are being obeyed, Brandt turns back to Barak.

The speaker crackles again. "Hey, Beagle," calls one of the two space-suited men.

"Yeah?" answers the other.

"Sounds like the old man is in a bitch of a mood today."

Across the bridge, startled faces turn to look at the screen. On some there are surprised grins. Brandt glances up again.

Beagle answers, "Maybe he didn't get any last night."

This time there are one or two quickly stifled chuckles—and a snort of obvious annoyance from Korie. But most of the men remain uncomfortably silent, surreptitiously watching the captain. Brandt touches the chair arm again. "Yes," he whispers into the mike, "I *am* in a

bitch of a mood today. However, *that* is not the reason
for it . . . and I will thank you to leave such speculation
for your off-duty hours." He cuts off.

The two bright figures on the screen stiffen in surprise; they cut off their suit radios hurriedly. A ripple of
laughter around the horseshoe underscores their embarrassment. Brandt turns again to his astrogator. "Now,
what about those fuel consumption factors?"

Grinning broadly, Barak says to him, "I think we can
control it, sir. I'll run some more checks."

The captain allows himself the hint of a mile—an unspoken acknowledgment of Barak's grin. "Fine," he says.
"You take care of that and let me know."

Barak nods and returns to his console. Brandt turns
his gray-eyed attention back to the screens, shifting his
position slightly, the better to see past Korie, who still
fumes impatiently in the pit.

Above, the two golems, heavy-footed, walk toward
the stern. Cameras and spotlights swivel to follow them,
marking their passage with slow uncurious stares. As the
men move nearer to the stern of the ship, the warp grids
loom ever closer overhead. The three giant grids are
mounted at the stern, but arch gracefully forward to en-
velop the ship in a fragile crystalline latticework. The
cruiser is a fat beetle in a silvervaned web.

The men move around the curve of the hull and disappear from view. The screen blinks as another camera
picks them up. For a brief moment, they are again dark
shapes against the star field, hunchbacked silhouettes,
bulbous heads and bulky yet slender bodies outlined in
white by the glare of unseen lights behind them.

At the base of one of the grids, a spotlight swings
around to point its wide flaring mouth at them. It throws
a sudden splash of white against the side of the ship and
outward too; the light shatters across the grids with eye-
glaring intensity—shards of it glitter and glint among the
vanes.

The men pause briefly—they lean back in order to
survey the bright-blazing frames overhead. Beagle seems
to sigh, then resolutely lowers a third and final filter
across his faceplate.

They bend to the hull and start unwelding the metalloid plates at the base of the number two grid. The magnetic welds give easily, exposing a gaping hole, an open mouth screaming in silent outrage at two gay-colored cyclopes. The cyclopes look silently at each other, then touch their great dark eyes together to confer without the use of radio. After a moment, they break apart and again bend to the task before them.

Satisfied that the work is progressing, Brandt nods to himself. Idly, he glances around the bridge. Most of the crew is following the operation on the screens, though one or two are still casually monitoring their boards.

Brandt nudges Korie, who has moved back to stand on the control island, just to one side of the seat. "Who's minding the store?" he asks.

"Huh?" Korie is startled out of his thoughts.

Brandt indicates the bridge with a sharp nod. For the first time Korie notices the distracting influence of the large viewscreens.

Taking the captain's remark as an indication to act, he steps down into the pit, calling angrily, "Let's keep an eye on those boards! We're not here to entertain you!"

The crew reacts as if stung; they turn quickly back to their control boards and pretend to be busy.

Korie's blue-gray eyes drift inevitably back to the huge forward screen. He folds his arms across his chest and relaxes into a more comfortable stance. A lean figure in a blue and gray uniform, he stands alone in the center of the pit and gazes resolutely ahead.

Around the bridge, behind him, the crew silently follows his example. One by one they turn away from their boards to again watch the progress of the work.

Brandt smiles—a tightening at the corners of his mouth. Abruptly he purges it in a quick flash of annoyance: annoyance at Korie for giving an unenforceable order, annoyance at the crew for lack of discipline. He makes a mental note to bring it up at the next briefing, knowing as he does so that unless he writes it down, he'll probably forget, but—

A sudden voice cuts into his thoughts. "Captain?!!"

Startled, Brandt looks up—it is Barak, a headset

pressed to one ear. "It's radec, sir. He says he's blown the bogie!"

Brandt straightens in his seat. Korie's head jerks around. "What was *that*?"

Barak repeats it. "*We can't find the bogie anywhere—he's dropped out of warp!*"

Three

The rocket made space travel possible; the energy field made it practical.

GUNTER WHITE,
The Economy of the Stars

The warp theory of my esteemed colleagues (and I am sure they will correct me if I am wrong) is based on the principle that two separate units of anything cannot exist in the same place at the same time; nor can they coexist without each having an effect upon the other. When the units are energy fields, the effect is supposed to be spectacular. (The effect is spectacular—I will admit that. As my esteemed colleagues have already so admirably demonstrated, the effect is certainly spectacular . . . though I somewhat doubt that this was the specific effect they had hoped for.)

Theoretically—at least, as their theory says—when two continuous fields are overlapped, it will cause a wrinkle in the fabric of existence. Unfortunately, the continuous energy field is only a myth—a mathematical construction. It is a physical impossibility and cannot exist without collapsing in upon itself.

Of course, there are still some members of this learned academy who insist on remaining doggedly skeptical of this fact of life. It is almost pitiful to watch them continue these attempts to *generate an energy field that is both continuous and stable. So far, the only thing that they have succeeded in doing is to convert several dollars' worth of equipment, buildings, and surrounding property into so much slag. (Oh, and incidentally, in doing so, they have also proven me correct.)*

DR. J. JOSEPH RUSSELL, PH.D., M.A., etc.,
comments to the Board of Inquiry
into the Denver disaster

Insufferable old windbag!

ANONYMOUS "ESTEEMED COLLEAGUE"

Dammit! It's like trying to stack soap bubbles!

DR. ARTHUR DWYER PACKARD,
remark overheard by lab assistant
and quoted by Duffy Hirshberg in
"Packard—Behind the Myth"

In light of events, it would be criminal to let them continue.

DR. J. JOSEPH RUSSELL,
comment to newsmen after appearing before the
Board of Inquiry

Actually, they were on the wrong track to begin with. The problem was not to create a continuous and stable energy field at all—but only to overload a section of space. Once they began thinking of it in those terms, the solution was obvious—and even practical, considering the then existing technology.

The answer lay in the use of a series of interlocking noncontinuous fields. The noncontinuous field gives the illusion of continuity, but like a strobe light, the field is actually a very rapid series of ons and offs. Several noncontinuous fields working in phase can create a stable continuous field. Each of the separate noncontinuous energy fields fills in the gaps of the others.

Three noncontinuous fields can dovetail their functions to make one continuous one, and two continuous energy fields can be overlapped to generate the much sought after warp.

When six field generators are working in phase and all on the same section of space, a great pressure quickly builds up. Something has got to give. Usually space does.

> HOWARD LEDERER,
> *Encyclopedia of 1,000*
> *Great Inventions*

Dammit! Why didn't I think of that?!!

> Remark attributed to
> DR. ARTHUR DWYER PACKARD

Because, I did.

> Remark attributed to
> DR. J. JOSEPH RUSSELL

The warp has no relation at all to normal space. It is a bubble, or miniature universe. Within it a ship still obeys all the known laws of physics, but it is totally separated from the outer universe.

The bubble, or warp, is made up of great energies locked together in a titanic embrace. The potential power inherent in that embrace is far greater than the sum of the component energy fields—not just because the bubble is a stable construct, but because it is a dimple in space itself. The very structure of existence is pressing against it, trying to restore itself to a condition of minimum distortion. With such an infinite store of unexpressed force to draw upon, the potential power of the system is almost unlimited. (In practice the limit is the size of the ship's generators.)

If a secondary set of fields is superimposed

across this point of pressured space—that is, the warp—it acts to liberate some of this great power and simultaneously provides a focus for it. As every second sees the warp restored to stability, the bubble cannot collapse; but this continued release of energy must be somehow sublimated—and it is; the effect is the introduction of a vector quantity into the system.

Because the shape of the secondary fields can be controlled, they can be used to produce a controllable velocity in any direction. The warp can be made to move at velocities many times the speed of light.

The Einsteinian time-distortion is neatly sidestepped, as the ship is not really traveling faster than light—only the warp is. The ship just happens to be inside it. It is the warp that moves, the ship moves within the warp and is carried along by it. Consequently, a starship has two velocities, one is the realized faster-than-light velocity; the other is the inherent normal space velocity. . . .

. . . For maneuvering within a planetary system, inherent velocity is an important resource; but unless it is compensated for, it can cause havoc to a ship in warp. . . .

JARLES "FREE FALL" FERRIS,
Revised Handbook of Space Travel

Finally, any system will automatically try to tune out external disturbances by introducing a compensating multiplex vibration. Disturbances will be interpreted by each element of the system in terms of the specific function which the element was designed to cope with, and that element will react in terms of its interpretation of that disturbance. When all elements in the system are functioning so as to introduce their own interpretive vibrations, the resultant multiplex vibration is often enough to cause undue strain on the system as a whole, and on the individual ele-

ments themselves—especially on those functions not designed to cope with such violent interplay of energies.

Undue strain means something has to give. Usually, it's the weakest part of the system. . . .

GUNTER WHITE
Mechanics of Government

There is a startled pause on the bridge. Heads turn to look at the astrogator.

"How far out is he?" asks Brandt.

Barak frowns in confusion. "They don't know—you'd better talk to him yourself."

Brandt thumbs his communicator to life. "Radec?"

"Sir?"

"What's the story on that bogie?"

"I don't know, sir. I can't find him."

"What do you mean you can't find him?" Korie steps in closer. Brandt flashes him a look of annoyance, but the first officer doesn't notice.

"Just that," answers the intercom. "I lost him during unwarp and I haven't been able to pick up a shimmer since."

"Could he be out of range?" asks Brandt.

"No, sir. Not a chance. It'd take him at least five hours at top speed to get out of range. Maybe six."

"Do you have any idea of his location?" Korie again.

"Well, it's kind of rough . . . approximately fifty-five light days away—give or take eight light hours in either direction."

Korie says thoughtfully, "It seems unlikely that we'd both have engine trouble at the same time."

"Mm." Brandt is silent.

Korie steps into the breach. "You never picked him up again at all?"

"No, sir. It must be that wobbly—during unwarp we picked up an electronic trauma. We had to clear our sensor fields entirely and then recalibrate as well."

Korie opens his mouth to reply, but Brandt cuts him off. "All right. We've got the picture. Keep watching for him."

"Yes, sir."

Brandt breaks the connection, looks to his officers.

Korie is frowning darkly, but Barak says, " 'Give or take eight light hours.' That's sixteen across—that's an awfully big area; bigger than the average star system."

"Not important," puts in Korie. "What we want to know is why he dropped out of warp in the first place."

"A good question," says Brandt. "A good question . . ." With a sudden motion, he heaves his bulky frame out of the chair. "Let's consider the possibilities here. . . ." He paces the bridge thoughtfully. "Either he's stopped by choice, in which case he's taking advantage of our inability to come after him; or he's stopped because he has no choice . . ."

Brandt comes to a stop behind the seat and rests his hands thoughtfully on the headrest. "Now, let's consider that latter—that he's had no choice. That'd mean that we've finally pushed him to his limit. His cells are exhausted, his engines are beginning to throw off sparks, his endurance is cracking. Sooner or later, he has to stop. Our wobbly just gave him that opportunity a little sooner. He could be trying to recharge his cells right now."

"Then let's get fixed and go after him."

Brandt looks at his impetuous first officer. "On the other hand," he continues, "there is the possibility that it's a trick. But I don't see what's to be gained by it. . . ." He moves away from the chair, continuing in a thoughtful monotone, "He knows we won't give up the chase willingly, so if *we've* stopped, it means we've blown something . . . He could be taking advantage of our handicap to lose himself in normal space."

The captain turns suddenly to the astrogator. "Can he do it, Al?"

Barak shakes his head. "Uh uh—it's too empty. There probably isn't a chunk of solid matter in the entire sector. There's nothing for kilometers in any direction but kilometers. All we'd have to do is scan the area at close range and he'd be as obvious as a fart in an air lock."

"And about as welcome, too," adds Brandt. A hint of a smile cracks his face. He shakes it away. "That means he'd try to sneak away at a lesser speed so we couldn't see his warp—but that doesn't make sense. He'd be cutting his own lead. We couldn't catch him without thirteen days of chase."

"Fourteen," corrects Barak.

"Fourteen, thirteen, what's the difference? We're still too far away."

"Only if it's a trick," puts in Korie. "We're too far away only if his engines are still in perfect working order. But his only reason for stopping is that he's in trouble too—and this could be our chance to move in for the kill."

Brandt nods. "It seems the most likely thing, that he's in trouble too. . . ."

"If he is," insists the first officer, "we might be able to get to him before he can recharge his cells."

The captain looks at him. "That is a possibility—however, that would necessitate that we repair our own engines first. . . ." He drops into his chair again, thumbs a switch. "Engine room, this is Brandt."

A pause, then, "Leen here." The chief engineer's voice comes filtered through the speaker.

"Status report, please." Brandt leans back in his chair.

"Uh—we're still searching. It's definitely something in the second phase circuitry."

"How long till you fix it?"

"Hard to say, sir—we've got to find it first. And then it depends on which component it is. Some of them are damned inaccessible. It could take two or three hours. Then again, maybe not."

Brandt looks at Korie—the first officer is frowning. "Let's hope not. Do you know yet how it happened?"

"Yes, sir, but you won't like it."

"Tell me anyway."

"Some kind of field interference—focused on the number three function."

"So?"

"So, the generator tried to compensate for it—introduced a reciprocal vibration."

Brandt ignores Korie's impatience. "That shouldn't have affected the warp."

"It didn't, not at first—but the thing was an unstable quantity. The generator couldn't match it. As it built up, we got a first-level resistance to the secondary fields. The warp was stable, all our fields were stable, but we weren't getting any push. That's why our speed started to drop when the vibration hit the red line. And because of resonance, all our other stress-field functions went wild too. Hell, Captain," Leen mutters, "it's such a piddling little thing—and it's practically crippled us! If they'd let us have those Thorsen generators when we asked, this thing'd never have happened. I could have simply cross-phased and outcircuited number three. We could have limped along on five and still maintained speed."

Brandt smiles, "If it can be done, Chief, I'm sure you can do it."

"Hell! I could do it with these, if they'd let me put in the override equipment I need—but if they ever found out I could run this ship on five generators, they'd take one out."

The captain grins at this. He glances up, but Korie is not grinning—he is glaring meaningfully.

Brandt's grin fades. "Listen, Chief; we may still have a chance at that bogie. He's dropped out of warp. Mr. Korie here is champing at the bit—so try and get your repair crew on the ball, will you?"

"Aye, aye, sir. I'll have the warp up again as soon as possible."

"Good man." Brandt disconnects; he looks to his pale first officer. "Well, Mr. Korie, I assume you still want to go after that bogie . . . ?"

"Yes, sir."

"Uh huh." Brandt turns to his dark-skinned astrogator. "What say, Al? Can we sneak up on him?"

"Why not just go after him at full speed?" interrupts Korie. Brandt looks back at him.

"He's got a point there," puts in Barak. "At top speed we could close with him in eight hours."

The captain looks at them both, clears his throat gruffly. "I don't like it," he says. "I don't want to give him eight hours' warning. He'd see our warp all the way in."

"He wouldn't be able to do anything about it, though," counters Korie. "His engines are blown. "Your way would only give him time to fix them."

"We don't *know* that his engines are blown," corrects Brandt. "And if we can fix our engines in the next eight hours, then maybe he can do the same with his. Whatever his trouble is, with eight hours warning, he would certainly be able to jury-rig something. Don't forget, we stopped because we *had* to. He stopped voluntarily. *Your way*, Mr. Korie, we stand a very good chance of picking up the chase right where we left off—*in a stalemate*. On the other hand, as it is now, he can't see us at all, any more than we can see him—let's keep it that way as long as we can and maybe we can get in close enough to attack."

The first officer is forced to agree; he nods reluctantly.

The captain turns to his astrogator again. "Now. Can you do it, Al?"

Barak frowns distastefully. It is obvious that he'd much rather do it Korie's way, but he just grimaces and says, "Probably . . . he must be watching for us pretty closely, but we could do it by keeping our warp speed low. The smaller our stress-field disturbance, the closer we can get to him before he can pick us up; but he is fifty-five light days away, Captain, and the slower we go means the longer we take getting there—and the more chance he has to escape."

Brandt nods warily. "But you *can* do it . . . ?"

Barak shrugs. "Well, we might try to come in as close as we can without getting picked up on his scopes— then when we're too close to avoid it, we could come down on top of him as fast as we could. Within a certain limit he will pick us up, but this would minimize his warning."

"And we could come in from an angle that he won't be expecting us from," suggests Korie. "It might throw him off balance."

"For a bit, anyway," qualifies Brandt. "But it's not a bad idea."

Barak shoots Korie a mock-sour look. "That's right;

make it harder for me. That means we'll have to sneak past his sphere of influence in order to come back down into it—that's like trying to graze a billiard ball from three miles away, bounce off the side board, and hit it square on the ricochet."

"What you're trying to say then is that you can't do it?" asks Brandt.

"Oh, I can do it all right. I just don't like it."

"You don't have to *like* it. All you have to do is *do* it. And if we're going after him at all, that course has to be ready and set up to go by the time repairs are finished."

"Aye, aye." Barak turns back to his board and his assistant. Brandt hits the chair arm and swivels forward. Korie steps out of his way as the chair swings around.

Ahead, on the screen dominating the forward wall of the bridge, the two space-suited figures have dismantled a large section of the hull at the base of the number two grid. The screen blinks to show a close-up of their work as seen by the helmet camera. Currently, they are checking individual blackbox components. One of the men is touching a sensor to various key points of the systems analysis network. In theory it should have already pinpointed the location of the malfunction, but so much new equipment and refittings have been added to the *Burlingame* since she was commissioned that the system has long since collapsed in its own complexity. Now, a malfunction in any part of the ship requires an additional on-the-spot check of the secondary analysis units. The second crewman has plugged into one of these units with a portable scanner. It is a flat plastic device and he watches the readings on it carefully while the other continues to probe.

Brandt glances right, at Korie's brooding shape. "What's your guess, Mr. Korie?"

Korie hesitates for a beat. "Multiplex adapter."

The captain weighs this possibility. "Hm, maybe."

A second later, the speaker crackles with electric life: "Fowles here—we found it! We've burned out one of the phase adapters."

Brandt looks at Korie, mildly surprised. "Good guess." Korie shrugs it off.

Another voice on the intercom. "All right, bring it in. We'll uncrate a spare."

At this, the first officer unclips a hand mike from his belt. "Engine room, this is Korie."

The same voice, Leen's voice, "Yes, sir?"

"You seem to be awfully free with the ship's stores, Chief Leen."

"Beg pardon, sir?"

"Do you know how much one of those adapters costs?"

"Yes, sir, of course."

"Good. Now let me ask you—why would one of them burn out?"

"I assume that's a rhetorical question, Mr. Korie. You already know the answer."

"That's a very astute observation on your part, Chief." Korie smiles thinly. "Yes, I do know. *Do you?*"

"Improper compensation of inherent velocity." The reply is quick and sure. "Either in the phase alternators or—"

"Or lack of compensation altogether," Korie says harshly. "It's an easy thing to overlook." He continues with staccato precision, "But somebody did overlook it. And because of that we may have lost a kill. From here it looks like somebody in the engine room has very little respect for this ship and its equipment. And that's something that I absolutely will not allow."

He becomes suddenly aware of Brandt's quiet gaze on him, continues quickly, "You're responsible for that engine room, Leen—and the people in it. Our lives depend on how well you and your crew maintain this ship!"

Leen is making apologetic noises. "It won't happen again, sir."

"It had better not."

"You have my word on it."

"Hm, we'll see." Korie glances at Brandt; the captain is expressionless. "All right, get on with the repairs."

"Yes, sir."

Korie disconnects and clips the hand mike back to his belt, grimly unsatisfied.

"Mr. Korie," says Brandt quietly, firmly. Something in his tone makes the first officer hesitate.

"Sir?"

Brandt gestures him closer; Korie steps up onto the control island. The captain lowers his voice to a whisper. "Try and take it easy on the crew, will you? We've all been in space a long time."

"Yes, sir."

Brandt lifts one thick hand, "Oh, I'm not chastising you, but I do want you to know that a delegation from the union called on me. They were complaining about your rigid discipline."

"There were—who?"

"That's not your concern, don't worry about it. It's me that you have to please—not them. And as far as I'm concerned, you're doing fine. You get results. Uh—it's just that—well, try to be a little more . . . tactful."

Korie brushes a wisp of blond hair away from his eyes. "I'll try."

"Good." Brandt leans back in his chair, once more turning his attention forward. It is his signal that the discussion is closed.

On the screen, the bright cyclopes have finished working their destruction—the ruined adapter has been pulled from its moorings. It is a simple black module—a naked piece of electronics. They examine it curiously with dark, expressionless stares.

Brandt drops his hand to the controls. "Quartermaster."

A voice from the speaker: "Yes, sir?"

"This is the captain. See that the engine room is charged for a multiplex phase adapter."

"Sir?"

"See that the engine room crew is charged with the cost of it. Take it off their EHD allotment."

"Yes, sir." But the voice is puzzled.

Brandt ignores it, cuts him off abruptly—he notices Korie staring at him curiously. "A captain always stands behind his officers," he explains.

Korie nods. "When they're right. . . ."

The captain nods. "When they're right."

Ahead, two more bright slender figures, this time in green and blue, float up and out of the air lock. One is carrying a duplicate of the burned-out adapter. They activate their gravitors and drop to the hull, the screen blinking to follow them.

The *Burlingame* hangs unmoving in the night. Or rather, it *appears* to hang unmoving. What motion there is is too slight to be perceptible.

Within—her crew also appears to be unmoving. They watch their screens in silence.

On the horseshoe, Rogers is staring morosely at his gravity meters—looking at, but not seeing. To his right, a blue-clad crewman is murmuring into a hand mike, "Maintenance? Oxy consumption is up 0.03."

Farther to the right, another crewman is adjusting the power levels of the ship's radiation shields. This far out from any star, there is no need for the power drain. To his right, a bored ensign is watching the progress of the repairs on a tiny glowing monitor.

Below them, Barak is sitting before his console, punching out possible interception courses. He looks at his glowing screen, frowns, touches a button, looks again, and sighs with satisfaction. The lines shift and change. Jonesy stands beside him, the everpresent headset pressed against one ear.

To the rear of the bridge, Willis is listening to an earpiece of his own. He drops his feet off the edge of his console, glances at his screens. "Uh uh, that's no good. Try camera hull-six."

Again on the horseshoe, the left rear, Korie is going over a shimmering graph with a reluctant crewman. Wolfe stands by, glowering. Below them, at the warp control console, an engineer is once more arguing with his counterpart in the engine room. "See," the speaker cries, tinnily triumphant, "I told you it wasn't our machines."

"Well, maybe that's why it burned out. You clowns don't consider the grids as part of your machines." He doesn't wait for the other to answer, disconnects instead.

And at the front, two officers slouch in their seats before the pilot console.

Not so long ago, all was dominated by an angry red

glow from the forward wall with a single shimmer of white in it. Now, four bright colored harlequins squat across that same screen, securing a replacement adapter into its moorings. The glittering lattice of the number two grid looms above them.

One of the space-suited figures touches a panel on his chest; his voice comes filtered through the speakers. "This is Crewman Fowles. We're going to have to degauss the grid."

The officer at the forward console bends to his mike. "Right." He turns to face Brandt. "Sir, they say they'll have to degauss."

"I know, I heard. Go ahead."

The officer turns back to his board, glances up to the horseshoe. "Rogers."

"Yes, sir?"

"Fade to free fall."

"*F-fade* to free fall?" he stammers. "But—"

"But *what*?" the officer demands.

"Uh—nothing, sir." Rogers swallows nervously. "Fade to free fall." He turns back to his console. Seconds later the raucous sound of a klaxon vibrates through the ship.

"Secure for free fall. Secure for free fall." Rogers' high-pitched voice squeaks loudly from the speakers. Two crewman exchange a smirk at its adolescent sound.

Brandt shifts in his seat, fastening a safety belt across his wide stomach. Korie, still on the horseshoe, takes hold of a convenient stanchion. Others on the bridge do the same: grab at railings or fasten safety harnesses in anticipation of the gentle falling away of weight.

"Ten seconds. Ten seconds." the voice quavers with inexperience.

The crew moves hastily to secure a few last styli and terminals. There is a pause, a single bell-like tone—a sudden painful wrenching at the gut—and then the floor drops out. Korie grabs at his stanchion with a sharp, stabbing vertigo.

Brandt gasps at the suddenness of it, finds himself unable to breathe. Half out of his couch, his safety harness binds tightly across his chest. Loosening it with one hand, he pulls himself back into the chair.

On the horseshoe, some of the men are sitting in mid-air and cursing softly. Others are pulling themselves down into couches and hastily fastening their belts. One man—Wolfe—grabs futilely at a floating stylus, shoots suddenly upwards, a look of annoyance on his face.

Another man—a husky man—doesn't pull himself back into his couch. Angrily, he seizes the railing on the inner edge of the horseshoe and pulls himself through the air, hand over hand, toward the gravity control board. "Rogers, you damned idiot! Where the hell did you ever learn—"

"*Reynolds! Get back to your post!*" The captain's deep voice thunders across the bridge. There is a sudden hushed stillness; silent white faces turn and look. Reynolds hesitates, caught in mid-air, hands still on the railing.

"Dammit, sir! He's—"

"Did you hear me? I do the disciplining here!" No one moves. Even Wolfe, floating at the ceiling, is motionless. His elusive stylus drifts across the bridge, drifts directly across the captain's field of vision.

Brandt ignores it; looks only at Reynolds. Abruptly the man realizes where he is. "Yes, sir."

He turns in mid-air and moves back along the railing to his own console. He grabs at his seat and pulls his big frame down into it. Fumbling with his seat belt he makes a point of fastening it with a loud magnetic click.

The captain glances around at the rest of the bridge; the men turn silently back to their boards. An expressionless ensign reaches up and pulls Wolfe back to deck.

"Thanks." He starts to add something else, but a cold look from Korie freezes it in his throat. He pulls himself into a couch instead.

Brandt locks eyes with Korie—the first officer is hanging airily off a stanchion, one foot hooked casually through a metal hole—and inclines his head sharply toward the front of the bridge. *Find out what happened.*

Korie nods, *message received,* unhooks his leg, launches himself across the bridge toward Rogers. Catch-

ing hold of another stanchion, he brings himself to an
awkward stop. "All right, Rogers. Start talking."

Shaking nervously, Rogers stammers out, "I—I don't
know, Mr. Korie, sir—all I did was hit the power cut-off
and—well, it was supposed to fade and it didn't—"

"Why didn't you use the dimmer?"

"The dimmer, sir?"

"You do know what a dimmer is?"

"No, sir, I—"

Korie's pale eyes narrow. "Haven't you done this before?" he demands.

"No, sir, I never—I was supposed to be a radec tech.
That's all they trained me for—"

The first officer stares at him unbelievingly.

"—It was the rush training course. They only taught
us our specialties; I mean, we had the basics, but they said
we'd learn the rest on ship—"

"Then why didn't you?"

"I did—I mean, I was. That is, I didn't finish."

"Then why were you on this board?"

"They told me to."

"Who did?"

"Uh—"

Korie cuts him off. "Never mind. I'll see who made
up the duty roster. Who was supposed to check you out
on this board?"

"Wolfe, sir; I mean Crewman Wolfe—but he said it
was all automatic. I didn't think that—"

Korie ignores him, swings around to face the still silent bridge. "Wolfe!"

Wolfe glances over fearfully. "Yes, sir?"

"Get up here!"

"Yes, sir." He starts to launch himself off the railing,
thinks better of it, and pulls himself along it instead. With
a quick hand over hand motion, he circles the horseshoe
to where Korie hangs in mid-air.

"Were you supposed to check this man out on the
gravity board?"

"Well, I—"

"Were you or were you not?"

"Uh, sir, I—"

"Yes or no?" Korie demands.

"Uh ... yes, sir," Wolfe admits, "I was supposed to check him out."

"Why didn't you?"

"Sir?"

"I said, why didn't you?"

"I did, sir."

"Then why doesn't he know what a dimmer is?"

"It wasn't necessary, sir."

"It wasn't *what*?!!"

"Well, sir, it's hardly ever needed. I didn't think—"

"You're damn right you didn't think!" Korie stares at him for a long moment, holding himself back. The captain is watching, expressionless. Korie says slowly, "You told this man this board is all automatic?"

"Yes, sir."

A pause. "Wolfe, I'd suspect you of being a saboteur if you weren't so stupid."

"Sir, I—" But the dark look on Korie's face tells him that any attempt at explanation would only be wasted. He trails off.

A communicator panel on the console beside and below them begins flashing angrily. Korie ignores it. Rogers starts to reach—

"Leave it," growls Korie, not taking his eyes off Wolfe. Rogers snatches his hand back as if burned.

Korie looks at Brandt, no help there. He looks back to the pasty-faced Wolfe, utters a single syllable, "Off."

"Sir?"

"Is there something wrong with your hearing, too? I said, get off—off the bridge. You're confined to quarters." Without waiting to see if his order is followed—he is sure that it will be—Korie turns to the console, reaches past Rogers, and hits the still-flashing button.

A gruff voice bellows from the panel speaker. "Bridge, this is the galley!"

Rogers moans softly, "Oh, no."

The gruff voice continues, "I thought I told you to control those goddamn G's! You ought to see the mess you've made in my kitchen! I ought to drag you down here and make you clean it yourself."

The first officer and the captain exchange a quick glance.

Korie starts to reach for his hand mike, but a gesture from Brandt halts him. Brandt unclips his own hand mike, thumbs it to life. "Cookie, if you call this bridge one more time to complain about the gravity, I will personally come down there and stuff you into your own garbage disposal!"

An angry "Who's *this*?!!" roars from the speakers.

"*This* is the captain!" Brandt bellows back, and the whole ship is suddenly silent.

Brandt lowers his hand mike slowly, now speaking to every man on the ship. "Goddamn it! Have you all gone crazy?"

No one answers. The captain looks around the room; the men are pale, unmoving figures, frozen in mid-air.

"In case you have forgotten," Brandt says in a slow and measured tone, "we are in a state of war. You are supposed to be fighting men. And that does *not* mean that you will fight with each other."

He pauses, fixes an eye directly on Reynolds, his own personal bane. "I have put up with it for as long as I am going to. From now on, if any of you have any personal differences, the gym is always open. Use it. Go in there and put on the boxing gloves and slug it out—but, by God, you will keep your arguments off my bridge. *Do you understand . . . ?*"

He looks slowly around the room. "If you can't remember that, then please let me know. I'm sure I can think of something to remind you. And if I can't, I know Mr. Korie can. Are there any questions?"

Silence. There are no questions.

"Good! I didn't think so. Now, get back to your boards."

The crew moves quickly; no one wants to find out just how serious the captain is. Blue-clad crewmen pull themselves quickly around to float once more over their quiet humming consoles, each trying to outdo the other in feigning nonchalance.

The captain clips his hand mike back to his belt and

stares resolutely ahead. He forces himself to concentrate on the progress of the degaussing.

At the horseshoe, Korie directs a wide-eyed Rogers back to his board, then turns and notices Wolfe, still floating beside him. The man is pale and nervous, and droplets of sweat are beaded on his skin.

"Are you still here?"

"Sir, may I just explain—"

"I gave you an order, Wolfe. I expect it to be obeyed."

Wolfe looks pleadingly into Korie's face, seeking one last chance—a spark of mercy. Finding none, his face sags. He drops his eyes. "Yes, sir." Shifting his hold on the railing he pulls himself along it toward the rear of the bridge. The door slides shut behind him with a swift and final *thunk*.

Korie glances quickly around the room. "Goldberg," he calls.

A short stocky man with incongruously red hair answers, "Yes, sir?"

"You know this board." It is a statement, not a question.

"Yes, sir."

"Sir?" Rogers, floating behind Korie, breaks in.

Korie twists in mid-air to look at him. "Yes?"

"I'd like to request permission to be relieved of duty on the bridge, sir."

"Denied." He starts to turn away—

"But, sir. I—"

Korie stops—he tries to stop—he writhes in mid-air. He catches a handhold, rights himself. Looking at Rogers, "*I said, denied.*" He stares at the man, as if daring him to speak.

Rogers submits. "Yes, sir."

Korie turns back to the pit. "Goldberg," he snaps. "Check this man out on his board." He indicates Rogers.

"Yes, sir." The red-haired man starts swimming across the bridge toward them.

"Next time," Korie mutters, "you won't have an excuse, Rogers, so you had better learn it right."

"Y-yes, sir."

Korie releases his hold on the stanchion and drifts toward the center of the pit. He grabs at the back of a couch, misses, grabs again. He pulls himself down into it and straps a belt loosely across his waist. Wiping his forehead with the back on one hand, he realizes suddenly that he is sweating. He slides his damp palms along his thighs to dry them.

To his left is Brandt. The captain is immobile; he ignores his first officer as he does the rest of the bridge. Korie follows his heavy gaze forward to where the bright, faceless figures are just now sealing up the gaping hole in the ship's metal back. All four are floating free, their gravitors turned off so as not to interfere with the degaussing. They are secured by safety lines to grommets on the hull. One of the men continually refers to a panel of meters that he carries, checking the progress of the degaussing operation. Slowly, the latent magnetism of the grids is neutralized.

Noting the captain's expressionless face, Korie stretches toward him and says in a quiet whisper, "I thought we weren't going to yell at them any more. . . ."

Without taking his eyes from the screen, Brandt mutters, "I changed my mind."

Four

One thing you should always remember when training your pet: be patient with him. Never strike the animal—especially in anger.

However, in some cases, a sudden sharp rap across the nose may be necessary to attract his attention.

J. H. HARRIS,
*The New Revised Guide to
Training Your Pet,*
abridged edition

Amidst the hum of the consoles, a communicator gives a sudden bleep. "Beagle here. We're just about finished."

"Right," answers one of the pilot officers. "We'll take it from here." He looks up to the horseshoe and nods to Goldberg.

Goldberg turns to Rogers, floating thin and nervous beside his console. "All right," he says, "do you understand it now?"

"I think so. . . ."

"You *think* so?!!"

"I mean, yes," Rogers corrects himself quickly. "This thing—I mean the dimmer—has to be patched in and slowly brought up to full. . . ."

Goldberg sighs. "That's right." He glances up at one of the screens above his head, checking to see that the suited figures are indeed finished with the degaussing. He turns back to Rogers. "All right, you can begin procedure."

Rogers nods, starts to reach, then hesitates. He sucks in his lower lip—his thin face is suddenly unsure. "Wait—let me go over this again . . . make sure I've got it right."

Goldberg sighs audibly, then stretches past him and flicks at a button. The sound of the klaxon screeches through the ship again. Thumbing another control, Goldberg rasps, "Secure for gravity. Secure for gravity." Looking at Rogers, "All right now, what's next?"

His thin face is still puzzled, "Ten second warning?"

"I meant after that."

"Bring up the dimmer?"

"Are you asking me or telling me?"

"Uh—I'm going to bring up the dimmer."

Sighing loudly, Goldberg says, "Thank you, Rogers. Thank you very much. All right, go ahead. Sound your warning."

He does so. His thin voice echoes through the bridge and through the ship. Around the room, crewmen hastily orient themselves into a generally vertical attitude. Some of the more skeptical ones pull themselves into couches and fasten safety harnesses.

Looking at his watch. Goldberg counts silently, "All right . . . *now*."

Rogers touches a button, patches in the dimmer, sounds a warning chime, and starts to bring the dimmer control up to full. Gradually, the falling sensation at the gut starts to ease: Wolfe's floating stylus starts to drift downward. The floor again becomes a floor. Goldberg poises himself above a couch, drops slowly toward it. . . .

Rogers pushes the dimmer switch slowly toward the top, slow. He sinks toward the floor, relaxing a bit, he takes his hand off the switch and—not thinking—taps it easily home.

The deck leaps up and bangs against the soles of his shoes, throwing him off balance. Crewmen sag under the sudden surge of weight and somewhere a stylus clatters loudly on the deck. Goldberg sinks—*oof!*—into his couch. He sits there despairing, covering his eyes with one freckled hand.

At the back of the bridge, Willis levers himself awkwardly out of his couch and silently hands a bill to Reynolds, who takes it, folds it once, and stuffs it smugly into a pocket of his tunic.

At his console, Rogers secures the dimmer switch, locks it into position, and clips a plastic cover carefully across it. That, too, he locks into place. Eagerly, he turns to Goldberg. "Well?"

Goldberg, hand still across his eyes, inhales deeply. Slowly he drops his hand and exhales with a tired sound. "Well . . . ," he admits finally, "it could have been better."

"Oh," says Rogers.

Silently, the redhead rolls his eyes upwards in despair. How did a wobblehead like this ever get through training? He spins around in the chair to look at Korie. He shrugs helplessly at the first officer; *I did the best I could, sir.*

Korie nods slightly, an acknowledgment.

Shaking his freckled head, he starts to pry himself out of the couch—

"Hey—," says Rogers. He stoops to the deck, comes up with a stylus. "Wolfe left his pencil here. . . ."

Goldberg pauses. "So?"

"Well, I mean, what should I do with it?"

"You really want me to tell you?" But the meaning is lost on the other; Rogers looks at him blankly. "I don't care. Give it back to him." He steps past the man and down into the pit.

As he crosses to the back of it, Korie nods to him, "Thanks, Ben."

"Don't mention it, sir . . . ever." Still shaking his head, he returns to his own post.

Korie leans back in his couch. It is on the right side and to the rear of the Command and Control Seat and can function as an auxiliary control in time of battle. Now, however, almost all of its functions are inactive. Idly, Korie begins punching a logistics problem into the ship's computer.

On the screen ahead, the four space-suited figures continue to reweld the metal plates back to the hull of the ship.

In the seat, Brandt notes this, swivels right to face his

astrogator. "Say, Mr. Barak, where's that interception course you promised me?"

The heavy-boned man spins in his chair to face the captain. "It's ready any time you are, sir."

"All right. Put it on the big screen; convince me that we can catch him."

Barak nods, gestures to Jonesy. The maintenance operation disappears from the forward wall and is replaced by a glowing grid. In the upper left-hand corner appears a small circular patch of haze with a larger white circle around it.

Barak moves up to stand by the side of Brandt's chair. "Now, that's our bogie—that haze is the locus of all possible points where he could be by the time we get there. It grows every second to allow for drift, his maximum probable inherent velocity."

"How big is that area?" Brandt asks.

Barak frowns thoughtfully. "Pretty big . . ."

"How big is *pretty big* . . . ?"

"Um . . ." He coughs into his fist, scratches abstractedly at his neck. "About sixteen and a half light hours."

"What's the white circle around it?"

"That's his sphere of influence. It's about forty-eight light hours in diameter. Actually, his sphere is only thirty-two, but we have to allow that extra sixteen because we're not sure of his position. He might be *anywhere* in that hazy area by the time we got there.

"Figure he can scan any ship within that circle before it can get to him—outside of it, he can only pick up the stress-field disturbance if the ship's speed is above a certain factor in relation to its distance to him. The dividing line occurs where our velocity quotient, a variable, sinks below our mass quotient, a constant."

Brandt gestures impatiently. "Right, right. Go on."

Barak gestures to Jonesy. A point of white appears in the opposite corner of the screen, on the lower right. "That's us," says Barak. "Now almost fifty-six light days away."

Jonesy touches another button; a long slow curve arches out diagonally from the lower point of light and rises toward the haze in the upper left corner. It passes close to the bogie's sphere of influence—almost touching that circle—then hooks sharply back into it. "And that's the course you asked for," adds Barak.

Brandt notes the wording of the astrogator's last sentence. Apparently, Barak is still unhappy with the idea of sneaking up on the bogie.

"Now, what you want to do," Barak continues, "is to approach him at the maximum possible speed while still remaining below the minimum speed at which he can detect us."

Nodding slowly, "Right, right."

"Now, we're pretty sure that that fellow is in the destroyer class, so he can't have any more power for his stress-field antennae than we do. I figure a detection factor of four over six should be safe—meaning that for every four light days distance between us, we can have six lights maximum speed. That should keep him from picking up our warp and as we come in closer we'll lower our speed proportionally. Initially velocity will be 82.5 lights and we'll cut that by one and a half lights for each light day we travel."

"All right. Now, what happens when we get to his sphere of influence?"

"It gets tricky there. First of all, our speed will be down to about one light—and the warp fields get hard to handle at speeds that low; the control is fuzzy. We'll have to generate a subwarp just to maintain.

"When we hit the point of closest approach—where our course grazes the circle—that's where we'll hook back into it. We'll boost our speed to maximum and come in hard on the center."

"Assuming he's in the center of that hazy area," rumbles Brandt, "how long will it take to close with him?"

"Um . . ." Barak's broad face creass into a frown. He pulls a hand-terminal from his tunic pocket and punches quickly at its buttons. "Eight minutes, twenty seconds—more or less. That's an approximate answer; it could be a few seconds either way."

Brandt waves it off. "And what if he's *not* in the center of that area? What if he's moved off to one side, or out of it altogether—how long will it take to locate him?"

"Uh—we'll have him right away—we'll probably get a fix on him on the way in, and we can come to an intercept course almost immediately."

"I'm talking about a search pattern," says Brandt. "How long will that take?"

Barak shakes his head. "I don't understand. We should still have him right away. Our scanning range is as good as his, and he'll be in that hazy area. I can't see why we shouldn't—"

"Mr. Barak," Brandt cuts him off. "*Why* does he have to be in that hazy area . . . ?"

"Uh—he won't have time to go anywhere else."

"Mr. Barak, *how long* will it take us to get there?"

Now the astrogator is confused. "To get where—you mean into his sphere of influence?"

"I mean to get *there* from *here*."

"Thirty-four hours."

"Uh huh," says Brandt. "Thirty-four hours. A lot can happen in thirty-four hours, Al. Probably he'll still be within that sixteen-and-a-half-hour radius you drew, but there's also the chance he might not be. By then he might be somewhere else entirely."

"It's not possible for him to be outside that radius, even allowing for error. We figured the speed of his drift and—"

"I'm not talking about inherent velocity! I'm talking about the fact that he'll probably try to *sneak away*—and if he does try that, I want to know how much longer it will take to find him."

"Oh," says Barak. He looks down, pretends to fumble with his hand-terminal. "Well . . . we'll be scanning for him all the way in, so we can distort the standard search pattern to allow for that. . . ."

Korie speaks up. "The primary search pattern will take forty-three minutes. The secondary search pattern will be one hundred eleven minutes, and the tertiary, six hours and twenty-seven minutes."

Both men turn to look at him, Brandt swivelling nearly 180 degrees in his chair. Barak scowls. Korie has been standing behind the Command and Control Seat, casually leaning against the high-banked autolog console. Now, in response to their questioning looks, he says, "I asked the computer. I wanted to know myself how long it would take to make the kill."

Brandt starts to relax—perhaps one of his officers is on the ball after all. He lets his big frame sink back into the padded chair. "How big an area does that last pattern cover, Mr. Korie?"

"Five light days maximum. I doubt that he'll be farther out than that."

"Why?"

"Uh, well—if he tries to hide himself any farther out, he'll have to go faster to get there—we'll see his warp—"

Brandt shakes his head, cuts him off with a sharp gesture. "You disappoint me, Mr. Korie. For a moment there, I thought you had it, but you're only making the same mistake Mr. Barak made: you're both assuming that he's going to sit out there waiting for us to sneak up on him. Well, he's not. He's going to get the hell out of there as soon as he can."

The captain rises out of his chair, stabbing at the air with a thick hand. "As soon as he gets his blown system repaired, he's going to *move*."

"If he does, we'll see his warp—"

"That's only if his speed is high enough and we're within range. Aren't I getting through to either of you? *that ship out there is trying to get away from us*. That's what he was doing when he dropped out of warp and that's what he's going to continue doing when he gets his engines fixed."

He pauses to swallow, continues in a slightly calmer tone, "Right now, we're fifty-five light days away. We don't know where he is—we don't know that he's still out there even now—maybe he isn't. Maybe he's already fixed his warp and moved off. If he kept his speed below eighty lights, we'd never know it. And remember, the distance is *his* advantage. The farther away he gets, the faster he can go without our seeing him." He pauses, looks at the two of them, almost as if daring them to speak. "Maybe he hasn't sneaked off yet, but he probably will do so in the next day and a half."

Korie says nothing, his pale blue eyes are expressionless. But Barak shakes his dark head thoughtfully. "I see your point, Captain, but it just wouldn't make sense for him to sneak away. He's got too good a lead on us already—why bother with subterfuge?"

"Al, you're a good astrogator, but you'll never be much of a general. You're still thinking in terms of right now—if he could effect immediate repairs, of course it wouldn't make sense for him to sneak away. But if he's stuck there for, say, ten or twelve hours, it's his only alternative."

Brandt turns to his first officer. "And you, Mr. Korie, I'm surprised at you—the scent of blood seems to have shortened your logic circuits. If the captain of that bogie is any kind of a captain at all, he's playing our side of the game too. While we're sitting here arguing about how to catch him, he's sitting there trying to outguess us. It won't take him long to figure out that our only chance is to try to sneak up on him. That'll leave him two choices. Either he can sneak off, or he can try to sneak up on us. . . ."

This time, Korie shakes his head. "Uh uh. His warp is no bigger than ours—that means destroyer-class ship, like us. Our destroyers are better armed and he knows it."

Brandt smiles. "Right. So, he's left with only the first alternative. At least, that's my guess. The captain of that ship has to be a fairly intelligent man. He'll assess the situation, size up his chances, and decide that his best course of action is to move off without being seen. It seems very likely to me that he'll be successful."

"Sir?"

Brandt looks at Korie. "Well, look at it—he's got a fifty-six light day lead on us. Whether we come in at top speed or whether we sneak in, he's going to have plenty of time to outmaneuver us. It all hinges on how soon he gets his engines fixed." He gestures at the diagram on the screen. "Like it or not, this thing is only a long shot. I doubt very much that it can be pulled off. It could turn out to be a very expensive waste of time and fuel."

"But that's a chance we have to take," insists Korie.

"Is it?" Brandt looks at him.

"We've come too far with this thing to go home empty-handed."

Brandt says nothing. Korie's narrow features are grim. Barak speaks, gently reminding the captain, "You did suggest this course of action, sir. . . ."

Brandt nods slowly, silently. His brooding gray eyes seem to focus on a point beyond the walls of the bridge. His wide mouth works with unspoken thoughts. Finally, he rasps, "All right. We'll go after him. Let's see if he's there or not."

Korie and Barak exchange a quick triumphant glance. Barak starts to step down to his console—

"Wait a minute, Al. One more thing. If he is there, he'll have eight and a third minutes to see us coming. If he can't run, he'll have to fight. That's still too much warning. He could have cross hairs on us all the way in."

"Well, I wouldn't worry about that too much, sir. We'll be scanning for him at the same time. As soon as I get a good fix, I'll set up a ten-second scramble pattern for when we unwarp."

"Good."

The big screen clears to show the four space-suited men just dropping down into the bright open hatch of the airlock. The repair operation has been completed. "All right," says Brandt. "Let's go. Set it up on the boards."

"Aye, aye, sir." Barak turns to his console, clears the monitor, begins snapping out orders. The crew of the bridge slips easily into the familiar security of the pre-warp routine. Voices crackle across the intercom:

"Request inherent velocity vector."

"Victor zero mark zero. Standard heading."

"Right, thank you. Warp control, polarity of secondaries, zero degrees—ninety degrees—one hundred eighty degrees."

"Setting polarity; zero degrees—ninety degrees—one hundred eighty degrees."

"Initial warp factor, 82.5."

"Initial warp factor, 82.5."

"Warp control, reset polarities."

"Stand by."

"Standing."

"Right. Ready to reset."

"On these coordinates: thirty-six degrees—one hundred forty-four degrees—ninety degrees."

"Christ! We're going in sideways."

"Confirm, please."

"May I have a repeat?"

"Thirty-six degrees—one hundred forty-four degrees—ninety degrees."

"Thank you. Confirmation; thirty-six degrees—one hundred forty-four degrees—ninety degrees."

"Right."

"Hey, what's Black Al up to?"

"Setting up a scramble. He wants to bounce off at an angle at unwarp."

"Gravity control, watch your power."

"Uh, yes, sir. Right."

"Prepare to warp in . . . what was that again?"

"Seven minutes. First optimum peak in seven minutes and fifteen seconds."

"Can I have a mark at seven?"

"Stand by."

"Standing."

"All right . . . three, two, one—*mark*."

"Got it. Thanks."

"Setting warp factor; 82.5."

"Eighty-two point five? Is that correct?"

"Eighty-two point five is correct."

"Are you sure? That'll take us sixteen hours to intercept."

"Thirty-three point seven. We're dropping speed as we go in."

"What the hell—?"

"Get back to procedure, please. Power consumption inputs?"

"Stand by."

"Standing. Ready for data."

Brandt drops the headphone on which he has been listening. The procedure may sound sloppy, but it is sure.

The ship will warp when it is supposed to and the warp will move in the direction it is supposed to.

"Ready to warp, sir."

Brandt nods. "Warp at will."

The pilot speaks to a mike. "Engine room, please confirm, frequency modules two, four, and six on phase reflex nine zero. Angle of adjustment—0.00012 . . ."

"Confirming."

"Thank you," says the officer and adds cheerfully, "and by the way, don't forget to compensate."

"Right," comes the laconic reply. "And up yours."

A warning bell chimes. Around the horseshoe, all secondary functions begin to shut down. Every bit of power available must be shunted into the generators for the initial strain of expanding the warp fields. The lights fade to a dark gloom; a speaker crackles, "Prepare to warp. Mark sixty seconds."

Brandt decides not to wait. He levers himself out of his chair. "Mr. Korie."

The first officer looks back. "Sir?"

"Take the helm."

"Yes, sir." Korie steps easily, familiarly, into the seat.

"I'll be in my cabin."

"Right, sir."

Brandt steps to the rear of the bridge and out. The door slides shut behind him. The corridor is narrow and cramped. It has a stale smell and the plastic panels of the walls are stained with the passage of years.

As he moves along it there is a warning bell, followed by an almost unfelt flicker of free fall. Brandt steadies himself between the walls, a hand on each one, then moves on as the lights come back to normal. The ship has enfolded itself into warp, a procedure that would be routine if it were not so complex.

Brandt pauses only once, to turn sideways and allow another man to move down the narrow passage. The crewman mumbles a quick but startled acknowledgment of the captain's presence, then hurries on.

The corridor runs the length of the ship; the captain's cabin is one-third of the way back. Brushing at the door, Brandt steps into it.

Traditionally, the captain's cabin is the largest on the ship, but even that is none too large on a destroyer-class starcruiser. The ship is built for only fifty-three men and space is at a premium. Even so, the cabin is roomy—twelve feet by sixteen—and it reflects the captain's taste for luxury.

For instance, there is a real bed instead of a sleeping web; of course, it is set into the wall where a cabinet should have been, but it is still a real bed with mattress and linen. The floor is covered with crisp red and gold foam—its incongruity betrays the recentness of its addition—and set against one wall is the captain's proudest possession: a table and two chairs.

Admittedly, the furniture is a shameful waste of space, but the pieces are of true Terran mahogany and were a gift from the Brazilian ambassador. After keeping them for a suitable length of time, Brandt found that he no longer wished to be rid of them. The cramped feeling that they had generated in his cabin at first has since worn off, and now he rather fancies the touch of elegance that they give his otherwise meager quarters.

Opposite the table, on the other wall, is a large painting—a silvery battle cruiser orbits below a swollen red globe. At other times, it is a viewscreen; but for now it remains an image of his first command.

On the shelf below is a typer. A single sheet of stiff gray paper sits in the machine. Abruptly Brandt remembers what it is. He steps over the typer and pulls the letter from it:

FROM: Georj Brandt
           Captain, U.S.S. *Roger Burlingame*
TO: Vice Admiral Joseph Harshlie
           United Systems Command
SUBJECT: Request for transfer

Admiral Harshlie,
    Again, I would like to repeat my request for a transfer to a less active command. As I have stated previously, I feel that my services could be more valuable in a position closer to home.

While I can understand the position you are in politically, I would like to point out that

Brandt lays the unfinished letter aside. Next to the typer are two other letters; the paragraphs are only blocks of familiar phrases:

FROM: Joseph Harshlie
          Vice Admiral, United Systems Command
TO: Captain Georj Brandt
          U.S.S. *Roger Burlingame*
SUBJECT: Request for transfer

Captain Brandt,

Much as I would like to honor your latest request for transfer, I regret to inform you that it is still impossible at this time. The situation as I outlined it to you in my last communication still has not changed appreciably, nor do I foresee any change in it for some time to come.

When a request such as yours again becomes practical, I will immediately let you know. Thank you for your continued interest and for communicating with us on this matter.

Cordially,
JOSEPH HARSHLIE,
Vice Admiral

And then the other letter:

Dear Georj,

You know there isn't a thing in the world I wouldn't do for you if I could. You know that. Certainly there is nothing more I would like than to be able to grant your request.

But, Georj, take my word for it—it is impossible. There are just too many starship commanders who have grown weary of the war, men who are every bit as qualified as yourself.

Many of them—too many—are long overdue even for Rest and Recovery. You at least are lucky enough to have both a ship and a crew in reasonably good condition. (I know of men who would gladly trade places with you.)

You are not the only one who has grown weary of this war. We have all grown tired of it. God, how I wish I could tell you what it is like to have a casualty report waiting on your desk for you every morning. (And the war doesn't stop on weekends either. Monday's list is always the worst.)

Other men get tired too, Georj, but if I were to give a transfer to every man who got a little tired, I would have a hundred empty ships on the docks tomorrow. I don't have to tell you we can't afford that.

I can't order you to stop making these requests, but as a personal friend I can advise you that you are only wasting your time. While the *Burlingame*'s record has never been substandard, neither has it ever been outstanding. There is nothing in your record to warrant a transfer.

In your present assignment, at least, we can depend on you to keep your ship aloft—and in that capacity, you cannot easily be replaced. (You yourself have said that your first officer is still not ready for a command of his own. Personally, I don't agree; but if you say he still needs more experience, I'll have to take your word for it.)

Once more, I ask you to please stop sending in these requests. You know as well as I that in your case a transfer would necessitate a promotion. While I (personally) would like to approve such a request, this office is not in a position to be able to do so. Your requests are creating no goodwill for you among the admiralty; they are most painful for me to read and even more painful to have to submit to a sure and certain negative answer. Georj, the board is hostile to these requests; please let this be the last.

I know it is hard for you, but think how
hard it is for me. My burden is already heavy.
Please don't make it any heavier.

With regrets

Joe

Abruptly, Brandt crumples the letters and shoves
them into the disposal incinerator reserved for the burn-
ing of confidential documents.

Five

Morality and practicality should be congruent. If they're not, then there's something wrong with either one or the other.

SOLOMON SHORT

Korie knocks gently on the captain's door. After a minute, he knocks again. A pause, then a muffled voice asks, "Who is it?"

"Korie, sir."

"Just a minute." Another pause, then the door slides open.

Inside, Brandt is just buttoning the top button of his tunic. His iron-gray hair is mussed; he brushes a hand stiffly through it. "Yes, what is it?" He sits down on one of his precious wooden chairs. He does not offer his first officer a seat.

The captain's cabin has a stale smell. Somewhat uneasily, Korie begins, "Sir, I was wondering what we were going to do about Wolfe."

"Wolfe?" A slight frown accompanies this echo.

"The crewman who was negligent on the bridge."

"Oh, yes. Him. Mmm . . ." Brandt's voice trails off; he focuses thoughtfully on the dark mahogany surface of the table. Idly, he brushes at a speck of dirt. "What would you suggest, Mr. Korie?"

Korie hesitates. (All right, if you won't say it, I will.) "Bust him." After an almost imperceptible beat, he adds, "Sir."

Still not looking at him, Brandt shakes his head. "Uh uh. I don't see it."

"Sir—?"

"It's not necessary, Mr. Korie." He glances up. "Just confine him to quarters for a week and dock his pay for the time off duty."

"Sir!" Korie is outraged. "Negligence is an offense requiring court-martial. And—it would demonstrate to the crew that we mean business."

"I'm familiar with the regulations," Brandt sighs. He wipes at his nose. "But in this case, we might find it very difficult to prove."

Korie allows himself the luxury of an oath—a single sharp syllable.

The captain raises a shaggy eyebrow. "Mr. Korie!" he says in mock horror. "Such language from an officer and gentleman?"

Korie ignores the jibe. "It's pretty obvious, sir, that Wolfe was negligent in not showing Rogers the complete setup on the G-control board."

"Can you prove it?"

"Of course—"

"If I were Wolfe's counsel," the captain puts in, "I'd plead that it was Wolfe's every intention to complete Rogers' training at a more opportune time in the immediate future."

"That's an awfully thin thread to hang a case on."

"Strong enough," Brandt counters. "After all, he doesn't have to prove it. But we—as prosecutors—would have to disprove it.

"Besides, Mr. Korie—and you'd better learn this now if you ever hope to have a ship of your own—convening a court is a headache. And the resultant upheaval in morale is an even bigger one." He cuts off the other's objection with a brief gesture and adds thoughtfully, once more staring into the table top, "So, rather than reach for a possibly untenable position, this gives us instead an opportunity to show that we are both just and merciful. The man saves face and we save ourselves one competent crewman."

"Competent?" Korie snorts.

"Relatively speaking," Brandt concedes. "I'm sure I don't have to tell you how bad the replacement situation is. We're at war. Everything has to be stretched a little, even regulations."

"Yes, but—"

"Ah, there's always the 'yes, but—' Isn't there, Mr. Korie?" A hint of a smile starts to flicker across the captain's face, but it dies before it has a chance to be realized. "Give him a chance, give him a chance. If he's smart enough to take it, we all benefit. And if not—if he turns out to be as big a wobblehead as you seem to feel ... well, then we'll only be giving him enough rope to hang himself."

"Then, if we do have to court-martial him," says Korie, "we'll have two incidents instead of one. . . ."

"I hope not," says Brandt. "Let's wait and see. . . ." Abruptly, he looks up, seems to notice Korie again. "You'd do better to concentrate on your—uh, *master plan*—to have the ship ready for battle. After all, that bogie is our main concern."

Korie straightens. "Yes, sir, but this would be a useful part of the psychonomic gestalt."

Brandt waves away the objection. He changes the subject. Psychonomy discomfits him. He is a captain of the old school. "Those battle drills you were running— how long has it been since you've held one?"

"Too long."

"Hmmm," Brandt says. "All right, I suppose you might begin a new series of them." He sighs. "I suppose this is as good a time as any—in fact, I can't think of a more appropriate one. Go ahead, Mr. Korie. Amuse yourself."

"Yes, sir. Any suggestions on what kind or how many?"

Brandt shakes his head. "No. Use your own discretion. I trust you."

"Yes, sir." He turns to go.

"Oh, and Korie—"

"Sir?"

"Remember what I told you before about overdoing it. Don't push them too hard."

"Yes, sir."

"All right, you can go."

For a long time, Korie stands in the corridor outside the captain's cabin, exploring a crevice in his mouth with his tongue, and the possible course of action as well.

There is nothing he can do about Wolfe at the moment. However, there will undoubtedly be opportunities in the future to take care of the matter. (Wolfe is too big a fool to disappoint me. All I have to do is wait.) It's only a matter of time—

Abruptly, he makes a decision. He turns on his heel and heads aft. Through the galley, bright, deserted, smelling of cleanser and coffee. Through the lounge, not as bright, its plastic furniture folded into the walls, leaving only an empty, carpeted room. Through the auxiliary control decks, dark and silent.

He comes to a ladder suspended in a no-gravity tube and downs it hand over hand. He'd rather go through the torpedo storage decks than the crew's quarters. Dull plastoid casings line the walls, cylinders secure in narrow racks. His steps are loud on the plastic deck.

The engine room is large and filled with the stasis engines. Korie finds himself on a sudden catwalk halfway up one wall. Nylon webs are strung throughout the room and across the generators; the webs are for easy access to the machines, but nobody is on them now. The stasis generators are six cone-shaped monsters set in a spherical framework; each cone points inward to the center and to another cone pointing back at it from the opposite side. Each pair of cones is mounted at right angles to the others. The north and south poles of the framework and every ninety degrees of its equator are marked by generator mountings. Great cables are strung from them.

This first spherical framework is itself set within a second. It is mounted on gimbals and can rotate into any desired position in relation to the rest of the ship. The direction of the warp field is independent of the direction of the rest of the ship. The whole unit nearly fills the engine room.

Korie glances back and forth. There are men on the other side of the room, but he can't see them past the blue haze of the generators, nor hear them over the hum. He lowers himself down another ladder, finds a bored-looking technician at a monitor console. "Where's Leen?" he demands.

"Gymnasium," grunts the other. "He's filling it."

Korie continues his journey aft. He gives wide berth to the stasis frames and leaves the engine room through the rear.

Now he is in "goblin country," the dark, dirty aft part of the ship. There is another section of crew's quarters here, but it is on the next deck up; he will not have to pass through it. This deck contains the access and maintenance equipment for the two life-shuttles on the deck below. There is also a well-equipped machine shop, complete with templates and synthesizers for hyperstate units.

Past it is a narrow chamber which functions as an observatory; but its sensory equipment has been locked away in its mountings. The chamber has a dual function—now it is being converted into the vestibule for the gymnasium.

Korie pulls himself into the cramped room, but only halfway; almost immediately he backs out to give the three men working inside more room. It is doubtful that they have even noticed him. Only Leen grunts, and that is a less than cordial acknowledgment of his existence. The chief turns his attention back to the job at hand.

The "gymnasium" is a balloon-like chamber. When deflated, it takes up no more than a few cubic feet; when inflated at the stern of the ship, it becomes a large, almost spherical, free-fall environment. Its storage closet becomes an alcove leading into it, but access to that is still through the observatory.

Air is slowly being pumped into the plastic bubble; one of the men is watching carefully for any sudden pressure drops. The gymnasium is supposed to be untearable, but there have been exceptions. An exterior webbing holds the mylar balloon firm. It is released slowly, only a bit at a time, preventing a too sudden filling. The alcove to the gym will not be opened to the ship until the last pressure check is made, but their concern is about possibly ripping or weakening the balloon by over-hastiness.

"Boy, I'll be glad when we get this mother up."

"Me too. One more watch on battle alert and I would have been ready for the rubber room. Watch it. It's pulling too hard on the bottom."

"I got it."

Slowly, majestically, the chamber puffs out, becomes a sphere. They can see into it through the glass door of the alcove. On the monitor board, all the lights stay green. All the dials remain at full. "It's at one-fourth pressure," says the man. "No leaks."

"No leaks *yet,*" corrects Leen. "Watch it for five minutes. If the pressure holds, bring it up to full, then drop a dozen Ping-Pong balls into it. If they don't cluster together within a half hour, you can open up for the crew. He turns to the door, "And what brings you down here, Mr. Korie?"

Korie steps inside, startling the two crewmen; they hadn't realized the first officer was watching. "Business," he says. "The captain wants me to set up another series of drills."

Leen's eyes are wary. "What kind of drills?"

"Battle alerts. Things like that."

The chief engineer nods slowly. "I'll set up the boards for you. Who're you going to be working on?"

Korie pauses for effect, he studies the other, "I was thinking that the engine room has been a little too loose lately."

Leen is a short man with a fatherly manner, but under the eyes of the first officer he begins to tighten up. He purses his lips, almost bites them. "Mr. Korie, my men have been doing the best they can—"

"It hasn't been good enough."

"I'll talk to them."

"*We'll drill them.* I'll tell you when they're doing their best."

"Yes, sir." Leen's words are clipped.

"I'd like to begin at—" Korie looks at his watch. "—six hundred hours."

"Sir—"

"Yes?"

"That's too soon. The men won't be ready—"

"But I will. The enemy doesn't schedule appointments, Chief. Neither do I. That's plenty of time." He turns to go. "They'll be ready." Then he ducks out through the door.

As he strides away from the observatory, a voice says, "That bastard! I'd like to—"

And another voice answers, "Who wouldn't?"

Korie scowls; he is tempted to go back and discipline the men, but he forces himself to continue on instead. *Let the damn fools work it out now. After the drill, we'll see if they need discipline.*

He retraces his steps forward, taking a side corridor instead of passing through the engine room. This time, the auxiliary control decks are lit as he passes through them. Two technicians are warming up the consoles.

In the lounge, some of the furniture has been unfolded, but there is a tenseness about the few men there. They stiffen momentarily as he strides through, but he ignores them.

The galley is the busiest. "Hey, Cookie, hurry up, huh?" A line of men waits impatiently to be served. None of them look happy, even though this is their first real break in days. Korie glances at his watch; this is a new shift coming up; these men will be the first to drill. Probably they already know about it. In just the time it has taken him to come forward, Leen could have alerted the entire crew.

He follows three of the men forward to the bridge; they will be relieving three of their shipmates. He steps through after them and down into the pit. He taps the officer there out of the Command and Control Seat and settles himself into it. (I'll only watch for a little while.)

On the horseshoe, Goldberg, Rogers, and one other man have just been relieved. Rogers has a stoop-shouldered gait and a downcast expression. As he walks, he watches the heels of the man in front of him. Just before exiting, he looks back at Korie—and is surprised to find the first officer studying him intently. Flustered, he hurries off the bridge. "Why does he look at me like that?"

"Huh?" asks Goldberg in front of him.

"Nothing," says Rogers, following. He leaves the other two at the galley and keeps heading aft, toward his bunk.

This particular section of quarters is a narrow room with bunks cramped up against each wall in layers of three. There are four stacks of three bunks each, twelve in all; they are hard plastic frameworks strung with wide nylon webbing.

At the end of the room is a double bank of lockers and a lavatory. There is also a sonovac; the only real shower on the ship is forward—for easier access by the captain.

Only two other men are in the room; both are asleep. Except for the lavatory, the crew's quarters are kept in perpetual semidarkness. Night and day have no meaning on a spaceship; they are only arbitrary designations of time and are discarded on all but passenger vessels. A cruiser operates on a twenty-four-hour clock, and it is up to the individual to schedule his eating and sleeping around his watch periods.

The room is hot and has a stale, sweaty smell. Taking care not to disturb the others, Rogers starts peeling off his clothes. His tunic is still clean and he hangs it carefully in his locker. His shorts he tosses into the laundry chute; his sock-skins go into the locker. Wearing only briefs, he closes the plastic door of the locker and pads back to the bunks. He starts to pull himself into one of the narrow webbed frames, then remembers something. He pads back to the locker, opens it, reaches in, and fumbles in his tunic pocket. He pulls out a tiny bottle of capsules, pops one into his mouth, and swallows it dry. As he returns the pills to his tunic pocket, something clatters to the floor. A silver stylus. Wolfe's.

He looks at it for a long moment, then picks it up. He starts to lay in on a shelf in the locker, then changes his mind. He pulls out a pair of shorts and a loose-fitting T-shirt and starts getting dressed again.

Six

Nothing exceeds like excess

SOLOMON SHORT

Wolfe stares at the bottom of the bunk above him. The webbing is only a few inches away from his face. It is so close he has trouble focusing on it clearly. He is wearing only shorts. His tunic and sock-skins lie in a crumpled heap at the bottom of his locker.

"Wolfe?" a voice asks, breaking into his thoughts.

"Huh?" Startled, Wolfe turns sideways—a bit too fast, he bumps his shoulder on the hard frame above. "What do you want?" Then he see who it is. Rogers. "Shit! What the hell—" He pushes at the webbed framework of the bunk above him, folds it flat against the wall, then sits up on his own bed to face the other.

"Uh, I came to apologize," says Rogers. "I didn't mean to—"

"Screw if you didn't mean to!" Mimicking the other's high-pitched voice, he echoes, " 'Uh, sir—Wolfe—I mean *Crewman* Wolfe was supposed to show me this board.' " In his own voice now, "You couldn't have torpedoed me worse if you had tried."

"It was an accident. It just slipped out that way. I didn't mean to get you in trouble. I didn't mean—"

"Yeah, that's right. You couldn't be smart enough to do it on purpose. Well, what do you want from me now? You want to make sure I'm staying in my quarters?"

"No. I—I—you left this on the bridge." He fumbles in the pocket of his shorts, produces the silver stylus.

Wolfe looks at it, looks at Rogers incredulously. "You came down here just to return that! Shit! You've got to be the stupidest dumb wobblehead—"

Rogers stiffens somewhat. "If I'm so stupid, how come you're the one confined to quarters?" He is still holding the pen.

Wolfe reacts as if playing to an unseen audience. He is breathing heavily and he looks around to see if anyone else has heard Rogers' last incredible statement—he wants to share his astonishment. There are several other men in the bunkroom, but they are trying to appear nonchalant. Wolfe looks to Rogers again. "I'm confined *because* of your stupidity, you dumb shit!" he explodes. "Don't you know enough to cover for a fellow crewman?"

"I've never had a '*fellow crewman*'! I've been on this ship four months and I'm still waiting for someone to say something to me besides 'you dumb shit'!"

"Well, you are a dumb shit! Face it, Rogers! You were born a dumb shit and you're going to die a dumb shit!"

Rogers' face is red, his body trembling. "At least, *I'm* not confined to quarters—!!"

"Aw, go to hell. Get out of here, will you? I don't want to look at you anymore." Wolfe lies back down on his bunk.

"No!" says Rogers in his loudest voice yet. "I came down here to tell you something and I'm not leaving until I say it. Nobody on this ship ever speaks to me or listens to me or anything—well, dammit, I'm tired of being treated like an idiot child! I have feelings too—"

"Will you get out of here—you're boring me."

"Not until I finish!"

Wolfe puts his hands over his ears. "Okay, you can talk all you want, but I don't have to listen." He fixes his gaze on the ceiling.

Rogers starts screaming at him. "If you want to be able to depend on me, you've got to start treating me like someone you can depend on! You've got to start being nice to me!"

Wolfe just smiles at the younger man. Smugly.

"I didn't get you in trouble. You did it yourself! You can't blame me! Wolfe! Are you listening, Wolfe? It's your own fault you're down here—but if you want me to help you, you've got to start being nice to me! Wolfe!"

Wolfe continues to smile, continues to pretend he can't hear him; his face is a leering grin. Rogers lunges at him, trying to pull Wolfe's hand away from his ears. "You listen to me, now! Just once, you're going to listen to what *I* have to say!"

Wolfe's silence is shattered—"Get off of me, you little shit head!"—he pushes the other back away from him. Rogers comes right back, flailing wildly. Again Wolfe pushes him away, then rolls off his bunk to face him squarely.

Rogers stops, looks at him. "Wolfe, listen—"

But Wolfe is angry and out of control—he steps into the other, sinking his fist into Rogers' soft belly. As the younger man doubles over, Wolfe kicks upward with his knee, at the same time pushing Rogers' face into his rising leg. Rogers staggers back, Wolfe punches hard at his head, slamming him suddenly against the opposite row of bunks. Rogers hangs on the plastic frames for a second, then slips to the floor, all the while making gasping sounds in his throat. He clutches his stomach in agony; his face is spattered with blood, and he curls into a writhing foetal position.

Wolfe stands over him, breathing heavily. Two or three other men in the bunkroom move up to stop him, but he's already through. The fight is over.

"Looks like you did a job on him, all right," mutters one, a husky engineer. Rogers is groaning on the floor, rocking back and forth in pain. He coughs once or twice.

"You really had to do that, didn't you, Wolfe?" asks another.

"Aaah!" Wolfe waves them off.

"How're you going to explain this? You know Rogers—he's going to go straight to that asshole Korie."

"No, he won't." Wolfe steps over to the fallen crewman, puts his hands on the other's shoulders. "You're not going to say anything—are you, Rogers?"

Dazed, Rogers shakes his head.

"There, you see. The dumb shit is learning already."
Wolfe goes back to his bunk, throws himself into it.

"Hey, Wolfe," says the big engineer. "You forgot
this."

"Huh?"

The other throws something small and glittery at
him. Wolfe snatches it out of the air. It is his stylus. He
starts to scowl in annoyance, lets it become a grin instead.
"Yeah," he says. He drops the pen onto a shelf next to his
bunk.

Meanwhile, the engineer, Erlich, is leaning over
Wolfe's victim. "Hey, Rogers, you all right?"

The youngster is still too dazed to be coherent. He
groans.

The man watches him for a moment, becoming more
and more concerned. He kneels by the other. "Come on,
can you get up? You can't stay here."

In reply, Rogers starts coughing. He is bleeding pro-
fusely from his nose. Erlich exchanges a glance with the
other crewmen. "Hey, Mackie, give me a hand—let's take
him down to sick bay."

"Sick bay! Are you crazy?" cries Wolfe, sitting up.
"You can't do that!"

"Shut up, Wolfe! Haven't you done enough?"

"Just take him to his bunk—he'll be all right."

"You hope!" says Erlich. "And what if he isn't—
what're you going to say then?"

"What're you going to say to the doc when he asks
how Rogers got creamed?"

"Nothing—and he won't ask. He's on our side."

"Shit if he is," Wolfe snaps.

The others ignore him. Erlich starts maneuvering
Rogers to his feet. "Attaboy, champ. Just hang onto me
now. Mackie, get his other arm." Struggling awkwardly
in the cramped bunkroom, the two men heft the bleeding
Rogers between them. "Come on. Mackie—"

"Yeah, yeah—the kid's not gonna die." To Rogers:
"Pick up your feet, dummy. You're not completely help-
less."

"Lay off him."

"Yeah, yeah."

They move down the narrow corridor toward the sick bay, leaving a white-faced Wolfe staring after them. The other men in the bunkroom turn back to their own business, pointedly ignoring him.

Holding the still-dazed Rogers between them, Erlich and Mackie continue forward. They pause once to let another crewman—Jonesy—pass them. He has to turn sideways to do so. As he comes abreast of Rogers, he says, "Jeez! What happened to him?"

"He ran into a bulkhead," answers Mackie.

"He must have had help."

"He had a running head start."

"*Suure,* he did. . . ."

"Move on, will you," Erlich growls.

Jonesy shrugs and disappears down the corridor.

They move on. "Well, now it's going to be all over the ship. Jonesy couldn't keep his mouth shut if he was hoarding diamonds in it."

"It's not going to be much of a secret anyway," Erlich snorts. "If Wolfe doesn't start talking about it, *this* idiot will." He indicates Rogers.

"Yeah, well—one look at his face and it won't be hard to tell. Wait till Korie finds out—"

"I can wait," says the other. "Here's the sick bay."

Seven

Even Murphy's Law doesn't work all *the time.*
SOLOMON SHORT

At precisely six hundred hours, First Officer Jonathan Korie steps into the engine room. "Mr. Leen?" His voice is firm, crisp.

"Sir!" Chief Leen snaps to attention. "The engine room is ready for inspection and drill."

Korie nods slowly, glances around the room with an almost forced casualness. At every monitor console, two men stand at ready attention; their uniforms are shining clean. Above, wearing bright-colored protective suits, the "monkey crew" hangs ready in the nets with an easy grace. Korie looks at Leen. "See, I told you they'd be ready."

Leen's mouth tightens, but he says only, "Yes, sir."

Abruptly, Korie's manner changes; his casualness is replaced by a brisk military air—his stance, his attitude, the set of his jaw, all become more direct, more business-like. "All right, let's get on with it." He steps over to one of the consoles and taps its technician aside. "I'll monitor from here. I have three men on the auxiliary control deck. They'll set up each problem there and feed it to your boards. As far as you're concerned, these are actual battle alerts."

"Yes, sir." Leen continues to stand at stiff attention. His whole rigid attitude says, "You bastard, I'll show you," which is exactly what the first officer wants to see.

Korie kicks at a pedal beneath the console; behind

him a seat unfolds from the floor and he drops into it eas
ily. From his position here at the corner, he can see almos
two-thirds of the engine room crew.

He turns his attention to the board in front of him
clears it of its routine monitorings. Leen stands by stiffly
If his crew has been properly trained, they will show it i
the drill; if not, that too will be evident. In either case, h
can do nothing but watch. From this point on, it is out o
his hands.

Korie taps the intercom. "Bridge? Are you ready?"

From the auxiliary control deck—the acting bridge—
comes the reply, "Yes, sir."

"All right. Let's go with Problem One."

A klaxon sounds throughout the engine room—th
sound of alarm. "Battle stations. All hands, battle sta
tions." It is an unnecessary command, the engine room
crew is already waiting. The lights on Korie's consol
snap to green as each station reports.

"Evasive maneuvers," notes the communicato
"Switch to autocontrol. Thirty seconds, pattern Twelv
Alpha; thirty seconds, pattern Six Lambda; thirty seconds
pattern Nine Theta."

Panel lights flick to yellow, back to green again, a
each station surrenders to computer control of its func
tion. If this were an actual battle alert, the speed and di
rection of the traveling warp would now start varying a
a rate of anywhere from one to fifty times per second
The patterns are random and preset.

The response of the crew is quick, but Korie's expres
sion remains fixed. The real drill has not yet begun. Th
screen in front of him begins tracing a complex three
dimensional pattern, the supposed zigzag course of thei
warp through the stress field. It is only a simulation; al
but the auxiliary monitors in the engine room have bee
disconnected from the ship's control system; the battle sit
uations flashing on the screens exist only in the mind o
the main computer. In the engine room, there is no way
to tell the difference between this simulation and an ac
tual battle.

"Prepare to collapse warp for missile firing," come
the order. "Neutralize the secondaries."

Next to Korie, a technician repeats the order; other men echo it.

"Remove the interlocks. Stand by to neutralize."

"Standing by."

"Come to new heading," orders the pseudobridge. "Eighty-three mark fourteen."

"New heading. Eighty-three mark fourteen." Quickly, it is punched into the controls. The great spherical framework of the generator mounting begins to move, rotating slowly into a new orientation; the ship is changing its heading within the warp.

On the screen, the warp is still zigzagging through the stress field. The ship's new orientation in space will not be apparent until the warp is collapsed. In actual battle, a ship in warp is practically untouchable; a warp is so ultramaneuverable that it is difficult to predict where the enemy will be when the missiles are fired, let alone where he will be when the missiles arrive. The missiles are equipped with warp fields of their own—short-lived units whose main purpose is to home in on an enemy ship and disrupt his warp by overlapping their own warps onto his. If the missile is on target, the enemy's stasis-field generators will be overloaded; both the warp and the ship within it will be destroyed. Instantly.

But in order to launch its missiles, a ship must drop out of warp. The missile must be jettisoned, activated, and into its own warp a safe distance away before the firing ship can climb back into the comparative safety of stressed space. For those few minutes, while it is firing the missile, it is vulnerable—hence, the compulsion to spend as few moments as possible in the unwarped state.

In battle, the warp's maneuvers are controlled automatically by the ship's computer; it is faster and more random than any human being could be. When the ship drops out of warp to fire its missiles, its motion is determined by its previously established inherent velocity. The ship's heading will be the same as its direction was within the warp—but that direction is always variable. A ship's velocity is meaningless within warp and can be redirected at will. The orientation of the warp generators remains the same; functioning like a gyroscopic flywheel, the generators remain stable and the ship "rotates" around them.

The direction of the *Burlingame*'s inherent velocity, therefore, is easily controlled by slipping into warp, changing the direction of the ship, then dropping out of warp again. The direction of the warp and the direction of the inherent velocity are independent of each other—in effect, the ship is bodily lifted out of the stress field and reinserted in a different direction, with no loss of kinetic energy. All that has changed is the direction of the vector.

A typical battle maneuver consists of several minutes or hours of complex evasive patterns of the warp in the stress field, interrupted by a sudden unwarping—with the ship bouncing off in a totally unexpected direction and at sublight speed—followed by the almost immediate launching of its missiles and the re-establishment of its warp. More evasive maneuvers follow this.

Such is the nature of the drill that Korie has set up as Problem One. Later, more complex maneuvers will be run, including false starts, false stops, feints, and decoys.

"Still standing by to neutralize secondaries," reminds a technician.

"Hold your horses," says the bridge. "Stand by to neutralize evasion patterns and cancel."

"Standing by."

"Cancel."

"Canceled."

"Neutralize secondaries."

"Neutralizing now."

"Cycle set at one-eighty. Begin phasing."

"Cycle set. Beginning."

"Inject compensators."

"Injecting."

"Cycling—five, four, three—"

"Injection achieved—"

"Cycle complete. Secondaries neutralized. Stationary warp."

"Unwarp."

"Right—"

Panel lights flash; on the monitors, the computer has simulated an unwarp. Almost immediately—

"Jettison missiles. Prepare to warp."

"Standing by." The engine room is not concerned with the firing of the missiles, but this is still the most important part of the drill. Korie wants to see how long it will take them to clear their boards, set up a new heading, and climb back into warp. Orders crackle over the intercom.

"Inherent velocity vector, eighty-three mark fourteen."

"Confirming, eighty-three mark fourteen."

"Warp control, polarity of secondaries, thirteen degrees—thirteen degrees—thirteen degrees."

"Huh?"

"You heard me. Thirteen degrees—thirteen degrees—thirteen degrees."

"Confirming; thirteen degrees—thirteen degrees—thirteen degrees."

"Missiles activated. Stand by."

"Standing."

"Initial warp factor, 135."

"Initial warp factor, 135."

"Prepare for resumption of evasive maneuvers after warp."

"Evasive maneuvers. Right."

"Power inputs matching?"

"Matching—"

"Compensators set?"

"Setting them now."

"Power inputs matched. Completed and confirmed."

"Compensators set. Completed and confirmed."

"Double-check that please."

"Will do."

"Frequency modules, one, three, and five on phase reflex one three."

"Got it. Angle of adjustment?"

"None."

"None?"

"Right."

"Lock in evasive maneuvers. Patterns Seven Gamma, Eight Gamma, Nine Delta; fifty seconds each."

"Locking in; Seven Gamma, Eight Gamma, Nine

Delta; fifty seconds each; to take effect three full seconds
after stabilization of warp."

"Can you cut it finer than that?"

"I'd rather not."

"All right."

"Missiles warped and away!"

"Go, baby, go!"

"Hey, man, it's only a drill—"

"Shut up, you idiot!"

"Prepare to warp."

"Prepared."

"All lights green?"

"Go!"

"Go!"

"Go!"

"Going!"

"We have warp!"

"Interlocks in?"

"Interlocks in! Cycle released."

"Evasive maneuvers resumed."

"Confirming."

"Right."

"All clear on C deck."

"Report status of missiles please."

"They're tracking—"

"Us or them?"

"Them, I hope."

A voice from the bridge: "Status of missiles—we
missed."

"Aw, shit—"

Leen looks at Korie. "You couldn't even give them
that much, could you?"

Korie is sitting before his console with his hands in
his lap and a bemused expression on his face. He looks
up at Leen. "Actually," he says, "the program was written so they would have a fair chance at it." He takes a
breath, loudly, not quite a sigh; then taps the intercom
button on his console. "Bridge, this is Korie. How much
were they off?"

The answer is laconic: "Forty-three per cent off optimum."

Again Korie looks at Leen. "You see? That's why they missed. The way I wrote it, you have to get it down to 15 per cent or better to make the kill."

"You think of everything, don't you?"

"That's my job." Korie straightens in his seat and clears his board. "All right, let's try it again. Bridge, set up Problem Two. Auxiliary engine control, did you have any trouble keeping up with us on the compensators?"

Eight

MEMO
FROM: Base Admiral Farrel
TO: Vice Admiral Harshlie

Joe,
    Just as we figured, the enemy has opened up a third front in the GY sector. I don't have to tell you the bind this puts us in. We can meet the challenge, but it's going to be tough.
    I want to move as many ships into that area as possible. We can pull some of them from GX and GV, but I don't want to leave those areas underdefended.
    What do we have on the docks here or at either of the advance bases that we can also throw into the donnybrook?
    Stephen

MEMO
FROM: Vice Admiral Harshlie
TO: Base Admiral Farrel

Dear Stephen,
    Nothing.
    Joe

MEMO
FROM: Base Admiral Farrel
TO: Vice Admiral Harshlie

Dear Joe,
   Come on now. I can look out my window and see six ships hanging in orbit—what are those, optical illusions?
   Stephen

MEMO
FROM: Vice Admiral Harshlie
TO: Base Admiral Farrel

Dear Stephen,
   Cruiser K-143 is the *Massion,* slated for advance duty in sector DL.
   Cruiser K-146 is the *Specht;* Tyler needs that for some special project of his own.
   Cruiser K-151 is the *Cutter,* slated to join its sister ship, the *Perry,* as soon as its interior fittings are completed.
   Cruiser F-93 is the *Burlingame.* 'Nuff said about that.
   Cruiser F-101 is the *Carver.* She's also for sector DL.
   Cruiser H-13 is only a hulk. She used to be the *Wilson.*
   Any other questions?
   Joe

MEMO
FROM: Base Admiral Farrel
TO: Vice Admiral Harshlie

Joe,
   What's wrong with the *Burlingame?*
   Stephen

MEMO
FROM: Vice Admiral Harshlie
TO: Base Admiral Farrel

Stephen,
   Surely you jest. I wouldn't use the *Burlin-*

game for committing suicide. That ship is older than I am, and we're both overdue to be scrapped.
Joe

MEMO
FROM: Base Admiral Farrel
TO: Vice Admiral Harshlie

Joe,
I don't care how old it is, I want to know if it's usable. Please authorize a status check.
Stephen

MEMO
FROM: Vice Admiral Harshlie
TO: Base Admiral Farrel

Stephen,
Okay, here's your status check, but you won't like it. I could have told you how bad a situation this ship is in.
Joe

MEMO
FROM: Base Admiral Farrel
TO: Vice Admiral Harshlie

Joe,
There is nothing wrong with the *Burlingame*. Its generators work and it's airtight. It needs some minor refitting, but we can use it.
Stephen

MEMO
FROM: Vice Admiral Harshlie
TO: Base Admiral Farrel

Stephen,
In battle? Are you kidding?
Joe

MEMO
FROM: Base Admiral Farrel
TO: Vice Admiral Harshlie

Joe,

I can't afford to kid.

Who said anything about sending the *Burlingame* into battle? I want it for the milk-run patrols in DV sector. That will free at least one good D-class ship for transfer to GY.

Stephen

MEMO
FROM: Vice Admiral Harshlie
TO: Base Admiral Farrel

Stephen,

ITEM: the *Burlingame*'s system analysis network is no longer fully operational. So many new pieces of equipment have been added to that ship since she was commissioned that the network has completely broken down. If something were to go wrong, they'd have to depend on their secondary analysis system and perform on-the-spot checks.

ITEM: the guide rods for the power and control cables to the stasis generators have been removed. That ship cannot change heading in warp without her cables fouling. We have no replacements for the guide rods because the F-class generator configuration has been obsolete for twenty years.

ITEM: the phase reflex system is partially deranged.

ITEM: the phase adaptive system is totally deranged.

ITEM: the injective compensators would have to be replaced before that ship could pass her safety checks. Where are we going to find F-class compensators here?

ITEM: do you want me to go on? I can—the

list is endless. The *Burlingame?* Uh uh, not even
for a milk run.

Joe

MEMO
FROM: Base Admiral Farrel
TO: Vice Admiral Harshlie

Joe,

We have no choice. We need that ship. We
need any ship that holds air and moves.

I have the *Burlingame*'s log tapes in front of
me. That ship has operated for six years without
a full systems analysis network. The longest
breakdown they ever had stranded them for only
ninety-three hours.

The stasis generator guide rods were removed four months before the ship was decommissioned here. They were removed by the
ship's chief engineer because they weren't working. According to the log, he put a "monkey
crew" in the webs and they guided the cables
manually. Apparently it worked; it says here
that the ship operated more efficiently without
the guide rods.

The phase reflex and phase adaptive systems are not considered "life-or-death" systems.
A ship can survive without them, if necessary;
the crew can do those operations manually. The
Burlingame proved that.

Have the injective compensators rebuilt. (I
don't care where or how, just do it.) They've
been rebuilt twice before; find out how they did
it and do it again.

And so on.

Listen, our ships are built in triplicate, with
fail-safe devices for every function and activity.
Stop worrying. The ship will work. We need her.
It's as simple as that.

Stephen

MEMO
FROM: Vice Admiral Harshlie
TO: Base Admiral Farrel

Stephen,
        All right, but you sign her papers, not me.
        Joe

MEMO
FROM: Base Admiral Farrel
TO: Vice Admiral Harshlie

Joe,
        Relax. It's not as bad as you think. But I
promise you that we'll decommission her again
as soon as we can.
        Now, who have you got to crew her?
        Stephen

MEMO
FROM: Vice Admiral Harshlie
TO: Base Admiral Farrel

Stephen,
        Attached is a list of available captains and
first officers. Pretty skimpy, isn't it?
        Of the three captains, Weberly is holding out
for a battle command. And I agree. I want him to
take the new *Roosevelt* when it's commissioned
next month. Also available is Yu. He's a good
man, but he's really not a space-going captain.
He's a—well, he's a paperwork man. He's at his
best where he is right now, on Base K-7.
        I think our best bet is to promote one of
these first officers to captaincy, let him get his
legs on an easy run. How about Korie, Perren,
Freeman, Yang, or Colen?
        Joe

MEMO
FROM: Base Admiral Farrel
TO: Vice Admiral Harshlie

Joe,
  How about Brandt? You skipped him. He's
an available captain.
  Stephen

MEMO
FROM: Vice Admiral Harshlie
TO: Base Admiral Farrel

Stephen,
  I wouldn't put Georj Brandt in command of
a floating outhouse.
  Joe

MEMO
FROM: Base Admiral Farrel
TO: Vice Admiral Harshlie

Joe,
  Yes, but how about the *Burlingame*?
  Stephen

MEMO
FROM: Vice Admiral Harshlie
TO: Base Admiral Farrel

Stephen,
  That's what I was talking about.
  Joe

MEMO
FROM: Base Admiral Farrel
TO: Vice Admiral Harshlie

Joe,
  I repeat: yes, but how about the *Burlingame*?
  What I'm getting at is that Brandt is starting to be an embarrassment to us. We've got to
get him out of the way somewhere. He can't stay
at Threebase much longer. It's starting to be a
source of gossip.

Put him on the *Burlingame*. He won't be
any trouble there. Trust me.
Stephen

MEMO
FROM: Vice Admiral Harshlie
TO: Base Admiral Farrel

Stephen,
Okay, but I'd prefer to put one of these first
officers in there instead.
Joe

MEMO
FROM: Base Admiral Farrel
TO: Vice Admiral Harshlie

Joe,
Sorry, but I'm saving those men for better
things. They're trained for battle and that's
where I want to use them.
On second thought, though, you could assign one of them to the *Burlingame* as a first
officer—kind of a backstop for Brandt. (That
way, we'll be sure there's at least one man on the
ship qualified to command her.)
See what the psych boys have to say. They'll
know which one will work out best.
Stephen

MEMO
FROM: Vice Admiral Harshlie
TO: Base Admiral Farrel

Stephen,
Attached is the report from the psych section on the command of the *Burlingame*. Best
choice for first officer would be Colen—but he's
already tapped to go out with Weberly on the
Roosevelt. Freeman's death and Yang's transfer
leaves only Korie and Perren. Psych recommends
Korie. Attached is his file.
Joe

MEMO
FROM: Base Admiral Farrel
TO: Vice Admiral Harshlie

Joe,

I approve of Korie. He has an interesting file; he shows promise of becoming a good battle commander when he grows up. Let's keep our eye on him.

At the very worst, we won't need the *Burlingame* for more than six or eight months. When and if we finally do get around to decommissioning her, please check Korie's record again. I'll want to see how he did.

After serving under Brandt, he'll have earned a ship of his own.

Stephen

Nine

An army travels on its stomach.
NAPOLEON BONAPARTE

The galley smells of coffee and ketchup. It is a bright room, but a small one. Divided by narrow tables and benches, it can serve a maximum of only twelve men at a time. Garish-colored condiment containers dot the tables. Three crewmen are brooding over their plates in a corner. In the opposite corner, with only a cup of coffee, is Korie.

As always, his appearance is impeccable. His light-colored hair has been parted with a ruler, his cheeks are plastic-clean, pink and shiny, no trace of razor stubble, his eyes are steely cold. He sips at his coffee thoughtfully. He stares at the table in front of him and at the opposite wall. The wall is pale green plastic, devoid of decoration; whatever Korie sees there remains his own private vision.

"This seat taken?"

Korie glances up. The speaker is Medical Officer Panyovsky; a thick man, wide Slavic face, broad chin, easy smile, clear eyes, thin brown hair.

"It is now," says the first officer, a hint of a smile on his face. "Sit down."

"I will. Just let me get something to eat first." He steps over to the counter, draws himself a tumbler of orange juice, some toast, and coffee. "Hey, Cookie—how about flashing me an eggpack?'

"Right," comes the answer. "Scrambled?"

"Yes, thanks." Panyovsky comes back to the table and sets down his tray.

"You always eat such a big breakfast?" asks Korie.

"Breakfast? This is a midnight snack for me. I haven't been to sleep yet."

"Oh. I just got up."

The other widens his eyes in mock surprise. "You mean you do *sleep*? The crew doesn't think you do."

Korie allows himself a grin. "Well, I don't do it much. It might be habit forming."

Over a mouthful of toast, Panyovsky mumbles, "If I were you, I wouldn't even admit an occasional nap—it'd spoil the image."

"You won't tell anyone, will you?"

"My lips are sealed."

"That's going to make it awfully hard to eat."

"For that I'll unseal them." The medical officer gulps his coffee noisily. "So, how's the first-officering business?"

A shrug. "About the same as always."

"Not really," he says. "I hear we've been having some excitement the past few days."

"Just an old bogie. Hardly anything." Korie says it sardonically.

"*Well* . . ." Panyovsky is expansive. "At least it's a break in the routine."

"After a year and a half," notes Korie, "*anything* would be a break in the routine."

"A year and a half? Has it been *that long*?"

Korie nods. "Actually, it's closer to two years. Two and a half more months and it will be."

Panyovsky grunts; he sucks at his teeth. "You're overdue for a ship of your own, aren't you?"

Korie shrugs again. "I suppose so, but I have a feeling they've stuck me on this tub to get me out of the way."

"Why would they do that?"

"I don't know—maybe I stepped on somebody's toes at Threebase without realizing it. I think the only way I'm ever going to get off is to prove myself in combat and make them notice me."

"The *Burlingame* is not a combat vessel, my friend—"

"I've noticed that."

"—and we are not in a combat area."

"I've noticed that too. We're here so that Callister Mines can't claim they're underdefended. Hmph. A fat lot of good we can do."

"It doesn't seem to me we've been doing that badly."

"We haven't had anyone to defend them against— how could we do badly?"

"I meant this bogie. You haven't been doing too badly with that."

Korie shrugs. "I have to prove myself to the top brass if I want to get off this ship. And I want to get off this ship."

"You're not alone."

"Who else—besides the rest of the crew?"

Panyovsky grins. "Me. Barak. The captain. This ship is as popular as Gristler's Planet during plague season."

"Hmph," says Korie. "I already knew the captain wanted off. It's no secret. He takes no interest in running the ship."

"There you see! You've got a ship of your own already. This one."

Korie's voice is like ice. "It's. Not. The. Same."

"Relax. I was only kidding."

They are interrupted by a bellow from Cookie. "Hey, Panyovsky! Come and get it—or I'll feed it to the hogs!"

The medical officer grins. " 'Scuse me a sec." He crosses to the other side of the galley, where a plastipak of scrambled eggs waits for him, steaming on the counter. Korie forces himself to relax, is even grinning when the big medical officer returns and slides into his seat. There is an antiseptic cleanliness about him that Korie finds refreshing.

"Y'know," Panyovsky says. "Sometimes I think the real captain of this ship is Cookie. Other times, I know it." He cracks open the pack, begins pouring ketchup over the eggs.

"The whole galley is an anachronism," says Korie. "I'd give a nickel for an honest 'mat unit."

"Well, this is a second-generation cruiser," explains the other. "And they weren't building them that way then. They thought that with artificial gravity, they could get away from the free-fall packs and return to a more traditional kind of food preparation—allowing, of course, for all the modern technical advances that have since come to the art and science of cooking." He cocks an eye at Korie. "So you see, my friend, what we have is something that is neither this nor that—but a little bit of each. We have a cook—whose main duty is to flash plastipaks. However," he adds thoughtfully, "I will admit his shish kebab isn't bad." He shovels a forkful of ketchup-covered eggs into his mouth.

"Besides," Panyovsky adds, "There are certain advantages to having a cook instead of a 'mat unit. For one thing you have more flexibility in your choice of meals. Look, no matter what kind of a galley you've got, the food is kept in stasis boxes and flashed by microwave. All you've got with a 'mat unit is portion control; big deal, nobody complains about getting more or less than anybody else—but on the other hand, there's no second helpings. At least not without heating up a whole new pack. Now, with a cook, you know there's always something cooking, and you have the backstop of the plastipaks anyway."

Korie is grinning. "Don't you ever think about anything but your stomach?"

"Huh?" Panyovsky looks at his belly, the slight bulge of a beginning paunch. "What else have I got to think about?"

"Doesn't anything ever happen in sick bay?"

The medical officer makes a face, a quizzical expression. "About as often as it does on the bridge. Today, I had to set a broken collarbone; it's the first real doctoring I've done in a month. It was getting so I'd almost forgotten how. Fortunately, there was a book in the ship's library—"

Korie ignores the other's glib manner. "Broken collarbone? Who?"

"Earlier today. A radec technician, kid named Rogers."

"Rogers—?" Korie is suddenly alert. "How did it happen?"

Panyovsky's manner is casual, but he glances both ways and waits until a passing crewman is out of ear-shot. "They said he fell against a bulkhead. I don't believe it."

"Why not?"

Panyovsky narrows his eyes meaningfully. "Do you know the kid?"

Korie is noncommittal. "I've had him on the bridge."

Panyovsky nods. "Then you know how the crew treats him."

"Yeah—like the neo he is."

"They you know how he got a broken collarbone. Somebody roughed him up."

"A broken collarbone is quite a 'roughing up.' Where'd it happen?"

"K Quarters on the afterdeck."

"That's a bunkroom," says Korie. He frowns. "Now, wait a minute—Rogers has no business there. He's assigned forward."

"Be that as it may, that's the story. Erlich and MacHeath brought him in and that's what they said. He fell against a bulkhead in K Quarters." He pauses to gulp at his coffee. "But is doesn't take a doctor to see that the boy's been beaten pretty badly."

Korie looks troubled. "I don't like that."

Panyovsky shrugs. "What can you do? These things happen. The crew has to settle their differences among themselves."

"Not like this, they don't—not if they're going to incapacitate each other."

"Oh, now I don't think it's that bad. He'll be wearing a brace for a while, but he'll be able to work."

"That's not what I mean. What if he weren't a radec tech, but were on the 'monkey crew' instead—or something else where he needed to be suited up—could he do that in a brace?"

The doctor fixes the first officer with a careful glance. "My job, Mr. Korie, is only to patch them up; not to run their lives. You should remember that yourself. What they do outside of sick bay is their own business. I try not to get involved because I'm caught in the middle already before I start."

"You know who did it?"

"I've heard rumors—"

"Who?"

"Let me tell you something. You may not have realized this, but it's not easy to be a doctor—at least, not on an F-class starcruiser. I probably know more about what's happening on this ship than any other two men aboard her, including you and the captain—or even you and the union representative. The crew tells me things; you tell me things—and everybody thinks I'm on his side. I'm not allowed to have a side of my own; so it's safest for me to just stick to business—keeping the rest of you fixed up so you can have your various sides."

"Uh huh," says Korie. "Now that you've issued the standard I-must-remain-aloof medical disclaimer, *who did it?*"

"My spies say that it was a fellow named Wolfe. You know him?"

"Yes. I know him." Korie starts to rise. Panyovsky pushes him back down.

"Wait a minute, my friend. That wouldn't be a good idea."

"*What* wouldn't be a good idea? You don't know what I was going to do."

"Whatever you were going to do," smiles Panyovsky, "it wouldn't have been a good idea."

Korie sits. "Why not?"

"Because," the doctor says slowly, "*even Rogers* says he fell against a bulkhead."

"Even though it was Wolfe that made him fall—?"

"Probably; but you won't get him to admit it. He's scared of retaliation. In any case, you have no way to prove there's been a fight. Nobody will admit to being a witness."

"What about the men who brought him in?"

"Erlich and MacHeath? Are you kidding? They're strictly crew, all the way."

"And you're sure Rogers won't talk?"

"Not to me, he wouldn't."

"I'll go see him myself." He starts to rise.

"No, you won't. He's asleep." Panyovsky looks casually at his watch. "Besides, you've scheduled another drill for the engine room, remember?—and you're already ten minutes late."

Ten

War is hell!
GENERAL WILLIAM TECUMSEH SHERMAN

Channel B, the all-talk channel on the intercom:
"He's late."
"So? Who's complaining?"
"Maybe we're lucky and he's dead."
"You dreamer—"
"Korie's the dreamer. He thinks this tub is a battleship."
"Maybe he knows something we don't."
"Maybe he's *on* something we're not."
"I wish he were on another ship."
"You know, if we ever get close to that bogie, we won't need any missiles. Korie'll put on a space suit and go after it with his bare hands."
"If he does, let's not wait for him to come back—let's just leave."
"Hear, hear! The man has finally come up with a worthwhile suggestion."
"Let's not even leave him the space suit."
"Aw, now—do I detect a note of hostility in these speculations?"
"Damn right you do!"
"Okay. I just wanted to make sure your hearts were in the right place."
"Hey, listen—you want to know what that asshole has done now?"
"Which asshole?"

"There's only one asshole on this ship."

"Oh—*that* asshole. What's he done now?"

"You know why we keep 'missing' on those drills?"

"Sure—because we're more than 15 per cent off optimum."

"Yeah, but do you know what Korie used as optimum when he wrote those programs?"

"Five million units of Hallucin-N?"

"Not quite, but you're close. The 'optimum' we're trying to hit is the battle efficiency of a K-class cruiser."

"Huh—?"

"You heard me. He's got us competing against K-class specifications."

"He's out of his tree—"

"He should have stuck with the Hallucin-N."

"Maybe he did and this is the result."

"You think we should tell him this is an F-class ship?"

"Naw, let him find out for himself."

"Yeah, but we're on it with him—"

"Unfortunately."

"Congratulations. You've just realized Korie's secret."

"What is?"

"That we weren't signing up for the space force, we were joining a suicide pact."

"*Now,* he tells us—"

"You should have read the fine print on your papers."

"Who can read? When I joined, all they wanted was someone who could stand up for five minutes without falling over!"

"Well, that explains the efficiency of *this* ship."

"Yeah, but what explains its *in*efficiency?"

"Hey, when we get back to base, what're we going to say when they ask us why we couldn't catch the bogie?"

"Our butterfly net had a hole in it?"

"That's very funny—hey, aren't you the guy who, when they start insulting your ship in the bars, you start nodding your head and agreeing?"

"Yeah, well—I don't like to argue with my own ship-mates."

"Has anyone ever noticed there's something *weird* about Korie?—Like he's always *calculating*?"

"There's something weird about everybody on this ship. That's why we're here."

"Hey, does anybody know what the penalty for mutiny is?"

"Last I heard, it was death by spacing."

"Hmm—that's getting more attractive every day."

"Forget it. The last one to try taking over the ship was Captain Brandt."

"And what happened to him?"

"Korie sent him to his room."

"That *bastard*—that's pretty harsh treatment for an old man."

"Yeah? Well, that's nothing compared to what he's got in store for us."

"Oh? What's he going to do to us?"

"He's going to make us stay at our posts."

"Aw, shit!"

Eleven

I have little hope that if the human race were more intelligent it would be an improvement. It would only enable us to make a higher class of mistake.

SOLOMON SHORT

A low whistle of surprise is the only signal—an officer has entered the crew's quarters. Someone turns the lights up, revealing the sagging griminess of the bunks, the chipped plastic panels of the walls. In the center of the room, First Officer Korie stands with a face like grim death. "Wolfe, stand up."

"Huh?"

"I said, stand up."

Surprised, startled, the shorter man levers himself upright—realizes abruptly that it is Korie and jerks to his feet. "Yes, sir."

"Wolfe, I'm only going to say this once, so you'd better listen—and if you miss any of it, I'm sure your big-eared bunkmates will clue you in."

"Yes, sir."

"Wolfe, I know what you did to Rogers. I know it as surely as if I'd been here watching."

"I don't know what you're talking about, sir."

"Of course, you don't—but just in case you do, you'd better listen."

"I repeat, I don't know what you're talking about, sir."

"Wolfe, you're interrupting me—"

"I don't know what you're talking about, sir. Rogers hit his head against a bulkhead."

"Wolfe—"

"I don't know anything about it—"

"Wolfe! Shut up!"

"Yes, sir."

Korie is breathing heavily. His usually pale face is flushed with anger. Wolfe stands stiffly at his bunk—at attention, but somehow still defiant.

"All right," Korie says, a little too quickly. "You don't know anything about it—but let me give you a warning—"

"Sir—"

"—*a warning* that you can give to the bulkhead that Rogers walked into." Korie is seething. "If I have any more trouble out of that particular bulkhead, I am going to personally rip it out. I am going to take it apart piece by piece and shove it out an air lock. And I am going to fully enjoy myself doing it—do I make myself clear?"

"I guess so, sir."

"There'd better not be a next time."

"Yes, sir. I'll tell the bulkhead that."

"You do that." Korie stares at the man for a moment, wondering if he should say any more. Wolfe is a pasty-faced slug; a sallow-colored muscle, layered with fat. His eyes are watery blue and hint of veiled meanness.

Korie decides he has said enough. Wolfe obviously isn't listening anyway. He turns on his heel and strides quickly out.

Wolfe waits until he is out of earshot, then exhales loudly and sinks to his bunk. "Wow! He is sure after my ass!"

"Yeah, well, that's a hard target to miss," calls MacHeath.

"Screw you."

"Face it, man," says Erlich. "You keep getting in his way. Pretty soon, the man's bound to trip over you. And then he's going to get mad. Just don't give him any reason to. That's all."

"You make it sound so simple," snaps Wolfe. He throws himself back into his bunk.

"Well, he sure didn't waste any time getting down here."

"Hey!" says MacHeath suddenly. "You think Rogers squealed?"

"No. I think that bastard's guessing—else he would have killed me for sure."

"You hope that's the case."

"It is. It is."

Twelve

Half the men don't know why we're fighting,
the other half don't care—they just like to fight.
MAJOR GENERAL JACOB ENDERLY,
Second American Civil War

"All right, let's go." Korie strides into the engine room and directly to his monitor console. "Leen, get your men in the webs." He drops into the chair and clears the board. "Bridge, we'll skip the first two problems and start with number three. Auxiliary control, you've got the red button. If you have any trouble compensating for any of these maneuvers, push it—I'd rather stop the drill than lose that bogie again." He swivels back then and looks at Leen. "All set?"

"Yes, sir. We've been ready for twenty minutes."

"My fault. I should have given orders for you to start even if I wasn't here. Oh well, no matter." He unclips his hand mike from his belt. "Now hear this," his voice is amplified throughout the engine room. "We're going to skip the two warm-up problems and go directly to the important ones. This first drill will be a series of hit-and-run missile firings to see if we can lay down a wide-spectrum barrage. We stand a better chance of getting that bas— that bogie, if we can drop a school of fish on him instead of just one. As soon as we master that, we're going to add a few extra touches—some evasive maneuvers and some programmed missile firings by our simulated enemy, so while we're 'shooting' at him, he's going to be 'shooting' back at us. And I promise you men—it's not enough to just kill the bear, we have to take his skin home and nail it to the wall. Uh—Chief Leen tells me I should compliment you men because you've trimmed your efficiency down to 22 per cent off optimum. I disagree. I don't think so. Not yet—let's get it down to 15 per cent and that'll be a job well done. If we can get it down to that, we may be able to make the kill. And, of course, that'll mean bonus money for us all, right?" He doesn't wait for an answer. "Okay, let's go."

He swings back to his board as the klaxon squawks across the room. The massive framework of the generator mounting fills the engine room like the bones of some Brobdingnagian beast. The conical black giants within the framework hum with a life of their own. Even from his position at the console, Korie can feel the tingling on his cheeks and hair that indicates the field pressure. "Chief?"

"Sir?"

"Static—I can feel it. Is everything all right?"

"Uh—" Leen steps to Korie's console, leans over him, and flicks a switch. He watches the monitor screen as it flashes a series of diagrams. "It's okay, sir. It's just routine discharge through the injective compensators. Auxiliary control must be doing it to prepare for the drill."

"All right. Thanks."

Leen straightens and moves away. Korie glances at his screen. The *Burlingame*'s warp is now moving at 28.5 lights. They have covered thirty-six light days, they have twenty to go.

He clears his board again, sets it up to monitor the drill. As an afterthought, he switches off the intercom, decides not to listen to the intersystem chatter this time. He will watch only the changing pattern of lights and diagrams.

Originally, he had thought his presence here in the engine room would allow him to pinpoint a specific cause for the crew's inefficiency—a man who was not doing his job properly or a procedure that was wasteful of time—but after running a few drills, Korie has realized that there is no one specific reason for the engine room's looseness; rather, it is a general sloppiness of the whole crew. The only way to tighten them up is to drill them—and drill them and drill them.

Korie narrows his thin lips in thought; they are almost bloodless normally and this slight pressure is enough to make them go white and disappear against the paleness of his skin. His eyes are veiled pinpoints of concentration.

Under ordinary circumstances, on their normal patrols, Korie would not have objected to a certain laxity in the crew's performance of their duties. This is an old ship and a tired one; if there is a noticeable lack of pride in her operation, it is not without justification.

But this is not a normal patrol—abruptly, they have been thrown into battle, and Korie is faced with the task of converting the lackadaisical crew of a middle-aged ship ordinarily assigned to backwater duties into a crack crew of precision military men able to compete with the best of them; they are equipped with inefficient equipment and they are underarmed, yet somehow he must make them meet—and exceed—the standards set by the finest ships in the force.

The bogie shimmering on his screen now is only a simulation—but somewhere out there, only twenty light days away, is a real bogie. An enemy ship, squat and deadly; its stress-field disturbance indicates it is a destroyer of much the same size as the *Burlingame*. Beyond that, its *capabilities* and armaments are unknown.

They'd picked up the bogie a little more than thirteen days ago in a supposedly "clean" area of space. There'd been a few scares in DV sector, though, and they had been warned to be on their guard. At first, Korie had dismissed the warnings. Threebase issued them with monotonous regularity—but when the first sensor flashes were picked up, he had been forced to change his mind.

They'd spotted the ship almost by accident—and at first, the radec crew couldn't believe there was actually something out there; after all, it was so unlikely. They kept checking and rechecking their instruments, but the bogie only became more and more substantial.

It was almost directly ahead of them and it was heading for their base on the same course they were—

presumably, the other ship was on a hit-and-run bombing mission. At first, Korie had thought it might be one of their own ships, but a check of the records and the bogie's behavior quickly negated that possibility. Its stress-field shimmer—as individual as a fingerprint—was totally unknown; therefore, it had to be an enemy.

As they increased their speed, so did the bogie. Apparently it had become aware of them at the same time they had become aware of it. The captain of the other ship must have decided to forsake his mission, for he bypassed their base. In hot pursuit, they did the same. The *Burlingame* increased its speed to maximum. The bogie did likewise; according to the computers, its warp had been boosted to 171 lights. But that speed was uneven, it kept slipping downward. Perhaps the other's cells were at their limit, perhaps his engines were unstable—whatever the reason, pursuit was feasible.

It was more than feasible—it was inevitable. Korie had been on the *Burlingame* for twenty-one months without seeing any action. The frustration had been building in him, gnawing at him like some deadly internal parasite. He'd been trained for battle, he'd been promised it, every part of his career had been oriented toward this one goal. His hands ached for the feel of the war, his eyes burned with it, his whole body had gone rigid with anticipation. He had given the order for pursuit without even thinking. In his mind, he had no choice. (And then, struck by what he had done, he had looked to Brandt; but the old man had only nodded and said, "This one is yours, Mr. Korie. Go get it." Then he left the bridge.)

For ten days, Korie had watched that bogie on the screen—and all during that pursuit, one thought had stayed uppermost in his mind. *When we catch it, will we be able to kill it?*

They had one advantage. The other captain obviously didn't know how badly equipped they were and how weakly they were armed—else he wouldn't be running. As far as that other captain knew, he was being chased by a K-class cruiser.

(Fine. Good. Let him think that. Let him go on thinking that at least long enough for me to fire my missiles and climb back into warp. Just that long, that's all I'll need.)

Korie had brooded on that, long and hard. (This is not a fighting ship; this is not a fighting crew.)

Drills?—he had scheduled a few during the strung-out agony of the chase, but his concern then had been to determine what his men were capable of so he could plan a battle strategy around that. Now that his strategy had been changed by circumstance, he had no choice. He had to try and whip them into shape. It was no longer a question of making the kill—it had become a matter of their own survival; they had lost their advantage. (That captain's going to know we're not a K-class cruiser by now; we've got to prove otherwise.)

Korie watches as the massive generators slide downward in their mountings, an important part of the drill; a bright-suited crewman scrambles to keep a cable from hanging up. The ship is changing her orientation within the warp, altering the direction of her inherent velocity. For a moment, the man teeters precariously in the webs; then the cable slides into its proper channel and Korie lets his breath out. The men know what they are doing, but still—

The man hangs there easily now, glittering in his yellow protective suit, dark goggles, and helmet. A cable runs from his left leg to a station on the engine room floor; should any of the generators throw off a massive spark of static electricity—as has been known to happen—the cable will ground it out. Dispersal of static electricity has always been a bothersome problem in spacecraft.

The warp generators are impressive units in their spherical framework. Each of the giant cones is eighteen feet long. The six big engines impress their fields one on top of the other in the narrow area at the center of the mounting sphere—creating a miniature warp there; that warp in turn is *resonated* through the three sprawling grids which surround the ship. In a sense, the warp is both within and without the starcruiser.

The grids expand the warp to enclose the ship and move it through the stress field. Every time the ship rotates, the orientation of the generators—and the warp within them—is changed in relation to the grids; but the shape of the *resonance* must be maintained in relation to the stress field—thus, as the ship and its grids swing into a new position, the phase reflex system adapts and adjusts the *resonance* throughout the grids, allowing the warp to maintain its orientation and stability.

The larger warp without keeps its relation to the smaller warp within; the ship turns between them. All the while, the injective compensators work to control any sudden energies thrown off by the phase adaptors. If the system didn't work this way, if the warp grids didn't change the shape of their *resonance* as the warp generators turned within the ship, the result would be a feedback, an overload, and a possible burnout—the latter would mean the destruction of the ship.

If a ship were to try turning without adjusting the *resonance* of its warp, it would—in effect—be trying to turn a piece of the stress field. The task is not necessarily impossible because that piece of the stress field is removed from the greater field surrounding it; but to do it would require more power than any one ship could muster.

It's easier just to turn the ship and leave the stress field alone.

The only other maneuver which involves the turning of the warp generators within their mountings occurs when the ship is *not* in warp. If a captain wishes to direct his inherent velocity along an axis other than the "usual" forward-and-aft orientation, he need only rotate his ship while in normal space. As there is always a small stable warp maintained within the generators, they function as a gyroscopic flywheel around which he can turn—in effect, bringing the generators into a new home position for warp control. The ship continues to fall along the same vector, but pointed now in a direction other than the one in which it is moving.

Once back in warp, operations proceed as before, only now the ship's inherent velocity might be downward, upward, sideways—whichever direction the captain has chosen. As before, he can alter the direction of that velocity by turning within the warp.

The main advantage of this procedure is in docking. If a ship's inherent velocity is already fairly close to that of its destination (and it is to the advantage of all ships and orbital stations to keep their velocities within an optimum range) it need only match the angle of its approach and the direction of its velocity. Both can be done by maneuvering within and without the warp.

Neat. Effective. Cheap.

And if one's inherent velocity is either too great or too small, he need only pick out a nearby planet and burn off some of his kinetic energy by fighting its gravity well, or pick up some more by diving into it. Most captains prefer to keep their inherent velocities low, however. It's easier on the compensators. Even when the ship isn't turning in warp, its inherent velocity creates a certain amount of feedback into the generators. The less the inherent velocity, the less the feedback.

The *Burlingame*'s phase adapter and phase reflex systems have only recently been rebuilt. If they had not been, this pursuit and stalking of the enemy ship would have been impossible. Without those two systems, the *Burlingame* would have lacked its necessary battle maneuverability. It would have been a "straight line only" ship, limited to only the simplest of spatial maneuvers. That the phase handling systems *have* been rebuilt is a point of pride with Korie; he is the one who had located the parts and technicians to install them.

He wants a ship that is as battle perfect as he can make it—if he can't get one through regular channels, then he will go outside them and build it himself. Throughout the *Burlingame* are scattered dozens of auxiliary devices and controls scavenged from scores of parts depots and decommissioned hulks. Korie wants his ship to work.

But most of all, he wants his *own* ship. He wants to be *Captain* Korie of the U.S.S. *Whatever*. At the moment, he almost doesn't care *what* ship they give him, as long as it's a ship. As long as it moves and holds air—

To be a starship captain, a man needs to master a

whole new order of physics just to navigate his ship; he must learn to think in two directions at once.

To be a starship captain, a man must know his ship inside and out; he must know every piece of equipment on her, how each piece works, and how it's taken apart, repaired, and put back together again. Before his training is complete, he will know every function of the ship; he he will be able to step into any job at a moment's notice and see why it isn't being done right.

A man must work the simulations again and again, so that his every split-second decision will be backed up by hundreds of hours of experience with comparable problems. Being a starship captain means taking full responsibility for a ship and her crew. A man must understand the decisions that will have to be made; he will have to make them and live with them.

To be a starship captain—

—is what Jon Korie wants.

To be a starship captain *at war* is what Jon Korie has trained for.

His hands are clenched on the arms of his chair. His knuckles are white. (So near. So near and yet so goddamned far!)

The drill is 24 per cent off optimum.

Thirteen

MEMO
FROM: Vice Admiral Harshlie
TO: Base Admiral Farrel

Stephen,
    I thought we were going to decommission the *Burlingame*.
    Joe

MEMO
FROM: Base Admiral Farrel
TO: Vice Admiral Harshlie

Joe,
    Sorry, but we still need her. Besides, there's no pressing need to decommission her now. That ship is no longer the wreck she used to be.
    Stephen

MEMO
FROM: Vice Admiral Harshlie
TO: Base Admiral Farrel

Stephen,
    If the *Burlingame* is in usable condition, it's Korie's doing. Remember our discussion about what would happen when you put a captain like Brandt on the same ship with a first officer like

Korie? Well, I was right—Brandt isn't running that ship, Korie is.
Joe

MEMO
FROM: Base Admiral Farrel
TO: Vice Admiral Harshlie

Joe,
He's doing a damn fine job of it too. The *Burlingame*'s efficiency has topped 70 per cent for the first time in years. I think we ought to give this kid a ship of his own.
Stephen

MEMO
FROM: Vice Admiral Harshlie
TO: Base Admiral Farrel

Stephen,
Sorry, but we can't pull him out without his captain's recommendation. Or, we could—but if we did it without Brandt's approval, it would look funny.
Joe

MEMO
FROM: Base Admiral Farrel
TO: Vice Admiral Harshlie

Joe,
Captain Brandt won't approve Korie's promotion? Why?
Stephen

MEMO
FROM: Vice Admiral Harshlie
TO: Base Admiral Farrel

Stephen,
Brandt wants a promotion to a desk job—fat chance—and until he gets it, he's not going to recommend anybody.

Of course, it's Korie who's running the ship and keeping her efficiency up; but Brandt doesn't mind taking the credit for it. Korie is keeping that ship aloft. Brandt knows it, and until he gets his own promotion, he's keeping Korie on that ship with him.

Brandt wants to be the first man off that tub.

Joe

MEMO
FROM: Base Admiral Farrel
TO: Vice Admiral Harshlie

Joe,

You're right, of course.

If there were a way to kick Brandt upstairs, I'd say do it and let Korie have the *Burlingame*—but I'd rather give Korie a ship he can fight with rather than an old wreck like this.

No, we have to keep Brandt on the *Burlingame*. (You might say they were made for each other.) And as long as Brandt's stuck on that ship, he'll keep Korie there with him to run it.

Kind of tough on Korie, but we'll make it up to him later.

By the way, take another look at Korie's file. Yes, he'd be good in battle—but I think he needs someone to keep him from going overboard; a moderate first officer perhaps. Have we got an experienced man to hold him back?

Stephen

MEMO
FROM: Vice Admiral Harshlie
TO: Base Admiral Farrel

Stephen,

Sometimes, I think we don't have an experienced man in our whole navy.

Joe

MEMO
FROM: Base Admiral Farrel
TO: Vice Admiral Harshlie

Joe,

After reading the report of the *Mitchell* disaster, I think you may be right.

Actually, what I was getting at was that Korie may lack discretion. He's an impatient young man.

While that might be good in battle, I think his first command should be on an outrunner attached to a major fleet or convoy. Having a larger plan to fit into would keep him from making rash errors in judgment. As most of our younger men are prone to do.

How soon can you get him off the *Burlingame*?

Stephen

MEMO
FROM: Vice Admiral Harshlie
TO: Base Admiral Farrel

Stephen,

I can't get Korie off the *Burlingame*. Period.

Every time I broach the subject, good old Georj brings up his own request for transfer instead.

He knows we want Korie, but he's not going to let us have him unless we take him too.

Joe

P.S. The union rep on that ship is one of my men. He confirms that Korie is really the one running it. And he's running it tightly too— unfortunately, because he's not the captain in name as well as in fact, there's a morale problem. The men don't think they have any real leadership.

P.P.S. We've had two or three battle scares

in that area within the past two months. I'd like
to get a couple more scouts into the sector. Do
you think the enemy could be opening up another new front?

MEMO
FROM: Base Admiral Farrel
TO: Vice Admiral Harshlie

Joe,
    A new front? In DV sector? I'd just as soon
start believing in fairies again.
    By the way, how did you work it so that
one of your own men is a union rep? And for
God's sake—if you could plant a man in the
union, what is he doing on the *Burlingame*?
    Stephen

MEMO
FROM: Vice Admiral Harshlie
TO: Base Admiral Farrel

Stephen,
    He's on the *Burlingame* because the union
knows he's one of my men. They requested it to
get him out of the way.
    Actually, he's a decoy. If I let them think
they've outwitted me there, I will find it easier to
plant other men elsewhere.
    By the way, one of the reasons for the
Burlingame's improved condition is that
she was able to refit some of her equipment
locally. It was Korie's doing, of course. He's
adaptable, that boy is, but I still think we
ought to reconsider our decision about a DV
supply depot.
    Joe

MEMO
FROM: Base Admiral Farrel
TO: Vice Admiral Harshlie

Joe,

There is no point in putting up a supply depot unless you have supplies to put into it.

Stephen

MEMO
FROM: Vice Admiral Harshlie
TO: Base Admiral Farrel

Stephen,

There was another battle scare in DV sector last week. I don't want to alarm you, but I really think we should move in some kind of support for the *Burlingame*. They've been there for more than twenty months now.

The *Burlingame* is not really equipped for battle—either physically or emotionally. You know as well as I what would happen to that ship if they ran into a serious crisis. Brandt would be incapable of handling it and Korie would have to take command.

That would hurt both men. Brandt would no longer be able to command his own ship after such an event. He'd have to be—removed. And he'd resent Korie's presumptuousness and ability; he might take it out on him by putting a black mark on his record.

Of course, all this is assuming that the *Burlingame* survives any contact with the enemy.

Joe

MEMO
FROM: Base Admiral Farrel
TO: Vice Admiral Harshlie

Joe,

Sure, I'd like to support the *Burlingame*. But what with?

The best I can offer you—or them—are some new armaments. I'll defer a couple of HE projectors and a half dozen new missiles into the DV pipeline for the *Burlingame*. If a minimum amount of their other equipment is working that should bring them up to workable battle strength.

The answer is still no on that supply depot. If Korie can jury-rig his repairs with local products, let him. We can't afford the cost of maintaining a new supply base while we've still got that trouble in sectors GX and GW.

About their psychological problems—they'll have to learn to live with them. Theirs is nothing compared to what I've got going on the *Sanders,* the *Appa,* and the *Goodman.*

Besides, if such a crisis should occur and Korie does prove himself in battle, it will be a good way to get him out from under Brandt's thumb. We need some heroes about now, anyway, for the home front. We could use Korie for PR and then get him a ship of his own. We could then give Brandt a lesser man; that is, if he's still on his ship.

All this is speculation, of course, but keep it in mind.

Oh yes—and increase the *Burlingame*'s tour of duty by another six months. At least. Sorry, but you know how strapped we are.

Stephen

Fourteen

There are countless velocities. Moons travel about planets. Planets circle suns. Suns move in relation to other suns and all of them spin within the galaxy. The galaxy itself is moving in relation to other galaxies and who is to say that the Universe itself is not moving in some vast unknown direction?

JARLES "FREE FALL" FERRIS,
*Philosophy and Relativity:
A Survey of Ideas*

Korie finds Rogers in the shower room. Like all shower rooms, this one smells of stale sweat and steam. Casually, the first officer drops his kit and fresh uniform onto the dry end of the plastic bench. He pauses to watch as Rogers struggles vainly with his tunic. It is caught on the bulky plastifoam brace across his shoulders.

"What some help?"

"Huh?" Rogers turns and notices Korie for the first time. "Oh, Mr. Korie, sir." He straightens—

"Relax. There are no regulations in the shower room." Indicating the brace again, "Do you need help?"

"Uh, thank you, sir, but I think I can manage." He resumes struggling.

Korie watches amused as the younger man tries to work his tunic over his head; he looks as if he is dislocating both of his arms in the process.

"Are you *sure* you don't need any help?—"

"Uh, pretty sure. I—"

"Bullshit." Korie steps over to the other. "Turn around." He unzips the tunic on both sides and pulls it over the other's head, like an adult with a small child. "There's such a thing as pride and there's such a thing as foolishness." He hands Rogers his shirt and returns to his own place.

Rogers watches him as he quickly strips off his clothes; his shirt is wet with perspiration and he has to literally peel it off. "Uh, thank you, sir."

Korie grunts in reply, rummages in his kit for his shampoo, and disappears into the shower, a doorless alcove behind two curved plastic baffles.

Rogers listens to the sound of water splattering against the floor. He lays his tunic down on the bench, begins to skin off his own shorts. He pauses then, decides to wait until the first officer is through with his shower. Sharing a shower is one thing—but sharing it with an officer is something else. Korie's voice, a surprising bass, comes caroling loudly out of the water. *"When I was a lad in Venusport, I took up the local indoor sport . . ."*

Rogers is startled. He hadn't known that Mr. Korie was human—the fact that Korie is singing this, the bawdiest of space ballads, is a surprise.

Abruptly, Korie pauses. "What's the matter, Rogers? Scared of an officer?"

"Uh, no sir, I—"

"There are four shower heads in here, Rogers. I can't possibly use them all. If you want to take a shower, you don't have to wait until I'm through."

"Uh, yes, sir." Glumly, Rogers strips off his tights. Naked, except for the brace across his shoulders, he steps to the shower, almost bumping into Korie, who is just exiting.

"However, it's all right," says Korie, continuing his earlier sentence, "because I'm through now, anyway."

"Uh, yes, sir." Rogers steps nervously past him and into the shower, still splattering hotly on the floor.

"I left it running for you," Korie calls.

"Uh, thank you." He adjusts the temperature more

to his liking, a pleasant tepidness. Perhaps Mr. Korie isn't so bad after all.

Rogers starts to lather himself. Self-conscious of his body, he tries to ignore the inherent luxuriousness of the sensation. He doesn't look down at himself at all, instead stares at the shower heads on the wall.

"Say—should you be showering?" calls Korie suddenly.

"Huh?" Rogers stops. "Oh, you mean the brace?"

"Yes," comes the reply. "I'd think that—"

"The doc says it's okay," Rogers answers a little too quickly. He raises his voice to be heard above the water. "It's only a broken collarbone. He says there's no reason at all why I can't fulfill my duties." And then, a little more tentatively, "You know, I'm off the gravity control board—"

Korie doesn't respond. Rogers starts lathering himself again. He adds, "The doc arranged it. He said if I'd trained as a radec tech, I should be a radec tech. Starting next watch, I go on the regular boards—" Abruptly, he realizes that he is being watched. Korie is standing in the door of the shower room, toweling his hair and eyeing him speculatively.

"Don't mind me," says the first officer. "I'm just watching."

"Uh—" Rogers half-nods, turns back to the shower, lathering himself madly, now acutely aware of his own bony awkwardness.

"I want to make sure," says Korie, "that you don't fall into any more bulkheads."

"No, sir. I won't," says Rogers as he drops the soap. It bounces and slides across the floor to stop at Korie's feet.

The officer picks up the slippery bar and hands it to the shivering Rogers. "Good," he says. "I wouldn't want you to get hurt anymore."

Rogers takes the soap from Korie's outstretched hand. "Thank you, sir, but that isn't necessary."

"Just the same."

"It isn't necessary," Rogers insists shrilly.

"You're awfully certain of that, aren't you. But your past record hasn't been too good on that score."

"Leave me alone, please. Will you! I can take care of myself." Rogers grinds his fists into his ears, but even that doesn't prevent him from hearing Korie's next words.

"I doubt that. Otherwise, you wouldn't be wearing that brace."

When he looks up, Korie is gone. Hastily, he rinses off and steps from the shower. Korie is just dressing. "I'm sorry I yelled at you, sir."

"That's all right—as far as I'm concerned, it didn't happen. We're all under stress."

"Yes, sir." Rogers picks up his towel, begins to dry his hair. The water drying on his body leaves him shivering.

"I am too," says Korie unexpectedly.

"Huh?"

"I said, I am too. I'm under stress too."

Rogers looks at the first officer curiously.

Korie says, "I don't suppose it ever occurred to you that I'm responsible for this whole ship and the men in it?"

"Uh, that's obvious."

"Is it? If there's something wrong somewhere on this ship, I'm supposed to know about it and see that it gets fixed—that goes for the men as well as the machines."

Rogers doesn't say anything.

"I'm a little disappointed in you, Rogers."

"Sir?"

"I know you're covering up for Wolfe. The whole ship knows it."

"I don't know what you're talking about, sir." Rogers starts rummaging through his clothes.

"I'm talking about the fact that you're not increasing anybody's respect for you this way—they still think you're a damned fool. Why should you protect Wolfe?"

"I'm not protecting anyone, sir."

"Not even yourself?"

Holding his tunic low in front of himself to cover his nakedness, Rogers looks at the other. "Sir, I'm in a low enough position as it is—why should I add 'squealer' to my list of offenses?"

"And why should you let a man who could be a danger to all of us remain on the ship?"

"I'm sorry, sir, but I can't help you."

Korie says slowly, "It could be done anonymously."

"Anonymous? On the *Burlingame*? The only thing more anonymous would be a billboard. There's only one person on this ship who can prove anything against Wolfe and that's me—and I'm not going to make myself any move unpopular than I already am."

"All right, Rogers. Is that your last word?"

"Yes, sir."

Korie turns to go.

"Sir—"

Korie pauses. "Yes?"

"There is one way . . ."

"Whats that?"

"Get me a transfer off this ship. Anywhere. Another ship. Another base. But off this ship."

Korie thinks about it. "No. Not a deal."

"Why?"

"All right. I'll tell you—you've made a mess of yourself on this ship, haven't you? You've fucked it up. Now you want to let them drive you out of here. And after you're gone, they'll think of you as Rogers the quitter."

"So what?"

"So, if you can screw yourself up on this ship, what's to prevent you from getting screwed up anywhere else we send you?"

"I'll know better. I've learned my lesson."

"Sure you have—all you've learned is that pain hurts. Well, let me tell you something, little boy—that's what they call you, isn't it, *'little boy'*?—and they're right, you know. They're right. You'll be a little boy until you realize one thing—you've got to be responsible for your own actions, just you and nobody else. If you make a mess, you've got to clean it up yourself. Now, this is your mess right here on the *Burlingame*. Nobody's going to just *give* you any respect for free, you have to earn it. If you act like a little boy, they'll treat you like one. But if you show them you're not afraid to fight back—"

"Sir—"

"This is your chance, Rogers. You can't have a transfer. Nobody gets off that easy. If you're going to be 'one of the men,' Rogers, you're going to have to do it here. You're not going to get a second chance."

"Yes, sir."

"Rogers, I'll tell you one more thing. You know I could bully the information out of you, don't you?"

"Sir—"

"Don't you?"

"Yes, sir."

"Keep that in mind. If I have to, I will." And with that, Korie is gone.

Fifteen

*To err is human—to blame the other guy is even
more human.*

SOLOMON SHORT

Feeling clean and crisp, still smelling of soap, the first
officer enters the bridge. He stands at the back of
it for a long moment, savoring the sensation of
power—inherent and implied.

At the consoles, the men display a visible tenseness.
Despite their easy familiarity with routine, their intent
watch of the boards betrays their nervousness. The usual
background murmur of conversation has disappeared.

Korie nods with satisfaction; he takes a step forward
and down into the pit. The ensign at the helm starts to
rise, but Korie waves him back down into the seat.
"Don't get up," he says, "I'm only watching, for now."

The man sits down again, somewhat nervously.

The screens circling the bridge flicker from one graph
to the next, but always returning to the empty and blood-
red grid of the stress-field scanners. Korie wanders a few
steps to his right, pauses at the astrogation console. He
taps Jonesy aside and snaps a button. "Radec? This is
Korie."

"Yes, sir?" The voice is Rogers'.

"Do you have any sign of my bogie yet?"

"No sir. Not yet. But we're scanning."

"All right." He snaps off, impatiently.

The rear door slides open with a *whoosh*. Korie
glances back, sees Barak.

The big black man nods, steps down into the pit and over to his console. "Nothing?" he asks.

"Nothing."

"Oh well, it's early." He glances around the casually tense bridge. "Captain isn't here yet?"

"Captain isn't up yet," Korie corrects.

"But he'll be here?"

Korie is noncommittal. "I wouldn't know."

"If he doesn't show—"

"I know, then it's my baby."

"How's it feel?"

Korie half-grins, "A little scary."

"Good," grins Barak. "If you weren't nervous, then *I'd* have to be." He drops into his chair, clears his board, and begins to bring himself up to date on the ship's position.

Korie steps up onto the horseshoe, moves slowly around it, pausing only briefly at each board, reassuring himself as to the battle-readiness of the ship. Occasionally, he suggests a correction, but for the most part he keeps his thoughts to himself. The men tense as he approaches, each one stiffening under the first officer's impartial scrutiny, then relaxing imperceptibly as he moves on.

"Approach minus sixty minutes," calls Barak.

At last, Korie steps down into the pit and allows himself the luxury of taking over the helm. The ensign there is glad to vacate.

The seat is firm and comfortable under him. Lovingly, Korie runs his hands across the smooth control surfaces on its arms. In a little while, all the action, all the meaning, all the importance of the *Burlingame* will be centered—*here*.

He punches for a control check; all his lights flash green—the seat is in proper working order. Good.

He swivels once around, quickly, to orient himself again and to see who is on station. He frowns as his glance strays across the rear of the horseshoe; three off-duty crewmen are standing behind the autolog console. He pauses. "You men. Clear the bridge, please." He swivels forward again. (This is a warship, not a pleasure cruiser; we don't need an audience—)

The sound of the door tells him that the men have exited. Korie relaxes in the seat. Idly, he begins running a series of systems-reliability checks. One by one, the panels flash to green. Diagrams appear in the monitors. What he sees pleases him, and yet—

He touches the intercom button: "All hands. Please see that your posts are in a state of readiness. We are not yet at battle stations, but I would appreciate another set of last-minute checks while we still have the time."

Another thought occurs to him, and he switches to a private channel. "Engine room, is Leen there?"

"Just a moment, sir." A pause, then the chief engineer is on the line. "Sir?"

"The gym," says Korie. "Have you collapsed it yet?"

"Uh—" Leen's hesitation is damning. "No, sir. I haven't."

"Why not?" Korie's voice is noncommittal.

"I haven't had the chance, sir. I've been readjusting the Hilsen units. I wanted to give the subwarp some extra stability. I'll take care of it right now, sir."

"That'll be fine," says Korie. "You were right to work on the Hilsen units: they're more important than the gym. Just be sure that the gym is down within the next fifty-five minutes."

"Yes, sir. It'll be down."

"Good," says Korie, and he means it. He switches off.

(Leen is a good engineer; he'll get the job done. The only time to ride a man is when it's necessary. All other times, show him that you have faith in his ability; treat him as if you know you can depend on him and he'll react to prove you can. If he doesn't, that's the time to ride him.

(Let's see now, I've got Rogers on the radec boards— well, he says he's a technician, let's find out. We've got Barak and Jonesy on astrogation, no trouble there. Goldberg is on shift now, that's good. Hm, who's on autolog? Oh, Willis—Christ, that man is a slob. Let's see, there's Harris and Reynolds—Reynolds, he knows his board, that's for sure—and that new man on warp control, I wonder what his name is. Two months he's been on the ship and I still don't remember him. Oh, well, I know he must be doing his job—I'd have noticed if he weren't.

(Who's on duty in the engine room? Leen, of course, Stokely, yes; O'Mara, Fowles, Beagle—yes, the "monkey crew" will be adequate. MacHeath riding the secondaries? No, we decided to put Eisely there and MacHeath on a console. Who does that leave in the power bay? Erlich, Petersen, Campbell, and Dover—yes, they're good; they can handle the stasis cells as well as anyone—not that there's that much to handle. Any good stasis technician could handle it. Hm. Erlich fixed Cookie's stasis boxes once, didn't he? And I thought I saw him working with Leen once too. I'd better check that; the man could be due for a bonus.

(I don't like the idea of Rogers on radec, though—who else is there with him? Keene? No, he's going to be riding auxiliary control to monitor the missiles. Bridger, yes, Bridger's on radec. That should be okay; he can handle his end of it. All I need is two good men on the radec—

(Rogers—?

(Well, I'll just have to wait and see—but dammit, radec is going to be the important part of this maneuver! That'll be what makes us or breaks us. That bogie'll see our shimmer the minute we start coming in—we won't see him till we get close enough to pick up his stationary mass. He'll see us first, he'll have more warning than we'll have, we'll be going in blind—we'll need the sharpest eyes possible. Who have I got I could replace Rogers with?

(Nobody, dammit—no, what am I thinking of? I can't replace Rogers now. If I pull him off his board, it'll look funny—it'll ruin him with the crew; they'll know I have no faith in him. Of course, he's already ruined as far as the crew is concerned, it wouldn't make that much difference—no, I've got to leave him on the board; I've got to let him have his chance to prove himself.

(Or do I? Dammit, I can't afford to lose that bogie again due to some chuckleheaded error—

(Oh hell, I don't have anyone to put in there, anyway. I have to leave him there whether I like it or not.

(—and I don't like it.

(Damn.)

"Thirty-five minutes," notes Barak.

Korie is slouched in the seat, chewing on a fingernail.

His expression is dark and brooding. His face seems flushed, but it is only the reflection of the crimson glare of the forward screen.

Brandt enters then. Korie looks up at the sound of the door, so does Barak. The captain catches both their glances, indicates with a nod that they should join him on the wide shelf at the rear of the bridge.

"Well, this is it," he says. "Ready for blood, Mr. Korie?"

Korie nods grimly.

"Scramble pattern worked out, Al?"

"It's in the computer. All we have to do is ride her in. As soon as we spot the bogie, EDNA will note its position and compensate the scramble for it."

"Fine." He turns back to Korie. "Your missile crews ready?"

"As ready as they'll ever be. The missiles are present anyway. All they need is the target; we've got them locked in to EDNA now; she's keeping a running update on their programs and she'll also charge and activate them."

"You almost don't need the missile crew," notes Brandt. "The rest of the ship is ready?"

Korie nods.

"Fine." Brandt eyes his first officer thoughtfully. "Well, in a little while, we'll find out for sure." He steps past Korie and Barak and down the pit, into the empty Command and Control Seat. Korie looks after him with distaste.

"Relax," Barak whispers. "We'll make the kill in spite of ourselves. It's a good battle plan."

"I'm glad somebody thinks so," Korie whispers back.

"Thirty minutes to approach," calls Jonesy.

"All hands. Attention, all hands." The captain's voice booms through the *Burlingame*. "I don't think it's necessary to tell you to go to battle stations. I've just walked through the ship and I've seen that most of you are already there. But for the log, we are now going directly to Condition Red."

The ship's lights flicker and dim. The bridge lights go out, flash to red overheads, then go out again, leaving only the flickering screens and glowing consoles. The red overhead lights seep in at a lower level.

Brandt smiles in the darkness. "Well, I'll say one thing, Mr. Korie—you've certainly gotten them to be prompt." To the intercom again, "In a little less than thirty minutes, we will begin our final approach into the area where our bogie disappeared. We will be going in at top speed and we'll be watching for him all the way. The minute we spot him, we're going to drop four missiles on him—nuclear-tipped in case he's not in warp.

"Now, I know Mr. Korie's been drilling you hard, and I know you're as battle-ready as you can be. I just want to say that I have the utmost confidence in all of you—if I didn't, we wouldn't be here now—I know you'll all do your jobs well and we'll be able to go home with a kill to our credit. There's not a man on this ship who doesn't want that, so—let's go in there and give them hell." He switches off, looks at Korie. "How's that?"

Korie shrugs. "Sounded fine to me."

Brandt lowers his voice to a whisper, Korie steps in closer. "You know, Mr. Korie, I have my doubts."

"Yes, sir. I know. So do I."

Brandt grunts. "Yes, you should—*you* should know better than anyone on this ship how well prepared—or unprepared—we are."

"Yes, sir. That's why I have my doubts. But if they perform as well as they did during the drills—"

"This isn't a drill, though. This is for real."

"That's why I drilled them so hard—I'd rather that the actual battle be less than they can handle, instead of more."

"This crew has never been in battle—"

"Neither have I," says Korie. "Neither have you, sir."

Brandt looks at him sharply, decides to let it pass.

"What I'm getting at is that they're untested in a crisis situation—any one of them could fly apart at a crucial moment."

"I've got my eye on a couple that might not be able to cope with their boards. Aside from them, I'm not worried."

"Hmph. Well, we'll see. You drilled the bridge as well as the engine room?"

"Yes, sir. The first set of drills was only engine room and missile firing. The second set were full simulations. We took it down to 19 per cent off optimum."

"That's not too good—"

"*Optimum* was a K-class cruiser."

Brandt raises an eyebrow. "Then the rumor was true—"

"Oh, yes."

"Then the 19 per cent isn't really as bad as it sounds."

"On the contrary, it's quite good. For this ship, anyway."

"Well," says Brandt. "I'm reassured. Perhaps we have a chance after all."

"I've never doubted it," says Korie.

"Minus twenty minutes," notes a voice on their right.

For a while, silence reigns on the bridge. Brandt, a shaggy gray chunk of granite, is immobile in the seat. He seems like a statue, perpetually frozen into one character-istic position—a position of casual rigidity. Beside him, Korie resists the temptation to fidget, but his nervousness seeps out around the edges, displays itself in the insistent tapping of his foot, the recurrent pursing of his lips, the sucking in of his cheeks.

Elsewhere, things tick, things hum, things click and clatter; a monotonous symphony of checks and re-checks, of ask-me-again and tell-me-three-times. The tempo is four-four time, punctuated by bursts of staccato sixteenth and thirty-second notes; the key is the key of fear, and the conductor is destiny—

"Fifteen minutes."

Korie forces himself to sit. There is an auxiliary seat just to the rear and to the right of the captain's. He perches stiffly on the edge of it. "Radec?"

"Sir?"

"Anything?"

"No, sir."

"Keep watching."

"Yes, sir."

(All right, relax, he tells himself. You don't gain anything by being nervous. When it happens, it'll happen. Rogers will tell me as soon as he's got something—) He takes deep breaths, long deep breaths, slow deep breaths. (Relax, just relax—)

"Minus twelve minutes."

Abruptly:

"Sir, I've still got a red light on my board—"

"What is it?" Korie is on the horseshoe immediately.

"It's the gym. It hasn't been secured—"

Korie reaches past the man, flicks at the console. "Give me a visual on that," he mutters. He snaps a few more buttons. "There."

On the screen, the hull of the ship is shown, a single splash of light illuminating it. A narrow line of black indicates a hatch not completely closed and a gentle bulge of yellow-shining mylar shows that the gym is escaping from its storage bin. As they watch, the bulge forces itself out even farther.

"Are we losing pressure—?"

"No, sir. Not yet. That ballooning must be residual gas."

Korie flicks a communicator. "Leen! Dammit—why wasn't the gym secured?!!"

A puzzled chief engineer, "Sir?"

"The gym! Why wasn't it secured?!!"

"As far as I know, sir, it was."

"It wasn't!"

"It wasn't—??"

"Take a look on your screen. Channel D."

"Yes, sir."

"I want two men down there immediately. Get that damn thing sealed—and fast."

"I'm on my way, sir—"

"You stay on station. Send someone else."

"Yes, sir."

Korie switches off. Almost immediately, he switches back on. "Why wasn't that secured in the first place?"

Leen again. "Sorry, sir. I don't know."

"Find out—who did you assign to do it?"

"No one, sir. I went myself."

"You—went—yourself—"

"Yes, sir."

Korie stops himself from speaking. (No, I can't put Leen on report—not now. I—we need him.) "Uh—Chief, we'll have to go over this later." Very quietly, he says, "Just get it secured now." He switched off, and very carefully, very slowly, steps back away from the board.

The crewman there looks at him. "Sir—?"

"Give them—five minutes—to secure it—"

"Yes, sir."

"—and if they can't get it secured by then—" He weighs his words carefully. "—jettison it."

"Jettison it. Yes, sir."

Korie steps back down into the pit, makes his way to his seat. He is pale and almost shaking. The sudden surge of adrenaline in his veins has left him quivering. (Leen, that bastard, I thought I could depend on him—)

After a moment, he straightens, forces himself to be firm again. (Come on, man—it's only the gym. The real thing is still to come—) He looks to his left; Brandt seems almost asleep.

"Eight minutes to approach."

(Eight minutes—they'll never get it in that time.) He bounces back up to the horseshoe, hovers nervously over the crewman and his board. On the monitor screen, something can be seen jerking at the plastic, but no progress is being made.

"They're not going to get it," he says. "Tell them to stand clear; I'm going to jettison."

The crewman mumbles something into a mike. After a moment, "They're clear."

"All right." Korie punches at the board. Red lights flash; he snaps two more switches. There is only one way to jettison the gym—inflate it quickly with a small charge of gas under high pressure, then release the pressure collar that holds it fast to the ship. On the monitor, the bulge grows quickly to a sphere.

Behind him, there is a mutter of voices. "What the—"

"Hey! They're inflating the gym—"

The interior hatch is closed. Korie breaks a locked

cover, turns a key—the exploding blots are armed. A quick check of the board and he presses the button. The gym is cut free; the giant bladder squirts away from the ship. On the screen, it can be seen as a ghostly blur of pale white, reflecting the glare of the single spotlight against the hull of the ship. Like some vast, slow-fluttering butterfly, it swirls out toward the edge of the warp and is gone.

"Damn! There goes the gym," someone says.

Korie ignores it; he clears the board, punches for a check. All lights flash green. "Your board is clear," he says to the crewman.

"Thank you, sir." The man steps back up to it; Korie returns to the pit.

"Four minutes to approach. All stations, stand by."

As Korie starts to sit down, Brandt whispers to him, "Was that necessary—jettisoning the gym?"

"I think so."

Brandt considers it. At last, he says, "All right."

Korie explains, "Perhaps it wasn't necessary from a security standpoint; the gym alcove and observatory are double-sealed. But it was necessary for disciplinary reasons—it will serve as an example."

"An example?" Brandt raises a shaggy eyebrow.

"If we're going to be a battle cruiser, we'd better act like one. Next time, they'll make sure the gym is secured."

"Hm," says Brandt. "An interesting point." He falls silent, allows Korie to return to his position behind the seat.

"Three minutes," says Barak. "All stations, prepare for auto-control."

"Standing by."

"Warp factor at 1.1."

"Right."

The screens are flickering rapidly; diagrams flash, only to disappear and be replaced by others.

"Ninety seconds."

"All systems. Last check."

"Warp control?"

"All green."

"Power bay?"

"Green."

"Life support?"

"Go."

"Engine room?"

"Go."

"Astrogation?"

"Right on."

"EDNA—?"

"She says go."

"Systems check?"

"All on."

"Go to autocontrol."

"Fifteen seconds to approach."

The forward screen remains empty. Red and empty.

"Ten seconds. Stand by."

"Standing—"

"Five seconds."

"Autocontrol is green—"

"And go—!"

Somewhere a circuit closes—the *Burlingame*'s warp alters its shape and—

Now the ship is hurtling down a corridor of space, 174 times the speed of light, visible only on the flashing graphs.

The monitors beep. The screens flicker with lines and streaks, imaginary boundaries drawn by computers, directed by men; lines to mark the range of the battle, lines to give the minds of men something to identify in an otherwise empty environment.

"Radec! Report."

"Scanning for bogie. No response."

On the screen ahead, the stress-field grid swells and hurtles past. Korie moves to the center of the pit. In the darkened bridge, the lines streak past him like bullets. He fingers his hand mike impatiently.

"Still scanning," comes Rogers' voice. "No response."

"Six minutes to center," says Barak. "Scramble pattern standing by."

The screens flicker-flash. Their bright glare is hellish.

"Still scanning. No response."

"Five minutes to scramble."

"No response."

Flicker-flash. Flicker-flash.

"Still no bogie."

"All right, already," mutters Korie, half to himself. "Where is he?"

Brandt is immobile behind him, strobe-lit by the screens. He rumbles. "He should be here—"

The streaking lines on the screens flash to red, then white again.

"What was that—?"

"Just a visual cue, relax."

The consoles make sounds of their own, as involuntary a process as the sound of a man's heavy breathing.

"Four minutes."

"Still scanning. No response."

"Missile control, stand by."

"We're standing—"

And still the lines streak across the screens. The garish images are scribed across the bridge, a shattering, splattering corridor of light.

"Three minutes—"

"Still scanning."

"Where the hell is that bogie?"

The question remains unanswered. The endless tunnel of emptiness continues to rush past the ship. Korie fumbles at his mike. "Missile crew—"

"We're still standing, sir."

The insistent beeping of the monitors digs at Korie's brain. "Give me a target, already," he mutters.

"Two minutes."

"Radec—?"

"Nothing, sir—*nothing*."

"We should have spotted him by now."

"Not if he's on the other side of the target." That was Barak.

Korie snaps back, "We're close enough to see that far—"

Barak doesn't answer; the empty flashing screen says it for him.

"One minute—"

"Stand by for scramble pattern. Just in case."

Korie drops into his couch, impatiently. The bridge is a silent tableau; only the screens give the appearance of motion.

"Thirty seconds. Thirty."

"Radec?"

"Still scanning, sir."

"Well, where the hell is my bogie, dammit?"

"I don't know, sir. I—"

"Sir—" Barak, speaking to the captain. "—there's no bogie—"

"Scramble anyway," says Brandt.

Barak stabs his console. *"Scramble!"*

For one brief second all the screens flicker-flash out of synch. Suddenly the wild, rushing gridwork is viewed from a dozen different angles; the *Burlingame* ricochets madly through it.

"Radec!"

Rogers' voice, almost panicky: "I'm sorry, sir— there's nothing here!"

"Mr. Barak—" The captain. "Cut the scramble. Go to stationary fields."

"Yes, sir."

The screens flash insanely, then—

"End of scramble. Warp velocity zero. Stationary fields."

The screens are empty. And still. The bridge is strangely silent.

Brandt rumbles, "All hands, stand by."

A pause; they listen to the stillness. From a dozen mocking angles, the monitors grin down at them, toothless and empty.

Korie is in the pit. He whirls about, staring from screen to screen. Futilely.

All empty. Silent and still.

He looks at Brandt. Brandt looks at Barak. Barak looks at Korie.

Brandt glances from one to the other, takes a breath. "Well, Mr. Korie—it looks like your preparations were in vain."

Korie opens his mouth; he takes an angry half-step toward Brandt—then stops himself. He looks at Barak. "Radec—?"

Barak looks at his board, then back at Korie. "Check it out—"

Korie says, "I will," and leaps to the horseshoe and out the back of the bridge—down the corridor and into the narrow radec room. Bridger and Rogers look up startled.

"Get up," Korie snaps. He drops into Rogers' seat, clears the board, and punches for a systems check. The panel lights up green.

He hits the intercom. "Systems reliability, I want a full check on all scanning systems—now."

"Yes, sir."

He turns his attention back to the board, begins setting up a new scanning procedure. "So help me, Rogers," Korie breathes, "if that bogie is there and you've somehow missed it—"

"Sir," the intercom cuts in. "Preliminary check shows all systems on and working okay."

"Cross-circuit and try again."

"Yes, sir."

"I'm sorry, Mr. Korie," says Rogers, "but there's nothing there—"

The board confirms this. Before him, six monitor screens grin emptily. Korie clears the board, sets up another routine. Still nothing.

Again, the intercom: "Mr. Korie, all scanning systems are within 91 per cent optimum efficiency. Scanning quotient is at ninety-nine."

Korie doesn't answer. He sets up one more scan. Impatiently, he waits while the console digests it. Then, one by one, the screens blink—but remain empty.

Korie looks at Rogers, as if seeing him for the first time. He glances back at the screens once more to reassure himself that he has not made a mistake too, then says to the other, "All right, Rogers. You can have your board back." He levers himself out of the chair.

Rogers waits until the first officer steps past, then

slips back into his position at the console. His expression is sullen.

Bridger, a quiet man with a bony face, leans over and touches his arm. "Relax, he didn't mean anything by it. He just had to see for himself." Rogers doesn't reply.

Back in the bridge, both Barak and Brandt look at Korie. "Well—?"

"Nothing." He slams himself into his couch. "The scanners check out okay."

"Then the bogie's gone—" Barak.

Brandt nods slowly. "While we were sneaking in, he was sneaking out."

"Do you suppose," says Barak, "that he might have been trying to sneak up on us during the thirty-four hours that we were trying to sneak up on him?"

Korie shakes his head at the thought. Brandt considers it. "It's possible, but—"

"Mr. Barak," says Korie. "In the computer, coded under BOGIE, you will find a set of preliminary search patterns, spiralling outward from this point. They'll cover the activities of this ship for the next nine hours. I would appreciate it if you would set them up on the boards, please."

Barak looks to Brandt; the captain nods.

"Also in the computer," Korie continues, "coded under BOGIE II, you will find a search pattern that will cover the next three days of ship's activities. Would you please set that one up on standby?"

Again Barak looks to Brandt; again the captain nods.

"Also," Korie adds, "you will find supplementary search programs coded under BOGIE III and BOGIE IV. Those are prolonged-search programs—I hope we won't need them."

The captain nods a third time. "Good thinking, Mr. Korie. I'm glad you planned ahead. Now, if I may see both of you gentlemen in my cabin—" He rises and leaves the bridge.

Korie and Barak exchange a glance. Barak pauses to give an order to Jonesy, then they follow the captain aft.

Sixteen

Morality—like velocity—is relative. The determination of it depends on what the objects around you are doing. All one can do is measure one's position in relation to them; never can one measure one's velocity or morality in terms of absolutes.

JARLES "FREE FALL" FERRIS,
*Philosophy and Relativity:
A Survey of Ideas*

The captain is standing by his table. "Come in, gentlemen."

Korie follows Barak into the room, a thoughtful, almost skeptical expression on his face.

"Close the door, please."

Korie does so.

Brandt looks from one to the other; the husky, heavyset black astrogator and the lanky, pale first officer. He weighs his words carefully. "We have made a—what you might call a valiant effort to catch this bogie—"

Korie snorts.

Brandt ignores it. "—But I think the time has come to assess the situation realistically. First of all, I should like to congratulate you, Mr. Korie—and you too, Mr. Barak—on the fine way you handled yourselves and the crew this morning. I'm impressed by the skill and speed that was displayed in the precision handling of the ship during the attack maneuver. The response to orders has rarely been as prompt as it was today. Uh, my compli-

ments to both of you for the fine manner in which you
have trained and prepared this crew and this ship. I am
entering a note of recommendation into the log."

Brandt drops his gaze to the table beside him, rear-
ranges some papers on it. "Now, as for the bogie—of
course, we will search for him." He looks up again,
abruptly. "There is certainly the chance that he is still in
the area. However—it is much more likely that we have
lost him for good. We should—be aware of that—and
consider it in our future decisions—"

Korie is looking at him strangely; Barak too. Brandt
hurries on. "I—I think we've won something out of this
experience—a moral victory. We've proven that the
Burlingame can be a responsible member of the United
Systems Fleet. The autolog, of course, will confirm this to
the High Command that we've—in effect, lifted ourselves
by our own bootstraps. We're more than just a backwater
patrol boat—and—and that's something that we can be
proud of.

"Now, we will, uh—continue the search long enough
to be sure that the enemy is not still in the area—and then
we will head for home. I trust that—"

"Sir—" It is Korie.

Frowning at the interruption: "Yes, Mr. Korie?"

"Sir, I would like it entered in the log that I opposed
this course of action to begin with."

"This course of action—?"

"The maneuver we have just completed—the low-
speed attempt to sneak up on the bogie. I would like to
go on record as having recommended an alternate course
of action from the one we followed. If you will remember,
I wanted to go in at high speed from the start."

"Uh, yes—" Brandt pauses for a moment, slightly
taken aback. He licks his lips carefully. "All right. Yes, of
course—uh, by all means, we'll enter it in the log. Who
knows? You may have been right, Mr. Korie, but—the decision was mine to make, and I believed I was acting correctly at the time. I chose the course of action which
seemed to me to be the best. There is no way of knowing
whether or not it was—"

"Except that we've lost the kill."

"There is that, but—"

"If we had gone in the way I wanted to, we would have taken only eight hours to close with him. It'd have been only one-fourth the time and we probably would have caught him trying to sneak away."

"Mr. Korie, we thoroughly discussed all of these possibilities on the bridge, thirty-five or thirty-six hours ago. I do not feel like going over it again. I chose the course of action which seemed to me the best—"

"And it was wrong—"

Brandt looks at him coldly. "I do not thing that either of us is in a position to make that kind of assessment. If any of my command decisions turn out to be *obviously* wrong, I will be the first to admit the error."

Korie meets his gaze firmly. "Yes, sir."

Brandt takes a breath. "Do you have anything to say on this matter, Mr. Barak?"

Barak's expression is noncommittal. "No, sir. My job is to execute the decisions, not make them."

"Mm," says Brandt, slightly displeased with the answer. "All right." His manner changes, becomes more abrupt. "Now, about this search pattern—"

"Sir—" Korie again.

Slightly annoyed: "You could let me finish, Mr. Korie."

"Sir. I would like to recommend—"

"Why don't you *first* wait to hear what I have to say?"

"Yes, sir."

"What I was going to say was that we should continue the search for as long as necessary to determine that the bogie is no longer in this area. I think the standard-pattern search procedure should do. Mr. Barak. At the end of, say twelve hours, if we still haven't picked up a shimmer, we can safely assume that the enemy has vacated this sector, and we can head for home. Mr. Korie—?" The captain indicates with a gesture, almost mocking, that now he may express his opinions, if any.

Korie does have opinions. "First of all, the standard-pattern search procedure *will not* do. That procedure is used mainly for rescue operations and rendezvous. It is not a battle maneuver. It can be consciously evaded. Now, the patterns I have set up—the ones already in the computer—are three-dimensional spirals with random deviations to allow for the enemy's evasive maneuvers.

"A standard search covers a limited area, one in which you know your target is supposed to be. My search patterns covers an ever-expanding sphere because—as you said yourself—we do not know where the bogie is. The point of my search patterns is to *find him*."

"I believe that the standard procedure should also suffice to fill that purpose—

Korie snorts. "And we'll lose the bogie again. Your standard patterns will allow you to put on a show for the crew and for the High Command—so they won't think you gave up too easily—but if that other captain is as clever as he's supposed to be, the only way we're going to find him is to be unorthodox in our searching." He stops abruptly. The captain's features are grim.

"Mr. Korie," he says slowly. "I am not 'putting on a show' for anyone, as you put it."

"Sir, you admit your first battle decision may have been in error—excuse me, too cautious—why not let me have a chance with this one? We still may be able to catch that ship."

Brandt starts to say something, then changes his mind. For a moment, his gaze is inward, thoughtful. "All right, we'll try your pattern for twelve hours—"

"That won't be enough."

"How much time *do* you need?"

"I don't know, I'm not sure," Korie says quickly. "The effectiveness of this procedure requires that we take the time to check a large area of space, as large as possible—that means we need as much time as possible."

"How *much* time?"

"As much as we've got—"

"Give me a figure, Mr. Korie. Two days? Three days?"

Korie says, "I don't know, wait a minute. Let me think—Al," he turns to Barak, "how far are we from home?"

Barak scratches his head. "Let's see, ten light days at 174 lights plus another fifty-six days—about five and a half light years."

"Eleven days' traveling time at top speed, right?"

"Right."

"And how many days of power do we have left in our cells?"

"Um, a little less than forty."

"All right—" Korie does some hasty figuring. "Let's say we need fifteen days of power to get home from here. I'll take half the difference—" He turns to Brandt. "—fifteen days."

"Out of the question. You leave us no margin for error."

"My search spirals won't take us fifteen days of travelling distance away from here—coming back won't take more than seven days, maybe less—there's your margin."

"Still out of the question. You're cutting it way too close."

"All right, not half the difference, a third—ten days."

Brandt considers it.

"Plus—" Korie adds, "one day's worth of power for the missiles. Eight hours' cruising range for each, plus time to unwarp, drop them, and rewarp."

Brandt looks at Barak; the astrogator remains noncommittal; he looks back at Korie. "I don't like it. You can have ten days, Mr. Korie. Ten days. No more. If you don't find your bogie by then, we head for home."

"All right," Korie says. "I'll take it."

"Fine," says the captain. "I don't want you to say I didn't give you a fair chance. You do think ten days is a fair chance, don't you?"

"Under the circumstances—yes."

"Good." He pauses, eyes Korie speculatively. Almost mockingly, he asks, "Would you go on record with that? That is, may we enter it in the log?"

The first officer exhales loudly. "Yes, sir."

"Fine."

"May I be excused now, sir? I'd like to go to the bridge and see that the search patterns are being properly initiated—after all, I assume my ten days have already started."

"Yes, they have. All right, you're excused."

"Thank you, sir." The door slides shut behind him.

Seventeen

There is no way to command loyalty. Like respect, it must be earned.

ROGER BURLINGAME,
The Officer's Handbook

Brandt looks at Barak. "You have something to say, Al?" Barak doesn't look back at him, he studies his fingernails instead. "I don't think so."

"But you're thinking it, aren't you—?"

Barak looks up sharply.

"I can see it in your face," Brandt explains. "There's something—bothering you."

Barak eyes the captain carefully. Brandt's face is hard-chiseled granite. The astrogator knows the appearance is deceptive, but Brandt's eyes are steely.

Barak says, "Well, sir—if you really must know, I think Korie is right."

"About what?"

"About the bogie, sir—about the best course of action to have taken. I think we should have gone in at top speed, too."

"Mmm," says Brandt, making a wry face. He turns slightly away. "You don't think I made the right choice." A statement, not a question.

"No, sir; I don't."

"Ah, tell me, Al," Brandt looks at him again. In a slightly sharper tone of voice. "Why do you think I made such a decision?"

Barak shrugs. "You—had your reasons—I guess—"

"And what do you think those reasons were—?"

The astrogator shakes his head. "I wouldn't presume to—"

"Take a guess."

"Captain, sir—" Barak's tone is suddenly stiff. "I learned a long time ago not to question the orders of my superior officers. Usually they have reasons I don't know about—"

"That's true, Al; but I want you to understand those reasons—"

"If you please, sir—I'd rather not. It might affect the performance of my duties to know such things. My job is to work out the mechanics of your decisions; I don't need to understand *why* you make them."

"And you're not curious—?"

"You might say I don't want to be involved—you might tell me something that would change my opinion of someone I have to work with—and that might affect my performance of my duties."

Brandt nods slowly, a careful understanding. "Sit down, Al." He gestures to a chair.

The astrogator crosses the room in three steps and takes a seat. The spindly wooden frame creaks under his weight. His gaze is on the captain; Brandt has moved to face him from the opposite side of the room.

"You know," he says, "your reasons for not wanting to know more are very perceptive—they indicate to me that you already suspect why I made the decision the way I did." He frowns thoughtfully, then says quietly, "What do you think of Korie?"

"Korie—? Why he's a—an intelligent officer and —and—"

Brandt looks at him wryly. "Go on . . ."

Brandt takes a breath. "Sir, Mr. Korie is a fine officer; a little too much by the book perhaps, but still a fine officer. He knows his ship better than any man I've ever seen; he has very high standards and he expects the men and equipment to live up to them."

"And if they don't?"

"Uh, Mr. Korie is a stern disciplinarian, sir—but again, he's strictly by the book."

"Come on now, Al." Brandt leans up against the shelf with the typer on it. "I asked you what you *thought* of him; I didn't ask for a textbook description."

"I'm sorry, sir, but that's all that's necessary for me to know about Mr. Korie—or think about him."

"You don't have any opinions of your own . . . ?"

"I don't know what more you want me to say, if that's what you mean."

Brandt brushes a speck of dust off the typing machine. "What I meant was—what do you think of him *as a person*?"

Barak shakes his head. "I . . . don't."

Brandt accepts that. He chews it over thoughtfully and accepts it. "All right." He straightens. "Would you like me to tell you what I think of him?"

"Uh, sir—"

"I think that First Officer Korie is the most dangerous man on this ship. He has a single-mindedness of purpose which is all-consuming and deadly. Everything in his life and everything in this ship is being sacrificed on the alter of his incredible ego—"

"Oh, now, that's hardly—"

"—and his manic determination to be a battle commander is perhaps the most dangerous of all—especially because of his violent temper. Have you noticed his fits of hyperthyroid nervousness? Have you watched him on the bridge? When in pursuit of that bogie, Mr. Korie becomes like a madman—"

"Sir, I must protest—"

Brandt is brought up short. "Protest?"

"Mr. Korie is not—that bad."

"Not . . . that . . . bad . . ." The captain hesitates. "You mean—you wouldn't mind following him into battle."

"No, sir; I wouldn't. Mr. Korie is—is a careful planner—"

"Al," says Brandt. "I *would* be afraid to follow Mr. Korie into battle."

For a moment, there is silence between the two men. Finally, Barak says, "Why, sir—?"

"Look around you, Al—you see this ship? The

Burlingame—an F-class cruiser. Do you know how old this ship is? Do you know the state of her equipment? Do you know the condition of this—this hulk?"

"I know it could be better," the astrogator says carefully.

"Yes," Brandt smiles at that. "It could be better—it certainly couldn't be much worse."

"You exaggerate, sir. There's been a lot of work done on the engines lately and Mr. Korie has had a lot of new equipment installed—"

"Ah, yes, that's another example of his—what did I call it?—his single-minded determination to be a battle captain. The *Burlingame* is his toy. He thinks he's going to turn her into a fighting ship—he thinks he already has."

Barak doesn't say anything. His expression is carefully neutral.

The captain is striding back and forth in the narrow room. "Al, this ship is not the fighting machine Mr. Korie thinks it is—these men are not battle trained. Korie has become so possessed by his vision that he's blind to the truth of the matter. The *Burlingame* is little better than a moving wreck—despite Korie's improvements. She was supposed to be scrapped three years ago. Instead, they recommissioned her." He slams his hand against the plastic panelling of the wall. "She's nothing but a hulk! A rotten, stinking hulk—"

Barak is looking at the floor. "I'm sorry you think that, sir. I—I like this ship."

Brandt looks at him, suddenly surprised. "You do?"

"Yes, sir."

"For God's sake—why?"

Barak shakes his head. "I just do. She's small and she's comfortable and she's easy to live with."

"Easy to live with?"

"If you know what you're doing and if you're not in too much of a hurry to get somewhere else. Mr. Korie wants to be a battle commander. I don't blame him for being impatient with the *Burlingame*. He want to get off. There are other men on this ship who'd like transfers off too—for one reason or another—I don't blame them for being impatient either—"

"Al," Brandt says in a sharply serious note. "I'm one of those 'other men' who wants a transfer off."

Almost a whisper, "I know, sir."

"You do?"

"Yes, sir. The whole ship knows."

"Oh. Well—I suppose it really isn't a secret anymore." He wipes at his nose. "Well, anyway, I want to get off too." He sits down on his bed, facing the astrogator. "I want a base job. I want to help them win the war where I can help best. You know they're fighting this war all wrong, Al—they're fighting to win. And that's not how to win a war anymore. Now, you win by—enduring."

Brandt pauses. Barak is leaning morosely forward in his chair, staring at the floor, his elbows resting on his knees, his head sunk low on his chest. He nods slowly to show that he is still listening.

"Al," explains the captain, "I don't want to fight. I don't want to meet the enemy. I just want to outlive him. In order to do that, I have to avoid contacting him. That's why I—"

Barak looks up sharply. "Sir, I figured as much. It seems to me when you said we should sneak up on him that you were purposely trying to give the enemy a chance to get away."

"Why didn't you say something then?"

"I—wasn't sure." He returns to his contemplation of the space between his shoes. "Besides, you explained it so well—"

"Mm, yes. I don't want that bogie, Al. I don't want it. I—I'm not afraid of him, don't misunderstand; it's just that I don't think we could survive a contact with the enemy. We're not that fast or that skillful, or . . ." he trails off. "I couldn't just give up the chase, turn around, and head for home, though. It wouldn't—be right. So I did the only thing I could. I let him get away.

"Al, I'm a career man. The navy is my life—I was running ships for years before this war broke out. Now, everything's changed and I—there are new kinds of officers now. They don't understand what running a ship is all about. Like Korie, they think it's some kind of game—they're possessed by the idea of war. They—

"Al, Korie thinks he's transformed this ship into something more than it is. But, he hasn't—and there's no way to tell him he's mistaken.

"Oh, look, I'll admit he's done a fine job in many respects. I'm pleased with the way he's tightened up the *Burlingame*. And I don't mind letting him have a free hand with the crew and the engines. It's one less thing for me to worry about—and it's good experience for him if he ever gets a ship of his own. But—a battle commander? No—I don't want to trust my life to his hands. The *Burlingame* is still a hulk. The best that can be said for her is that she moves and holds air. Al, we're going to survive this war. We're going to endure. We're going to do it by not chasing after the enemy and looking for trouble. Is that such a terrible thing?"

"I don't know, sir—" Barak's voice is low, almost inaudible, "—but Threebase sent us out here to do a mission. We're supposed to do it—or die trying. I think this ship—Korie too—deserves a chance to prove itself. I think you're wrong for holding us back and not letting us have the kill."

A pause. "All right. That's your opinion. My opinion is otherwise. Korie isn't ready, this ship isn't ready, and this crew isn't ready for battle. I did what I did to keep us from making contact with the enemy and I'd do it again." He stands abruptly, crosses to the opposite side of the room. "Al, tell me, don't you want to live? Why are you so easygoing? How do you get along with Korie? Why do you like this ship?"

"If you have to ask, you don't understand. I just do. I'm that kind of a person."

"All right. Well, what do you think, Al—I mean, about what I've just told you? Don't you see that I'm right?"

Barak doesn't move. He is shrunken into himself and staring at the floor. His face is troubled; his eyes are almost moist. "Sir, I don't know. I don't know—I've always depended on my captains to do my thinking for me. I—I don't like to see them—show signs of weakness."

"You think I'm being weak."

"I don't know—I think so. I wish you were running this ship instead of Korie, but—you're not—I want to serve a captain I can support 100 per cent, sir."

Brandt looks at him for a long time. "What's that supposed to mean?" His voice is stiff.

"Nothing, sir—I—"

"Go on, Al. You can say it."

"I already have, sir," Barak's words are choked. "I respect the captain you should have been—so does the crew. But it's Mr. Korie who gives the orders now—"

"He does it by my authority!" insists Brandt, a little too loudly.

"I wish you were right, sir—but he does it by his own authority. The crew obeys him."

Brandt is stiff. "They obey *me*. I'm the captain." He repeats it. "*I'm* the captain." His mouth forms the words again. "I'm the captain."

Barak stares. There is silence.

Brandt returns his gaze. "Well?" he demands.

"Yes, sir." Barak is resigned. "You're the captain."

"Thank you, Mr. Barak."

Barak lowers his eyes. "May I be excused, sir?"

"Yes, Mr. Barak. You may be excused."

Eighteen

The only constant in the universe is change.
I Ching

The opposite of change is not resistance to change, but change in the opposite direction.
I Ching

The only thing you can be sure of is that you can't really be too sure of anything.
TOM DIGBY, twentieth-century
American philosopher

On his way back to the bridge, Korie stops at the radec room. "Rogers, Bridger—"

Bridger looks up; Rogers keeps his gaze fixedly on his monitors.

"I just wanted to tell you to keep your scanners wide open. We're starting a prolonged search for the bogie—you two are the key part of it. If you don't do your job, we might as well not go. But you'll do your jobs; I—have confidence in you." He looks from one to the other. "You haven't let me down yet." He looks at Rogers in particular, his eyes narrowing thoughtfully. The boy is rigid before his console; the brace across his back gives him a bulky, hunchbacked appearance. "Well, carry on—" The first officer continues on to the bridge.

He drops into the Command and Control Seat familiarly. "Donnelly," he calls, even before he has settled himself; the officer at the pilot console looks up. "What's our warp factor?"

"A hundred lights."

"Increase it to a hundred and thirty. Continue on the same search patterns."

"Yes, sir."

Korie checks the controls of the seat then; satisfied, he begins to reassure himself as to the ship's operational status. Everything is still at workable levels—fine ...

He taps the intercom. "Engine room—"

"Yes, sir."

"Put Chief Leen on the line, please."

"Yes, sir." After a pause, "Lean here."

"Chief, this is Korie."

"Yes, sir?"

"I just wanted to compliment you and thank you."

"Sir?"

"Your crew did a fine job during this morning's maneuver. We didn't catch the bogie, but your men seemed to be at peak efficiency. I'm pleased with them."

"Thank you, sir."

"You'll tell them for me, won't you?"

"Yes, sir—but if you'd say a word to them yourself, it might be better appreciated."

"Yes, of course; you're right. I'll try and get down there later."

"Mr. Korie—?" The chief's voice is cautious. "About the gym—"

"Chief," Korie cuts him off. "Let's forget about it." He chooses his words carefully. "I'm sure there's a good reason why it wasn't properly secured."

"Yes, sir."

"We have more important things to concern ourselves with. We're still going after that bogie; we're in a search pattern now. We're going to keep searching until we find him. I'm only concerned now that you keep your generators running tightly and your crew on top of every situation; so let's not worry about the gym. If the engine room crew continues to perform as well as they did this morning, there won't be a word said about it."

"Yes, sir. We'll do our best."

"Fine—uh, Chief, there's one more thing."

"Yes, sir?"

"We're not through with the drills. I'm scheduling a new set of them. Three hours a day for each watch."

There is silence from the other end. When he does answer, Leen's voice is noticeably colder. "Yes, sir."

"These will be full battle simulations, but they'll be a different kind of problem from the ones we were working before. These will be discovery and attack maneuvers, a little more complicated and difficult."

"Yes, sir. We'll be—ready."

"Good. Thank you." He switches off. For a moment he relaxes in the chair, fingers tapping on the arm of it. The bridge hums to itself around him.

Forward, the big screen shows the stress-field lines flickering steadily past, but at an odd vector. Instead of plunging headlong through it, they are moving diagonally downward across the rectangular gridwork.

Korie makes a decision; he touches the arm of the chair. "All hands, now hear this. This is First Officer Korie." He pauses for a second—as if to catch their attention—then continues, "As you know, we lost the bogie this morning—but we haven't stopped looking for him. He may still be in the area and we're going to keep searching until we find him. Even if he's trying to move out of the area, we're going to catch him.

"I want to congratulate all of you—and thank you— for your fine performance of your duties. And I hope I can continue to depend on you as this search progresses. We still have a very good chance and we're going to make the most of it. With your continued support, there's nothing we can't do together. Again, I thank you." He switches off.

Jonesy is standing at his right, waiting to talk with him. "Yes?"

"It's about this search pattern. I have a couple of questions."

"Yes?"

"We've increased our speed by thirty lights, but that'll add another twenty light days of visibility to our warp. Are you sure you want that?"

Korie looks at him. "You're right, but we don't have much choice." He swivels to face the other. "It's like this—we have a time limit; we have only ten days in which to find that bogie, but we also have a certain amount of area to cover. Ordinarily, I'd say we should keep our speed low so the enemy doesn't know where we are any more than we know where he is; but in this case, we have to find him fast.

"Now, I'm pretty sure that he's keeping his speed low—so we'll have to get fairly close to him to see him. With our speed so high, he'll be able to see us before we see him. We'll be like a dog thrashing around the bushes— maybe we'll scare him into making a run for it; in which case, we'll pick him up again. That's what I'm hoping for."

"Yes, sir. But, what I'm concerned about is the effect of our increased speed on the search pattern itself. The way you have this set up, we won't actually be covering every part of the suspected area; but if I understand this correctly, we will be moving the ship's detection radius through as wide an area as possible so as to intersect any possible course that the other might be on."

"That's right. We're travelling on the surface of an expanding sphere of possible locations."

"Well, with the increased speed," points out Jonesy, "we'll be hitting some of these areas too soon. Also, there's the greater chance that he'll see us in time to veer out of the way."

"You're right," Korie realizes abruptly. "Uh, we'll have to decrease speed until we can work out an alternate set of patterns for the higher warp factor—"

"I've already done that, sir. I had EDNA recompute your patterns for warp factor 130. I hope you don't mind—"

Korie looks at him, pleasantly surprised. "No, no, of course not. I'm delighted that you're so far ahead of me. Go ahead, set them up on the boards and implement them."

"Yes, sir." Jonesy starts to go.

"And Jonesy—," Korie adds. "Thanks."

"You're welcome, sir—but I want to make this kill *too*." And then the assistant astrogator is back to his board.

Nineteen

There must be an easier way to make a living.
Remark attributed to His
Holiness POPE GREGOR II

The first officer's cabin is close to the captain's—at least physically if not mentally. Rogers glances at the man with him, then knocks at the door; timidly at first, then with a resigned, let's-get-it-over-with attitude.

"Come in," calls a muffled voice.

Rogers enters, followed by Reynolds, the union representative. The room is dark, Korie is lying on his bunk. "Turn on the light," he mumbles. As Rogers does so, he winces and puts his hand over his eyes. "What do you want?"

"I want to talk to you, sir—"

"Uh—" Korie yawns and rubs his eyes; notices Reynolds for the first time. "What's he here for?"

Reynolds and Rogers exchange a glance. Reynolds opens his mouth to speak, but Rogers blurts out, "I asked him to come with me, sir. It's my right."

Korie makes a face, stifles another yawn.

"I've been thinking about what you said, sir—"

"Said about what?"

"What you said in the shower room, sir."

"Oh that—what about it?" Korie levers himself up on one elbow. "Have you come to tell me about Wolfe?"

Rogers straightens; the brace is stiff across his back. "No, sir." He hesitates, but when he does speak, his voice is controlled. "Uh, you said that you'd bully the information out of me if you had to."

"Uh huh . . ." Korie's tone is guarded. "And—"

"Well, I've decided—" Rogers looks to Reynolds again, but the union representative is carefully expressionless. "—I've decided that if you want, then that's the only way you're going to get anything from me. I mean, I'm not going to change my story."

"I see. Did you talk this over with Mr. Reynolds before you came to see me?"

"Sir," puts in Reynolds. "Mr. Rogers only asked me to witness this conversation, nothing more. As far as I know, he's acting on his own."

"I *see.*"

"No, sir," says Rogers. "I don't think you do."

"All right," Korie sighs and pushes himself into a sitting position. He rubs the sleep from his eyes. "Tell me about it." His tone is bored, almost impatient.

"Well, it's like this. You told me I have to be responsible for my own actions. And, uh, you're right; so this is where I have to start being responsible. I have to tell you no."

Korie exhales. Loudly. "An odd place to start."

"Don't you see? Telling you anything wouldn't be taking on my own responsibilities at all. It'd just be shifting them to someone else."

The first officer nods slowly.

"If I told you what happened, you'd use it against Wolfe—but I'd be the one who gets blamed for telling you. So this is where I draw the line and accept my responsibility. I have to say no to you. You'll *have* to bully me, sir."

"All right, I'll make a note of it." Korie suppresses another yawn. "Is that all there is to your reasons?"

"—There is one other thing."

"Yes?"

"Well, uh—we both know what happened. Everybody on the ship knows it. But unless I'm willing to testify, it can't be proven. And I'm not going to testify. And Wolfe knows it. In fact, the whole crew knows it. Thereore, I've got a certain degree of power over Wolfe, ight?"

Korie just looks at him. "You're awfully naïve, Rogers."

"I don't think so, sir. Their attitude has changed; Wolfe's attitude has changed. I don't mean they're being ice or anything like that, but at least they're leaving me lone. And that's an improvement over what it was be-ore."

Korie scratches his head, rumpling his pale hair even more. He looks over to Reynolds. "Is this true?"

Reynolds' tone is neutral. "I couldn't say, sir."

"You're really a big help," Korie mutters. He looks back to Rogers. From this angle, the young man seems unnaturally broad-shouldered. "Well, I hope the bit of backbone you're showing now is more than just that brace on your back—because that's coming off pretty oon. Right now, you think you're standing up to me; I hope you can stand up to the crew when the time comes."

"I'm—not at war with the crew, sir. I'm supposed to be one of them."

"Oh, yes; that's right." Korie stretches and stands, moves to a nearby chair. "I'll tell you, Rogers," he says, lowering himself into it. "I don't really care anymore whether you tell me anything or not. I don't need your help to bust Wolfe—it's all right if you hear this, Reynolds; Wolfe is your responsibility too. He's going to be back on watch soon enough, and I expect he'll do something else just as stupid within a few days. So, I don't really need your help. And I really don't feel like—bullying you. So, if you want to think you're one of the crew now, well go ahead and think it."

"I don't know if I am or not, sir. But you told me I'd have to make or break on this ship and no other. So I have to do what I think is right."

Korie waves it off. "All right—look, I don't care what you do. All I want is that bogie. If you do your job and keep out of my way, I'll be"—he snorts it—"happy."

"Yes, sir."

"Now, get out of here, both of you. I want to go back to sleep."

"Yes, sir."

As the door slides shut behind them, Reynolds look at Rogers. "You know something?"

"What?"

"You're *still* an asshole."

"Oh, well—" Rogers looks him in the eye. "That' just *one* opinion." Then he turns and walks away, leavin the other snorting in contempt and shaking his head.

Twenty

The trouble with having power if that you have to use it—and once you start using it, it's very hard to stop.

STEPHEN-JAMES WATLING,
Forty-sixth President of the
United States

Channel B, the all-talk channel:

"What is it? Five days now?"

"Yeah."

"You think we'll find the bogie?"

"Naw."

"Korie does."

"Well, we all know about Korie, don't we?"

"Aw, say what you like—I'd still rather have Korie on my side than against me."

"How can you tell the difference?"

"No, I'm serious—I'd rather have him on this ship than on that bogie."

"Not me—I wish he was on that bogie right now."

"No, listen a minute—we stand a little enough chance as it is. One thing you can say about Korie, he's a killer—"

"Of his own men, yeah. Christ, one more drill and I'll apply for the straightjacket myself; they won't have to come and get me."

"Yeah, but if Korie was on that other ship, he'd be after us so fast—"

"If Korie was on that other ship, Brandt would have

turned this one around and taken us home long befor
this. We wouldn't have come this far and we wouldn't b
searching this long."

"It's not the searching that worries me."

"Huh?"

"Was anyone paying attention to that last set o
drills?"

"No, why? Should we have?"

"I'll say. Do you know what he was rehearsing? A
Valsalva maneuver."

"Never heard of it."

"It's never been done—except in simulations. They
can't find anyone who's stupid enough to try it for real.'

"Huh? Why?"

"You dump your load *before* you unwarp—"

"Shit!"

"*Now* you've got something to worry about! Tha
asshole may want to try it for real!"

"Woops! Speak of the devil. Here we go again—"

Twenty-one

Once you give an order on any subject, you are accepting the responsibility for that area of authority. The lesser-ranking individual will usually be glad to relinquish that responsibility to you—thus, once you give an order on any subject, you are committing yourself to give orders in that area from that point on.

Never accept the burden of trivia that lesser-ranking men will want to put on your shoulders. Insist that each perform to the utmost of his abilities; insist that each man take the responsibility for the job he is supposed to fill.

You can't run the ship yourself; you've got to trust these men anyway—why not trust them all the way?

ROGER BURLINGAME,
The Officer's Handbook

Of the twenty-six human functions that must be performed to move the *Burlingame* through space, fully twenty-two of them are information-moving functions—a man sits at a console and sees that (a) this piece of informations is (b) moved to (c) this place at (d) this specific time. The more important a man is, the more information he has to move; he moves it from one bank of computers to another, or from the computers into the control network, or from the sensors into the computers; always there is a computer either receiving or sending the information.

The man in the Command and Control Seat is the most important man of all, he reviews the information. When the ship is in operation, his function is simple—he has to decide whether to let the information flow continue or whether to interrupt it. If he interrupts it, the *Burlingame* stops.

When the *Burlingame* stops, it is his responsibility to get it moving again. That means examining the information responsible for the stoppage in the first place, deciding what needs to be done about it, re-programming and redirecting where necessary, and finally, giving the order to start the information flow again.

The job of the man in the seat is to see that the right information is being handled in the right manner. If it isn't, then his job is to correct it. Usually, this means sitting long hours in the Command and Control chair, listening to monotonous chatter on the intercom, and watching abstract diagrams on the screens. But this is his responsibility; he can't slough it off to a lesser man.

The computers hum, the consoles tick and click, the monitors beep. The screens flash with lines and curves, yellow, green and blue. A full-scale battle simulation is indistinguishable from the real thing. The same images appear on the boards, the same patterns of lights and numbers. The same information moves from place to place.

The only difference is that the information is hypothetical. The control network has been disengaged and is being monitored in the auxiliary control deck. The vectors and velocities depicted on the screens of the bridge have no correlation to reality.

If there were a correlation, it wouldn't be a drill.

Korie has an earphone pressed to the side of his head. Voices—blurred one into another—rattle from the tinny speaker.

"Monitor alpha—nine six three."

"Got it."

"PL reading: zero zero two."

"Zero zero two, right."

"DTR at delta three zero."

"Delta three zero. Cycling."

"D Channel on."

"D Channel is overing. Let me take it on R."

"R Channel, right."

"I need a stability count."

"Mark seven minutes—"

"Stand by for new polarities."

"Standing by."

"Forty-five degrees—180 degrees—120 degrees."

"Confirming: 45 degrees—180 degrees—120 degrees."

"Hold for execution."

"Holding."

"Interrupt evasion maneuver."

"Stand by—evasion maneuver disengaged."

"Execute new polarities."

"Right."

A massive framework turns on its gimbals in three directions at once. Two sets of cables slide smoothly along their silicone-greased channels to follow the motion of the generators; the third set—

—fouls on a mounting, hanging up another cable, a lesser one. The thing on the end of it screams as it is jerked from the webbing; a yellow-suited doll—

Instantly, the generators stop their motion. The yellow thing swings—slams into a stanchion. Red lights start flashing on all the boards—

The sound of the scream is enough. Korie hits the red button on his chair arm: all the lights, all the panels, all the boards go red. All the information is stopped. The drill is interrupted.

—But when one flow of data is diverted, another begins; requests for reasons why, followed by hasty answers.

"Status report—What's the emergency?"

"Something in the engine room—"

"—The 'monkey crew'. Someone got tangled in the—"

"Sir, this is auxiliary control. Do you want us to shut down?"

"Wait a minute," snaps Korie. "Bridge, to go normal operation; re-engage control network. Report status of ship. Auxiliary control, stand by to be relieved."

"Yes, sir."

"Engine room, what's going on—?"

"We've got a man caught in the generator cage—"

"Is he hurt—?"

"Don't know yet—"

"Are the generators maintaining warp?"

"Yes, sir. Not a flicker."

"Good. Stand by."

Korie glances quickly around the bridge; the red lights are vanishing off the boards. Only the engine room is still paralyzed—

"Goldberg, take the helm." Korie is out of the seat.

"Yes, sir. Do you want me to wake the captain? Call him to the bridge?"

"No, not yet. Let me see what it is first." And he's out the door.

Korie races toward the rear of the ship, once crashing into another man who hasn't moved out of the way in time. His headlong rush is punctuated by the PA system: "Medical Officer Panyovsky, come to the engine room, please. Medical Officer Panyovsky, come to the engine room."

Korie thrusts himself down the no-grav tube, disregarding all safety regulations. He hits the bottom with a thump, stumbles, and keeps going.

The engine room is a scene of controlled confusion. Most of the men are still at their boards, but Leen and several others are in and around the webbing. Two of the men in the "monkey crew" are just lowering a third to the deck. A fourth suited man, his helmet removed, his ground cable dangling, stands by to receive the unconscious figure. He and Leen grab the body and keep it from slumping to the floor. Two other men move up with a stretcher.

Korie waits until the figure is laid out on it, then moves in. "Who is it?"

"MacHeath." Leen is removing the man's helmet; Korie kneels down and begins to help him. The chief looks at him coldly. "If you don't mind, *sir*—"

Korie returns the stare. "This is no time for that, Leen. He's my man too." He unsnaps the last seam and pulls the hood off. He unzips the front of the suit and puts his ear to MacHeath's T-shirted chest.

"All right," Leen pulls his hands back. "You do it." He stands. "You men get back to your posts. Clear those boards. I still see red lights. You too, Beagle. Get back up in the webs. Fowles—" He strides around angrily, snapping orders. "—and where's the doc, dammit?!!"

Korie snaps at him. "Leen! Shut up! I can't hear anything!" He lowers his head again to MacHeath's chest. He still doesn't hear anything—Korie reacts without thinking; he thrusts his face up against MacHeath's and begins mouth-to-mouth resuscitation. His hand on the other's chest feels the gentle rise of the lungs as Korie breathes warm air into his throat—blow gently, lungs rise; suck gently, lungs fall; blow gently—

"That's it, keep it up—" The speaker is Panyovsky. He drops to his knees, pushes Korie's hand out of the way. He listens first with his ear, then with a stethoscope.

Korie pauses to look at him—

"Don't stop!" Panyovsky is rummaging in his bag; he begins laying things out—a hypodermic spray, an electrode unit, an oxygen bottle—

"Move a second. Let me get this suit off him." Panyovsky jerks it free, exposing a section of bare arm. He presses the hypodermic to it; there is a hiss—

"Adrenaline," he explains. He picks up the oxygen bottle, snaps the plastic cover off the mask, and turns a valve. "Here—give him this."

Korie does so; he fumbles the mask into place over MacHeath's nose and mouth. Panyovsky puts his stethoscope to the man's chest again, frowns—

—reaches for his electrodes. With scissors, he cuts open MacHeath's T-shirt, then smears a light salve on the man's chest. "Watch out," he cautions. He presses the electrodes to the spots of salve, then thumbs the control on one of them. MacHeath jerks—

"Again!" says Korie. MacHeath jerks—

—jerks and gasps—

Panyovsky drops the electrodes, listens with the stethoscope again. He relaxes slightly. "Hold that oxygen bottle steady. He's going to need it."

"He's alive—?"

"He's in shock." Panyovsky begins pulling at the seals of the yellow protective suit. "He's got other injuries too. Leen, come here. Help me get this off him."

The chief is there almost immediately, pulling and tugging with Panyovsky. "There. Got it." MacHeath's burly form lies naked between them. Leen stares across the body at Korie. "I thought this was supposed to be a full simulation, sir—why don't you continue the drill? Pretend this is a real casualty—"

"Shut up, Leen." Panyovsky, pulling a blanket up.

Korie says, "You're right, you know. I shouldn't have stopped the drill. If this had been a real battle, we might all be dead now—"

Leen's face is incredulous. "You're serious, aren't you—?"

"Shut up, both of you!" Panyovsky tucks the edges of the foil blanket under MacHeath's form. He plugs it in at the end of the stretcher and sets a temperature control. "Give me two men to take him to sick bay." He moves up, straps the oxygen mask to MacHeath's pallid face. "I won't need you anymore, sir. Thanks."

Leen taps O'Mara and Fowles for stretcher duty. With Panyovsky staying close to the side of the stretcher, they move out of the engine room. Korie and Leen are left behind.

Leen looks over at the tall first officer, bitterness and anger etched across his features. He opens his mouth to speak, then thinks better of it. He bites back his words instead, and turns away—

"Leen."

"Yes, Mr. Korie?"

"What was MacHeath doing on the 'monkey crew'? He's a console man."

"Yes, sir. I asked him to."

"Why?"

Leen straightens. "I wanted him to help me run some checks on the generators—"

"During a drill?"

"Yes, sir. Because that's the only time we'd be turning the generators, and that's what I wanted to check."

"You were checking the way the generators turn?"

"No, sir—I was monitoring the phase adapters." He spits the words, "I don't want to burn out any more."

"I see," says Korie. He surveys the other carefully.

"Is that all, sir? May I go?"

"No. I'm not through."

Leen stiffens, his jaw jutting forward. His whole attitude says, *All right, you bastard. I can take whatever you want to dish out.*

"Chief," Korie says slowly. "If you're expecting me to chew you out, you're mistaken. You haven't done anything wrong. You've done exactly what you should have done."

Leen's jaw drops—

Korie adds, "I might fault you for snapping at me, but considering the circumstances, it's forgivable. Everything else you've done down here has been exemplary. You and your crew have been handling your jobs to the best of your abilities, and if you felt you needed to check the phase adapters—I can't fault you for that. Just keep it up, please. Thank you." He turns on his heel and exits, leaving an astonished chief engineer staring after him—

Outside the door, Korie pauses; slams his hand against a panel. (Christ, I'd like to take him apart—but I can't. I still need him too much. First, I've got to get that bogie. Then, I'll see about Leen—)

Twenty-two

The design of the machine, the nature of its use, the principles by which it operates, all have an effect on the men who come in contact with it. Our ships exist in isolated bubbles, temporary prisons moving alone through a resistant stress field: our warps are generated by pitting energy against energy—and we superimpose a secondary conflict on them to give them motion.

Then we put human beings inside those ultra-stressed pressure chambers.

Doesn't the nature of the tools they are working with affect the way they use them, indeed, even the very way they think and live?

JARLES "FREE FALL" FERRIS,
Electric Philosophies

Korie starts for the bridge—but his communicator bleeps insistently.

He thumbs it to life. "Korie here."

"Mr. Korie, this is sick bay. Panyovsky would appreciate it if you could come down."

"Right. I'm on my way." He goes at a half-run, the excitement still coursing through his veins. By the time he reaches the medical compartment, he's walking slower and panting slightly.

He enters without knocking. "How's MacHeath?"

The orderly looks up. He starts to shake his head that he doesn't know, when Panyovsky comes out of the other room. "He just died."

The sensation is like being kicked in the stomach. Korie gasps for air. "He—he—can't be. He was alive when you left the engine room—"

Panyovsky pushes him into a chair; he closes and locks the door. "Sorry, Jon—" Korie starts at the sound of his little-used first name. "But you can only revive a body so many times. His heart stopped again while we were putting him on the table. I couldn't restart it—" Abruptly, the doctor crumples, sinks down onto the bench opposite Korie. "Oh, Christ!" He buries his face angrily into his hands. "Goddammit all anyway! Son of a bitch! Shit, shit, shit—hell, hell, hell! Aw, *shit*!" For a moment there is silence, then he looks suddenly up at the first officer; his eyes are red. "Dammit. There aren't enough words. Dammit. Mike, bring me my bottle." To Korie, "Want a drink?"

"Strickly medicinal?"

"No—strictly alcohol."

Mike, the orderly, produces a flash of whiskey. He puts it on the desk by Panyovsky. "Get some cups—get one for yourself," the doctor says, opening the bottle. He looks at Korie. "Mackie was dead before they got him on the stretcher. I—couldn't have saved him."

"But his heart—"

Panyovsky waves that aside. "Reflex reaction; I don't know—I don't think he died all at once. He, uh, was pretty well broken up inside. He wouldn't have survived. Cracked sternum, ruptured lungs, ribs shattered in three places that I know of, burst spleen, and kidneys, too, massive hemorrhaging—he was lucky that the electric shock knocked him out first; he didn't feel a thing—" He takes a plastic cup from Mike and pours himself a drink. "—Uh, the shock alone would have been enough to kill him anyway. I mean, we restarted his heart once, but uh—" Panyovsky shakes his head, "—but we shouldn't have been able to. He's pretty well scorched up inside. Sorry." He sips at his cup morosely. "I think what happened was that his heart didn't realize the rest of him was dead."

Korie takes a cup from the orderly. "Do you know how it happened?"

"Fowles said he got his ground cable caught in the generator cage. When it moved, he was pulled from the webbing and into the mountings. He fell onto a stanchion."

The liquor burns Korie's throat; he makes a face. "That must have been quite a drop."

"According to Fowles, ten meters."

Neither man says anything for a bit. They stare at the floor and listen to the sound of each other's breathing. Occasionally one takes a pull at his cup.

Panyovsky mutters, "Hell of a way to go . . ."

Korie nods. "At least it was painless—it was, wasn't it?"

The doctor shrugs. "I don't know. He had time to scream, didn't he?"

Korie exhales loudly. "Yeah, I guess so—" He rises and steps to the wall communicator. "Bridge."

Goldberg's voice, "Yes, sir?"

"Everything all right?"

"Yes, sir."

"Keeping tight on those search patterns?"

"Yes, sir."

"Good—listen, I want you to wake the captain. Ask him to meet me down in sick bay. Tell him it's—serious."

"Sir—can I ask? How bad is it?"

"Very."

Goldberg hesitates. Korie can almost see him phrasing the next question. "Uh—"

"You'll hear about it later," he interrupts. "Listen, that drill we were on—set it up on the boards again. We'll start over in two hours. It's important; it's the missile evasion exercise."

"Yes, sir—anything else?"

"No, just keep her steady and wake the captain for me."

"Aye, aye."

Korie switches off, turns around, and looks at the doctor; he slumps one shoulder against the wall—he leans, his posture is wry, skeptical, tired.

Panyovsky makes a toasting gesture to him with his cup, as if saluting his courage in continuing, but he shakes his head sadly. "That isn't going to make you very popular with the men."

"You mean the drill?"

"Yes," he sighs. "I think you've pushed them about as far as they'll go."

Korie sits down. "Possibly—but they still need it."

"I don't know, Jon, I don't know." Panyovsky stares down into his cup. "I'm just a little—worried, I guess. You know they don't like you."

"I know—but when has a crew ever liked their officers?"

"Oh, I've seen a few." He takes a drink. "But there must be something about this ship—it's as if the brass purposely assembled a group of people that would hate each other." He puffs his cheeks thoughtfully, blows out the air. "Oh, I know it isn't really like that; all crews get a little sticky every so often; but this one—" He shakes his head again. "—I don't know, it just seems like this one is always angry."

"I've noticed that myself," Korie says. "I think it's the ship. None of us wants to be on this particular tub—the bridge is too cold, the bunkrooms are too warm, the engine room is too loud, the food is bad, the lavatories smell—"

"She's an old ship, Jon. There's not much we can do about that."

Korie shrugs, finishes his liquor in one gulp.

"You could ease up a little."

Korie meets his gaze. "Pan, you're a good doctor, maybe even a good psychonomic analyst—"

Panyovsky holds up his hand. "Jon, listen to me for a minute. I know you want a tight ship, but a good crew is like a violin string. You can only tighten it so much and then it breaks. You reach a point where there's nothing more you can do—except leave them alone."

"You think we're at that point?"

"Close to it."

"Well—I don't know." Korie puts his cup on the desk; Panyovsky refills it. "I keep looking at our efficiency ratings—they're way down; we should be able to

do better. We'll have to do better if we're going to meet
that bogie—"

"Perhaps—but I don't think you're going to get any
more out of this crew now."

"I've got to try."

"You could always give up the bogie instead—"

Korie just looks at him. Coldly.

Panyovsky drops his gaze. Embarrassed, he refills his
own cup. "Anyway," he says, "they don't like you, Jon.
They're going to like you less after today, just because
you're you."

"There's little I can do about that."

"Funny thing," muses the doctor. "I got my training
during the uprisings on Shaleen. That was a civil war, and
we knew who the enemy was—you always knew who
you had to hate, who you had to kill. Here—" He shrugs.
"—it's different. We never see the enemy, we never even
get close to him. It's all done by buttons; all we see is the
shimmer on the screen. He might as well be a simulation."

"So—?"

Panyovsky shakes his head. "This kind of fighting
isn't right, Jon—there's nobody to hate. If we're going to
be at war, we should be able to come face to face with the
enemy; we should be able to experience the actual act of
killing, of taking a stun pistol and pointing it at a man
and pulling the trigger—feeling the awful hum of it;
watching him as his eyes roll back in his head; all his
blood vessels rupture, and his limbs start quivering in pa-
ralysis. All his nerve cells discharge at once, and at
random—it's like an epileptic fit. He gasps, he groans, he
froths at the mouth, he falls down and shakes. If you
keep firing, he'll start hemorrhaging inside, pretty soon
blood starts coming out of his nose and mouth, sometimes the ears too. It takes a long time for a man to die
that way. I don't think it'd be a pleasant experience. I
know it isn't very pretty to watch—" He looks at Korie,
"But if you hate someone enough—"

"Is that what you used on Shaleen?"

Panyovsky nods. "There were times when it was
pretty bad." His manner changes, he straightens and ges-

res at the ship around them. "This is wrong, Jon—
e've denatured the war. We've taken all the horror out
f it. All we have left is the killing, sterile and clean and
uick. And supposedly painless." A pause. "It's no won-
er they hate you, Jon—they've nobody else left to."

Korie is staring off at a corner; the doctor's words
urt—but he won't let it show. "There's only one thing I
an do, Pan. I can try to be the best possible officer I
now how. That means I have to do what I think is right,
ame as you have to do what you think is right when you
et a man on the table."

"Yes," agrees the doctor. "But I can only lose one at
a time—"

Korie looks at him sharply. Panyovsky amends the
ought. "I don't envy your job, Jon—you have no mar-
in for error. You can't afford to be wrong. Ever." He fin-
hes his drink hastily. "Want another?"

Korie shakes his head. Panyovsky caps the bottle.
Well," he says, "I have a body to wrap up for burial. I'll
ave to autopsy him first—" He stands, his motion is
ow, almost tired.

At the sound of the door, he turns. Korie looks up as
randt enters. The captain looks from one to the other.
What's the matter?"

"We've had a death in the engine room."

Brandt goes pale. "Oh, God, no—who?"

"MacHeath," says Korie. "He fell into the generator
age—"

"How? He's a console man—"

"Leen had him on the 'monkey crew' so he could
onitor the phase adapters."

Brandt sags with the weight of it; he turns to
anyovsky. "Has the crew been told?"

"No, not yet."

The captain rubs his chin; his cheeks are unshaven
nd gray. "Oh, Christ," he says. The thought of breaking
ie news—

He looks at Korie. "You want to tell them?"

The first officer nods slightly. "I was thinking that
ight be best."

"All right—I suppose there'll have to be an investigation. It happened during a drill?"

"Yes. We've got the tapes."

"All right. Uh—I guess I'd better get reports from
you and Leen—and from any witnesses."

"That'll be the whole engine room crew."

"Yes," says the captain, his manner deepening. His
eyes seem to focus on something far away. "MacHeath
was a good man."

Korie and Panyovsky look in different directions; neither replies.

Brandt stares at the door behind the doctor. "He's in
there now?"

"Uh huh." Panyovsky.

His gaze still on the door, Brandt says, "You'll take
care of everything—?"

"Yes. I still have to—autopsy him, and then I'll put
him in a stasis box."

"I was thinking," says the captain, "of burial in
space."

Out of Brandt's sight, Korie catches Panyovsky's eye
and shakes his head slightly. Panyovsky sees it and nods
with a flicker of his wide-set eyes. To Brandt, he says, "I
don't think that'd be a good idea."

"Why not?"

"—Uh, I'm thinking of the crew. It might not have a
good effect on them. I'd rather wait until we return to
base."

"I agree," puts in Korie. "For one thing, it'd mean
dropping out of warp—and that'd mean stopping the
search."

Brandt turns to look at him. "I should think you'd be
willing to abandon that by now."

"I still have four days left in which to find that
bogie—"

Brandt doesn't reply. He shakes his head, almost in
pity at Korie's stubborn persistence. "All right," he says.
To the doctor, "You might sound out the men a little and
see how they'd feel about a burial after the search con-
cludes, but before we start back. Otherwise—we'll take
him home."

"You might want to check," says Korie, "and see if e has a will on file. There might be something in there."

"Yes, there might. I'll have to do that."

"Also—"

They are interrupted by a beep from the communica-or. "Sick bay, this is Leen."

The three men exchange a glance; Korie steps to the vall. "Yes, Chief?"

"Uh—" Recognizing the first officer's voice, Leen esitates. "Sir, I called to find out about MacHeath's con-lition. Is he all right?"

"Chief—" Korie's tone is careful. "—MacHeath died ust a little while ago."

There is an audible gasp from the intercom.

Korie continues quickly, "Ah, don't say anything to nyone yet. We were just about to announce it to the rew, and it would be better if you let us do it."

The intercom remains silent, except for a sound like omeone sobbing or choking. Korie looks to Panyovsky, elplessly.

"Sir—" Another voice on the intercom. "What's the natter with Chief Leen?"

Panyovsky steps up. "Why? What happened?"

"He just sort of crumpled up—"

"I'll be right down." He reaches for his bag. "Mike, lon't let anyone else in here till I get back."

"I'm going up to the bridge," says Korie. "I'll make he announcement from there."

"Hold off till I find out about Leen," says 'anyovsky, then darts out the door.

"Right," Korie calls after him. To Brandt, "Do you reed me for anything else, sir?"

"No, You go on up to the bridge. I'll—I'm going to tay here for a while."

"Yes, sir." Korie is already on his way.

—leaving Brandt, staring at the door to the other oom. (My God, what have we done?)

Twenty-three

It isn't power that corrupts; it's the use of it. After a while, a person loses his perspective.

GUNTER WHITE,
Mechanics of Government

Channel B, the all-talk channel:

"Attention, all hands. This is First Officer Korie. About an hour ago, an accident occurred in the engine room, interrupting the drill then in progress. Crewman Randall MacHeath, while on duty on the 'monkey crew,' caught his cable in the generator cage. He was pulled from the webbing and fell more than twenty feet onto a stanchion." Korie pauses, carefully he chooses his next words. "MacHeath's injuries were severe; so severe that Medical Officer Panyovsky was unable to revive him. He was pronounced dead just a short while ago." Again, he pauses.

"There will be a memorial service later this evening. We will hold it in the ship's lounge and broadcast it through the PA system for those of you who will be on station at that time.

"Let me add that both Captain Brandt and I share the grief and shock that every member of this crew must be feeling. MacHeath was a good man. It is our decision that we will dedicate this bogie, this kill, to the memory of Crewman MacHeath. It is no longer for us—it is for him.

"Thank you."

Twenty-four

If he's wrong, he'll be a dead fool—but if he's right, dammit, he'll be a hero.

> JACK MACAULEY,
> mule skinner for General Custer

Chief Leen is sitting on a bench in the cabin he shares with three other men. Captain Brandt is sitting on a chair opposite him. "Are you feeling better now, Chief?"

"Yes, I think so."

"Good."

"I'm sorry. I didn't mean to—break up like that."

"It's all right. It's understandable."

Leen looks around, as if familiarizing himself with his own room. His eyes are red-rimmed and move nervously, at last stopping on the communicator panel. "That didn't help any," he says. "His announcement, I mean."

"He meant well," soothes Brandt.

Leen shakes his head—insistent and quick. His reddish-brown hair is thick and wavy. "Uh uh—*uh uh*. If he'd meant well, he wouldn't have been driving us so hard. Drills and drills and more drills—" He focuses fiercely on the captain. "You know, that's what killed MacHeath—those drills. If he hadn't been so tired—"

"Chief, don't think about it. We can't change the past—" Brandt cuts himself off abruptly; the words sound so banal.

"We ought to try to change the future though." H
meets the captain's eyes.

"Of course," says Brandt. "That's what gives u
hope—the thought that we can make tomorrow better.'

"That's not what I mean—"

"What do you mean?"

"Stop him—stop Korie. Stop the drills and let's g
home. This is mad, this search is—futile. It's alread
killed one man. We're not going to find that bogie; h
must be light years from here by now—"

Brandt doesn't reply. He shifts his position in th
chair, looks off beyond the walls, the floor—"Chief,
don't know—you don't know either. There are—
aspects—to the situation—"

"You're still the captain, aren't you?" Leen's questio
is cutting.

Brandt stiffens. "What do you mean by that? O
course, I'm the captain. *The captain*. But I gave Korie
promise—I told him he could have ten days to search—
He looks at Leen; the chief's eyes are bitter and accusing
Brandt adds hastily, "I don't think we'll find it; we can af
ford the few extra days of patrol—"

"At least make him stop the drills—he's killing us—
And then he realizes the truth of what he has said an
lapses into moody silence.

"I'll talk to him," Brandt promises. "I'll see what
can do, but—I did say he could have the time and tha
means I have to let him maintain battle-readiness too—

"Bullshit!" Leen blazes suddenly. "You're the cap
tain! You can do anything you want to—you can chang
your mind if you want. Korie's becoming the Ahab of th
great wide nothingness—he's using this ship and everyon
in it for one thing only: to chase that bogie—and you'r
just as bad as he is for letting him get away with it
You're supposed to be the captain—"

Brandt stands, cutting off Leen's bitter fury. "Chie
you're right about one thing—I *am* the captain—"

"Then why don't you start acting like on
goddammit?" Leen is close to tears again; his voic
catches and breaks.

Brandt answers gently, "I have to do what's right b

his ship—but I also have to do what's right by the war
nd by the High Command—"

"But you're not—" Leen sobs. "You're not doing
—Korie is. He's acting in your name. Do you approve of
vhat he's doing? Do you?"

Slowly, Brandt says, "No, of course not—but—"

"Then, stop him!"

"—I can't stop him! It goes in the log. Every time
ve go back to base they check that log—and if there's
nything in it they don't understand, they investigate—
nd—"

"Do they know that Korie's running this ship?"

"They know that Korie's been given as much respon-
ibility as he can handle; they know that he's responsible
or putting this ship back into shape; they know that he's
cting under my approval—if I suddenly go back on my-
elf, they're going to want to know why. It would—it
vould look bad for Korie and—"

"You've let him get out of hand," Leen accuses.
You can't control him anymore, can you?"

"Yes, I can. I'm the captain! Korie used to be a fine
irst officer, then this business with the bogie began and
verything seems to have fallen apart. This ship was run-
ing so well before—"

"We never had any contact with the enemy
before—"

"—But we're in this situation now, we have to let
—"

"No, we don't!"

"It's only for a few days more—"

"A few days, a few years—what's the difference?
You're still letting him get away with it—"

"No, I'm not! *I'm* the captain. I have to think of my
hip, my crew, my men—I have to think of the High
Command; I have to think of—"

"You're right—you have to think of your ship. Save
t from Korie!"

"I am thinking of my ship! I have to save it—but it's
ot in any danger, is it, Chief? That bogie isn't there any-
nore! So there's no danger to us—we can let Korie have

his search patterns and it looks good on the record. W
have to do something to look good—"

"You're afraid of him too," Leen says suddenly.

Brandt is abruptly quiet.

"It's true, *isn't it*—?"

Brandt's reaction confirms the accusation. He oper
his mouth. He closes it. He looks away. He looks at th
floor, the ceiling, the walls—

Leen's gaze is shocked. "I knew it . . ." he breathe
"The crew kept saying it—but I didn't believe it. I didn
want to—"

The captain's eyes are unfocused. He forces himse
back to reality. He tries to force himself back—

"Captain—" Leen stands. "I'm sorry—I didn't mea
it. I—I—" But it's too late; the pieces are too widely sca
tered.

Brandt mumbles something. "I'm the captain. I'
pretend you didn't say it. I'll pretend—you didn't—" H
turns abruptly, fumbles at the door. "—didn't say it—
He lurches through it; it slides shut behind him.

Leen stares after him with unseeing eyes. "—Dam
them! Damn them! Bloody damned son of a bitch—" h
murmurs. "—Ass-licking, brown-nosing, hypocritica
shit-headed fools—damn them all!"

He goes on like that for a long time.

Twenty-five

MEMO
FROM: Base Admiral Farrel
TO: Vice Admiral Harshlie

Joe,

I have just finished reading your report on the *Burlingame* incident. It is very disturbing.

Naturally, we will want a full investigation. I will appreciate seeing tapes of the testimony as well as a more detailed report from you. Please implement this as soon as possible.

We are fortunate in one respect, in that the situation was not worse—thanks to the quick thinking of at least one of the officers on the ship. As you suggest, the man should be commended.

I agree with you that the incident should be hushed up as much as possible—it would not be good for general morale and the situation at home is such that an incident like this would not go down well at all.

By the way, please circulate a memo to all other F-class ships concerning the mechanical details of this incident. Point out the precautions necessary to prevent a repetition. For God's sake, once is enough.

Stephen

Twenty-six

I am suggesting that just as we psychoanalyze individuals to rid them of their neuroses, we do the same on a global level—that we psychoanalyze the characteristics and behavior patterns of the human species. I am suggesting that homo sapiens needs to become self-aware as a race.

If we don't the alternative is to rattle down through the cage of history, continuing to enact only our self-destructive games of blind aggression: the little aggressions of individual against individual, the medium-sized aggressions of group against group, the big aggressions of nation against nation, the massive aggressions of planet against planet—until finally, the race shatters and destroys itself in genetic chaos because it was too mixed in its schizoid games to look up and see that God is not a condition that all humans are born with, but one that all humans must aspire to earn.

JARLES "FREE FALL" FERRIS,
Electric Philosophies

Korie sits alone in the galley; his usual place is in th corner, away from the noise and clatter of the ser ing counter. Generally the crew leaves him alon keeps to the other side of the room as much as possible-

—except that this morning, Crewman Wolfe is con ing back on duty; his one week's restriction to quarters ended. When he comes into the galley, it is with a smu

ess that he makes no effort to conceal; he fills his tray
d purposely chooses a place at Korie's table. With a
nirk, he calls out, "Good morning, sir." Across the
om, one or two of the men watching him shake their
ads.

Korie looks up at Wolfe and a sour frown crosses his
atures, but he returns his attention to the cup of coffee
front of him. Wolfe snickers, half to himself, half for
e benefit of his audience. He slides his tray noisily
cross the table, makes a great production out of thump-
g and banging the various condiment containers; his
esence is gratingly obvious.

Every bite Wolfe takes, every mouthful of food,
unches loud and annoying—it is as if Wolfe is saying,
You can't touch me, sir; you can't touch me." He slurps
his coffee and he chews loudly on his toast.

Korie looks at him again. His expression is strained,
most on the verge of annoyance—anger. Wolfe returns
e glance; expectant, mocking, smug—

It is a conversation without words. Wolfe is saying,
m here, Mr. Korie, and there's nothing you can do about

And Mr. Korie is answering with his look, *You'd bet-
r watch yourself, Wolfe—you'd better not push too
ard.*

And Wolfe is replying, reiterating, *But I'm immune
 you, now. Rogers won't talk and I'm no longer con-
ned to quarters and there's nothing you can do about it.*
nd he says it all with a look and a smirk.

Abruptly Korie puts his coffee cup down, almost a
ttle too hard. He stands and brushes at his tunic. For a
oment, he looks down at the other, "What board are
ou going to be on, Wolfe?"

"Power six, sir."

Coldly, Korie says, "I'll be watching for it." He turns
nd disappears into the ship's head.

"You do that, sir," Wolfe breathes to himself, and
en wonders, *Now why did I do that? He wasn't both-
ring me any.* He turns around and looks for the reaction
f his shipmates, but at the moment, they seem to be
oking elsewhere. He returns his attention to his food.

The klunk of a tray makes him look up. Rogers
just sitting down at the other end of the table. Wolfe lee
sardonically. "Hey, little boy—" he calls. "How ya doin
How's your back?"

Rogers ignores him.

Wolfe calls, a little louder, "I hear you've been ge
ting awfully chummy with Mr. Korie. I thought I told yo
that wasn't a good idea."

"No," says Rogers, not looking up. "I'm not."

"I didn't hear you—what was that?"

Rogers concentrates on his soup.

"Hey Rogers—I'm talking to you."

"I'm listening." Another mouthful.

"But you're not answering—"

"Hey, Wolfe!" Erlich, from the other side of th
room.

Wolfe looks up. "Yeah?"

"You're awfully loud."

"I didn't realize you were listening."

"I'm not—you're making too much noise."

"I'll lower my voice."

"You'd do better to shut up."

Wolfe turns back to his table, looks speculatively a
Rogers. In a softer, but no less hostile tone, he says, "
hear you're off the gravity board, these days. Tell m
how's the radec business? Seen any good bogies lately?
you can find a few more, you'll be Korie's friend fo
life—"

He suddenly realizes that the room is silent. He look
up, sees the first officer standing in the door to the lava
tory, still wiping his hands and looking thoughtfully a
him. Korie glances scornfully at Rogers, then back t
Wolfe. "*Carry on,*" he says. He tosses the towel into
disposal and exits.

Wolfe stares after him, then whistles softly. "Well, I'
be damned."

Twenty-seven

Of course, the wicked people control the world—they deserve it.

SOLOMON SHORT

When I was ten years old, one of my friends brought a Shaleenian kangaroo-cat to school one day. I remember the way it hopped around with quick, nervous leaps, peering at everything with its large, almost circular golden eyes.

One of the girls asked if it was a boy cat or a girl cat. Our instructor didn't know; neither did the boy who had brought it; but the teacher made the mistake of asking, 'How can we find out?' Someone piped up, 'We vote on it!' The rest of the class chimed in with instant agreement and before I could voice my objection that some things can't be voted on, the election was held. It was decided that the Shaleenian kangaroo-cat was a boy, and forthwith, it was named Davy Crockett.

Three months later, Davy Crockett had kittens. So much for democracy.

It seems to me that if the electoral process can be so wrong about such a simple thing, isn't it possible for it to be very very wrong on much more complex matters? We have this sacred cow in our society that what the majority of the people want is right—but is it?

Our populace isn't really informed, not the

majority of them—most people vote by the way they have been manipulated and by the way they have responded to that manipulation—they are working out their own patterns of wishful thinking on the social environment in which they live. Though a majority may choose a specific course of action or direction for itself, through the workings of a 'representative government,' they may be as mistaken about the correctness of such a choice as my classmates were about the sex of that Shaleenian kangaroo-cat.

I'm not so sure that an elected government is necessarily the best.

ROGER BURLINGAME

"All right, what's your problem?" says Barak.

"I'd better tell it to you from the beginning," answers Leen. "Then you can see if you agree with me." They are in the tall, uneven area behind the engine room, an area that seems both cramped and roomy—roomy because of its height, cramped because of the great number of pieces of equipment hanging from its walls and lashed to its floor. This is the ship's workshop; most maintenance and repair functions are performed here. A massive synthesizer and its smaller cousin sit against one wall. Other plastic-working machines are spaced around the room. One whole side of the shop opens onto the life-shuttle maintenance deck, which also opens onto the large cargo hatch; at the moment those large doors are closed.

Chief Engineer Leen leads Astrogator Barak over to a worktable where parts of an intricate-looking device lay scattered across its plastic surface. "Remember, I was working on the Hilsen units? Well, I discovered something that made me start thinking. After I retuned the units, I opened them up again and looked at them a second time. That made me take another look at the phase adapters."

"This one?" Barak indicates the device on the table.

"This is the one we burnt out."

The astrogator pokes at it; but he shakes his head.

"Chief, it might as well be a ham sandwich sitting there; I wouldn't know one end of it from the other."

Leen waves that aside. "No matter, just let me tell you—I had just started to take this apart when Korie called me down to deflate the gym. I was so engrossed in what I was doing I hadn't realized how close we were to the attack maneuver—that's why I screwed up the gym, my mind wasn't on it. I was still thinking about what I'd seen in the Hilsen units and what I suspected was in the adapter."

"Uh huh—what did you find in the adapter?"

Leen takes a deep breath. "Look, do you know the way the adapter works?"

"Chief, I don't even know how the warp works. I'm an astrogator."

"Right. I forgot. Well, let me give you the two-minute cram course. You know the warp is a closed universe, right?"

"That much I've got."

"Ever wonder how we see out of it?"

"Why, I thought—"

"We can't, you know. Once we fold into warp, it's like being on the inside of a big sphere, and the inner surface of it is a mirror. No matter what direction you look you're only going to see yourself. It's a closed, unbroken universe—you've heard the stories about a guy dropping a wrench over the side, only to have it come back from the opposite direction a couple of weeks later?"

"Yeah—all right, how do we see out?"

"With the secondaries—they make the warp move by altering its shape within the stress field, but they also function like a window, through which we can look at the rest of the universe. Using the secondaries, we pick up vibrations off the stress field and the computers interpret them into the shimmers of other ships' warps or the gravitational masses of planets—it has to be a massive singularity for us to detect it in the stress field. Okay, turn off the secondaries, you close the window; what's left—?"

"Only our own reflection, right?"

"Right—only very much distorted, spread out all over the inside of the warp. The only time we ever look at it is when we want to read the shape of our own warp; the rest of the time, the radec boys try and tune it out."

"Yes, I know. They've had some problems with that recently—"

Leen looks at him sharply, "Then you know what I'm getting at?"

Barak shakes his head.

Leen goes on, "Anyway, I got curious when the Hilsen units kept slipping out of tune; those are the units that watchdog the secondaries and help us maintain shape. I figured they were getting some kind of feedback or vibration off the phase-handling system but where was the phase-handling getting it? That's why I put MacHeath on the 'monkey crew'—to find it. We needed to plug right into the generators because the systems analysis network is dead right there—I wanted him to monitor the phase adapters through a couple of maneuvers to see if that was the source of the vibration or not."

"Was it?"

"I don't know—and I'm not going to risk another man finding out." He pokes at the adapter on the table. "That's why I've taken this baby apart, but, uh—so far I haven't found anything. You want to know what I think? We didn't burn it out through any failure to compensate for inherent velocity—we watch that. It's such a stupid and easy mistake to make that it's on our checklists seven times. I think we burnt this out because it *wasn't able* to compensate. It wasn't designed to operate with our present equipment, so the vibration is inherent in the way the pieces work together. *At prolonged bursts of high speed,* it'll become magnified throughout the system."

"Have you told Korie?"

"No." Leen's features are craggy and not unfriendly, but at the mention of the first officer's name, his lips tighten.

"Why not?"

"Because of the phase adapter—you know where we got it?"

"Some parts depot or something—?"

"Uh uh. Korie scavenged them off an F-class hulk. Remember the *Calvington?*"

"No."

"No matter, but that's the ship that Korie got these phase adapters off of. Uh, let me tell you about them. The *Calvington* was one generation before this ship—pre-Hilsen; she used Grier units instead—"

"Uh, Chief, you're losing me."

"Sorry. What I'm getting at is that these phase adapters are not necessarily complementary to our equipment. I had to jury-rig a lot of control systems. It was none too neat a job, but Korie wanted phase adapters—"

"I can understand that. I prefer a ship with a phase-handling system."

"We don't need 'em, though."

"Well—" Barak is skeptical on that. "It depends on your point of view. To go from one place to another, no, we don't need them. We just fold into warp and go—but because we can't maneuver our inherent velocity without phase adapters, we're really not an independent ship. We're at the mercy of tugs."

"For the kind of patrolling we're supposed to do," asks Leen, "do phase adapters make a difference?"

Barak considers it. "Not really. DV base moves in a steady orbit. We kick off from it, go on patrol, stay in warp the whole time—when we come back, we only have to come up behind the base to unwarp and we're still moving in the same direction and at the same velocity as when we started."

"Right—so why do we have phase adapters?"

"So we can turn the ship in warp—"

"Because *Korie* wanted them!" Leen's voice is suddenly loud.

Barak pauses after the other's outburst; he says quietly, "We had the basic phase-handling system to start with, Chief. All it needed was some rebuilding and some new adapters."

"But don't you think that if Threebase had felt they were necessary, they would have given them to us?"

"I think that if they'd had a better ship, they would have given her to us; it's no secret that the *Burlingame* was rescued from the scrap heap at the last minute."

Leen doesn't answer right away. "Look, Al—that's

the whole point. This ship is a mess; I ought to know better than anyone. The phase-handling system that Korie had me jury-rig is—well, it's not a regulation system. We've got parts in it cannibalized from three or four different ships. None of them was specifically designed to work with the others, so we get distortions, interferences, vibrations—the thing has to be nursed." He leans across the worktable and switches on a monitor screen. "I want you to take a look at something." Punching buttons, "There. That's a simulation. If the phase adapters are magnifying the vibrations of our inherent velocity against our warp, that's the kind of pattern we'll get."

Barak stares at the screen for a long moment—the shimmering lines on it are disturbingly familiar. A thought starts to take shape in his head—he shakes it away. "No, Chief—it couldn't be."

"The way the Hilsen units were tuned," says Leen, "they could have acted as a focus."

Barak goes silent. His gaze remains fixed on the screen, his face is creased into a dark frown. That shimmer is all wrong; its shape—

"Oh, look," says Leen. "I could be wrong about this; but what if I'm not?" He says intently, "What about the spare that's in there now? What do I do?"

"You say you're not sure—?"

"Not without monitoring the actual adapters—"

"No, don't do that. It wouldn't look right, not now. What about the Hilsen units—are they back in tune?"

"Yes, but I don't know how long they'll stay that way—"

The astrogator is troubled and thoughtful. "And you haven't told anyone—not Korie? Not the captain?"

Leen shakes his head. "You're the first. I can't talk to Korie—or Brandt—" He breaks off without explaining. "Al?"

Abruptly, Barak makes a decision. "Chief—there's only a day or two left to the search; then we'll be turning home. Let's just leave things like they are—you stash this adapter away and forget about it. I won't say anything to anyone, neither will you. The search will end and we'll go home. You can recheck the adapters at base and no one will be hurt."

Leen's eyes are skeptical. "You really think so, Al?"

The astrogator says slowly, "No, I don't. But I don't want to consider the alternative." He reaches over and switches off the monitor.

Twenty-eight

In each ship there is one man who in the hour of emergency or peril at space can turn to no other man. There is one alone who is ultimately responsible for the sage navigation, engineering performance, accurate gunfire and morale of his ship. He is the commanding officer. He is the ship!

Bronze plaque, Office of Chief
of Fleet Operations

At zero three hundred hours and seventeen minutes, when the ship is at a low ebb of activity, an alarm—an electric and raucous scream—startles the crew into life.

Lights blink in confusion, fade out abruptly with just as much puzzlement, fade in again, then switch to battle-alert orange. Hurried footsteps, muffled curses, confused mutterings—men pad-pad quickly down corridors. "What the—?" followed by others, swearing, "Come on! That's an alarm! They've found something!"

Doors slam shut; there is the whoosh of air as compartments seal themselves off and pressurize. Emergency panels flash in indecision, then abruptly a voice—Barak's—on the intercom: "All hands, battle stations! All hands, battle stations!"

"Dammit! I thought we weren't going to have any more drills—"

"Shut up, you idiot! This isn't a drill!"

"Huh—?"

"That's Barak on the com. Let's go."

And suddenly, Korie is sliding through the tumult and confusion like an eel. Unruffled, he hurries surely down the narrow corridor to the bridge, still buttoning his tunic. Other men shoulder past him, some in various stages of undress, rushing to their battle stations. Korie starts to bark an order, then checks himself. If they don't know what to do by now, it's too late to teach them.

The bridge is a bowl of organized confusion. Men stand before their boards, but are staring at Barak. The dark-skinned astrogator is standing on the command dais, one hand on the seat's controls, but he is looking toward a still-sleepy Jonesy on he astrogation console. "Where is it now?"

"Still flashing on the edges—"

"What've you got, Al?" Korie drops into the seat.

"Not sure—we're picking up a persistent flash on the edge of our sensibilities. It's too definite to be a will-o'-the-wisp, but—"

"Then it's the bogie," Korie snaps; he smiles—a thin flash of triumph. *I knew it. I knew it.*

"I'm not so sure," says Barak. "It's still too vague to have a pattern."

And then Brandt is on the bridge. "What is it?"

"The bogie!" Korie says exultantly, "I've got him."

Brandt steps toward the seat, but Korie ignores him. Brandt covers by turning to Barak. "Let's get it on the screen."

Barak shakes his head. "It's too vague to show in the gridwork. We've got it on the high-gain sensors; still too fuzzy to pinpoint."

"We're going in after it," says Korie. He raises his voice to give the order. "Go to full warp."

The officer at the pilot console looks back at them, the first officer, the astrogator, the captain—*but Korie is in the seat.*

"Go to full warp!" Korie repeats.

Puzzled, the man glances at Brandt—why didn't the captain give or confirm the order? But he turns back to his console and obeys. After a moment, the gridwork begins flashing by faster.

"You getting it any clearer yet?"

"No, sir," Jonesy says, "not yet. They could be running."

Korie hits the chair arm. "Radec. What've you got?"

Rogers' voice: "I don't know, sir. We can't make out a pattern—it's a moving singularity, but that's all—"

"All right. Stand by." He switches off. To Jonesy, "How far is it? How long will it take to close with him?"

"Can't say—it depends on a lot of things—I won't be able to tell you until we get a clearer fix."

Brandt interrupts, "Mr. Korie, that bogie may be beyond our reach—"

"We don't know that yet—"

"He's too far away for a clear scan."

"Not for long—"

"And your ten days are almost up."

"We can do it!" Korie insists. He stands suddenly. "I'm going back to the radec room. *I'll* get a fix on him." He darts from the bridge.

The radec room is flickery-dark; only the screens are bright. Korie lunges in and stops. Rogers is setting up a new routine on his board; the monitors flash with the shimmering vagueness—he clears them, cross-circuits, and starts again. Again, the same shimmer, no larger, no brighter. He sets up a third routine—"Nothing, sir." He is curiously exultant, as if the elusiveness of the bogie is a personal attack on the first officer. He clears his board and starts over; every new scan he programs digs that much deeper into Korie.

The first officer watches with nervous impatience. Rogers' able hands move skillfully across his console. "Can't you pump more power into that scan?"

"Sorry, sir—I'm at maximum now. He seems to be maintaining his position in relation to us. He must be running. Wait a minute—" He adjusts a knob. "—No, he's not quite maintaining his position. We're gaining on him—I think—but very slowly."

Korie mouths a curse under his breath—"Damn! This is where we were twelve days ago—" He turns to go. The corridor back to the bridge is troubled and oppressive.

"Well?" says Brandt, as Korie steps down into the pit.

"We're gaining on him," he replies, "but only slowly."

Brandt lets his gaze meet that of Korie—the first officer is grim and pale. "I guess you know what that means—we're going to have to let him go—"

"We can't! Not after all this time! We've almost got him—"

"With what?!! You've got nothing left to fight him with—"

"We do!" Korie insists. "We have that extra margin—"

"We need that to get home—"

"We have enough for that and to catch him. He's not as far as he was before; we can close with him in a few days."

"And be left here without the power to return to base," rumbles Brandt. "No, Mr. Korie, we're going to have to let him go. You were given ten days to make the kill; they're almost up. I can't extend that deadline—we don't have the power."

"We have twenty days of power left in the cells! We're only thirteen days of travel from base."

"We can't throw away our safety margin!"

Korie glances at the captain; abruptly, he crosses the pit to the warp control board. He leans across the technician there, Wolfe, and stabs angrily at it. Above, a screen flashes with a bright blue graph. Korie takes a step back and looks at it. "Now, look—we can do it—"

The captain raises his voice, "I'm not going to argue, Mr. Korie!"

"If you don't believe me—ask you own engineers." Korie grabs at Wolfe, standing by the console, pulls him toward the captain. "Tell him."

Brandt looks at the man. "Well?"

Wolfe looks from Korie to Brandt and back to Korie again. The first officer's upper lip glistens with tiny beads of sweat.

"Well?" asks Brandt. "Is there power or not—?"

"Uh—" Wolfe is fascinated by the intensity in Korie's

face—by the power he suddenly holds over the man. It is too much—abruptly, he looks at the captain. Brandt is every bit as intense, but there is something disturbing there—"Yes, sir. There's power."

Korie's exhalation is a sharp, "I told you so."

Wolfe adds, "There's a five-day margin for error over and above the one that shows on the screens. We're not supposed to count on it—"

"But it's there, isn't it?" demands Korie.

Wolfe nods. "Yes, sir; it is."

"Thank you, Wolfe." (Thank you for giving me back my bogie.) He turns to Brandt. "We can do it—we have to do it. If necessary, we can cut back to half power on the way home. We can spare five more days that way—six, even—"

"Korie, didn't you hear him? We're not supposed to count on it—" To Wolfe: "Why not?"

"Uh—because that's the power that's necessary to maintain threshold levels in the fields. If we had to unwarp for any reason, we wouldn't be able to put them up again." Wolfe mumbles the answer: he didn't want to give it.

Brandt says to Korie, "You knew that, didn't you?"

"Yes, sir, but—"

"Never mind." To Wolfe: "Go back to your board."

Korie advances on Brandt. "Why don't you want to make this kill, dammit?!! We can do it!"

"Only if you get him on the first shot—and I don't care how well you've drilled this crew. They're going to need more than one shot!"

"At least give me that one shot!"

"He'll be shooting back at us, dammit! Evasive maneuvers cost power!! Your one shot could take us five or six days—once battle is joined, you have to make the kill or be killed yourself. One shot wouldn't be enough for you, Mr. Korie. If you could have caught him before your ten days were up, you could have had your chance, but I can't risk the safety of this ship—"

"This is a battle cruiser, Captain!! Certain risks are supposed to be taken—"

"I'll decide when!"

A pause—one of those endless moments when two sets of eyes lock. And then—the moment is snatched away from them—

"Heavy distortions! The pattern is dopplering—he's coming in!"

Korie whirls to stare at Jonesy; Brandt too. At the astrogation desk, Barak starts stabbing at buttons. "Dammit! He's not coming in clearly; he must be using some kind of scrambler to disguise his warp—" To the intercom: "Radec, what are you doing?"

"I'm scanning, sir—full power! But he seems to be all over the stress field—"

Korie steps in close to listen, to watch.

"—and he's coming in awfully fast."

"How much time, Al?"

Barak looks at his board. "Six minutes. Maybe less."

"Can you give me a target?"

"I'll try—" To Jonesy: "Patch in EDNA to the gunnery crew."

"Right."

Korie steps back up onto the control dais; he pulls out his hand mike. "All hands, stand by for target information. Prepare for evasive maneuvers, patterns Three Beta, Six Gamma, Nine Delta. Stand by to—" The captain's hand cuts him off.

"I didn't give you permission to order us into battle."

"You didn't tell me not to—we've got to be prepared—"

"We're not going to meet that other ship in battle!"

"You gave me ten days—I still have five hours left—"

"I've changed my mind. We're heading for home."

Korie is incredulous. "We're going to run—??"

Brandt ignores him. To Barak: "Al, stand by to reverse polarities; set up an emergency course for home."

"We're being attacked, damn you—*let me meet it!*"

Brandt steps past him to the pilot console. "Reverse polarities; maintain full warp."

"Aye, sir—"

"*Belay that order, mister—*" Korie's voice is knife-edge sharp. Into his hand mike: "Missile crews, stand by." To Barak: "Al, go to those evasion patterns—"

Brandt turns to stare at him; Barak too. Other men on the bridge look up. Brandt says, "What do you think you're doing?"

"I'm going after that bogie—"

"Still closing," calls Jonesy. "Four minutes to contact."

"There's no time to argue this, Korie—" To the pilot, Brandt says, "Reverse polarities."

The man looks from Brandt to Korie to Brandt again. One is the captain—but the other gives the orders. "Sir—??" He looks to Korie helplessly.

"Do it!" Brandt growls at him. "I'm telling you to do it—*I'm* the captain."

And still the man hesitates, waiting for Korie to confirm the order.

"Hold course!" snaps the first officer. "Al, go to those evasive patterns—"

Watching from his console, Barak remains motionless; but beside him, *Jonesy punches at the board*. It is a signal. Follow Korie. Around the bridge, the men snap to orders.

And Brandt realizes. He stares about in confusion. "*I'm* the captain—!" He takes a step toward Korie. "Don't be a fool! You can't risk the ship this way."

"We've trained for this," says Korie. He continues to watch the screens around the bridge. "Missile crews—stand by to lay down a spread of three."

"Right, sir—"

"Listen to me, Korie! This ship isn't in as good a condition as you think! Neither is the crew—I don't care how well you've trained them. We'll never survive a battle encounter!"

Korie ignores him. To Wolfe, he calls, "Stand by to charge the missiles."

"Aye, sir."

"Two minutes to contact—"

"Korie! Stop it!" The first officer ignores him. Wildly, Brandt crosses the bridge. "Al, stop him! Stop him for me—"

Barak grabs the captain by the shoulders. "Sir!" He looks from Brandt to Korie; the first officer is standing coolly by the seat, watching the forward screen.

Brandt babbles at the astrogator, "Al, that emergency course for home—have you got it?"

"Yes, sir—yes, I've got it."

"Prepare to implement—" He lurches away from Barak, toward the pilot console. Except for the astrogator, every other man on the bridge is too busy to pay any attention to the captain.

"Missiles ready and charged. Standing by."

"Ninety seconds to contact."

Brandt grabs one of the officers at the pilot console. "Reverse polarities," he says. "We're going home—"

The man ignores him, raises one elbow to keep Brandt's hands away from the board. And then Barak is tugging at the captain—"Sir—?"

"Jonesy, stand by," said Korie. "We'll unwarp thirty seconds before contact, drop our missiles, and run."

"Right, sir."

"Don't do it!" cries Brandt. "Head for home!" Barak is holding him back. "That's an order! I'm the captain!"

"Get him out of here!" It is Korie's first notice of Brandt.

"Don't unwarp—we'll never survive it!"

"We've got a pattern!" says Jonesy. Both Brandt and Barak holding him turn to the screen—the whorl of white lines is sharp and familiar. "Coming in fast! EDNA's targeting."

"Sixty seconds to contact, thirty seconds to unwarp."

"Missiles targeted and ready—"

"Al!" screams Brandt, struggling again. "We've got to stop them!"

Barak is still frozen to the screen; his face is ashen and gray. That pattern—

"Al! Stop them!"

—is too familiar. Barak releases the captain; he turns to Korie, to Jonesy. "Go ahead," he says, quietly, "Unwarp."

Behind him, Brandt is stricken. "Al—what are you doing—"

"Fifteen seconds to unwarp."

Korie flashes a triumphant glance to Barak. "Thanks Al—"

Brandt lunges at the astrogator, hands like claws; he bounces off, lurches toward Korie—Barak grabs him knocks him to the floor. He sobs, "I'm sorry, sir—" Brandt continues to struggle. Barak hits him again.

"Five seconds—"

"All lights green—"

"Stand by—"

"*Unwarp!*" calls Jonesy, then confirms, "We have unwarp."

"Drop missiles—"

"*Hold it!* I have a red light—"

"Fire, dammit! Fire!" shouts Korie.

There is a pause, then—"At what, sir? The target's gone—" The screen is empty.

"Huh?"

Snap. "Radec! Where's that bogie?"

"I don't know, sir! We unwarped and it disappeared—I've cleared the board three times already—"

Jonesy breathes, "Do you think they could have unwarped at the same time?"

"No—they couldn't have—" Korie whirls, "Al—?"

Barak rises; he has been holding the captain down at the center of the pit. He ignores Korie and concentrates on helping Brandt up; he guides him to the seat. "Take it easy, sir. You'll be all right."

Korie stares at them amazed; he grabs his hand mike. "Missile crews, stand by. Radec, get me that last known position—maybe he's playing dead duck again—"

"You want to just drop the missiles and let them hunt?"

"We might do that too. Radec, have you anything yet?"

"No, sir—I've got the scanners full open—"

"Keep trying—"

"Mr. Korie!" It is Barak, standing on the control dais at the center of the pit. "You're wasting your time. *There is no bogie.*"

Korie whirls to look at him. So does Jonesy. So do most of the other men on the bridge.

"There's no bogie," he repeats. "It never existed."

Korie takes a half-step. "What're you talking about? I know it's there. I saw it—you did too!"

"You saw a stress-field shimmer, Korie, not a ship—and that shimmer was only our own reflection. The Hilsen units have been focusing a projection of our own vibrations against the warp—we've been chasing our own shadow! There's nothing there!"

"You're lying, Barak—that bogie moved! We gained on it!"

"The vibration was progressive; as it got larger, so did the projection we were chasing; the computer said we were getting closer."

"No—I won't believe it—"

"You have to believe it, Korie—it's true! And it's your fault. It's your phase adapters—those damned jury-rigged phase adapters! They keep throwing off vibrations because they're not right for this ship. Ask Leen about it; he'll show you—"

"—No—!!" Korie shakes his head, wildly, frantically. "No—no—it's not true, it's not! That bogie is there, we can get it—" He turns to Jonesy, "Aim those missiles—for its last known—last known position—"

"Forget it, Jonesy," Barak countermands the order.

"No—" shouts Korie.

Jonesy looks from one to the other. The astrogator says, "Check your console."

The assistant astrogator casts a despairing glace at Korie, "I'm sorry, sir—" then turns to his board.

Korie stares at Barak. "Al—what are you doing to me? My bogie is there—"

Barak looks down at him from the command dais. He shakes his head sadly. A moan from the captain distracts him.

"Radec!" says Korie. He leaps for the door, stumbles through it. Only Jonesy looks after him.

In the seat, Brandt shakes his head confusedly. His eyes wander from side to side. "Al—Al—"

"It's all right, sir; everything's all right." Into the intercom, Barak says, "Medical Officer Panyovsky, come to the bridge please."

"Al—I—I—"

Barak turns to the older man, the gray-haired man, the slack-jawed man—the man with the shattered expression. "Sir, just relax. The doc will be up to see you in a minute. He'll give you something to make you feel better. The ship is all right."

"I—I—" The eyes are unable to focus.

"Just relax, sir, just relax," Barak straightens; abruptly, he looks around. "Where's Korie?"

Jonesy says, "He—he left. I think he said something about radec—"

Barak gestures impatiently. "Goldberg, watch the helm—" He darts out the door.

In the radec room, Rogers is lying on the floor, blood flowing from one corner of his mouth. Bridger is tending to him worriedly; the plastic brace across Rogers' back has been shattered into fragments, and the youth is moaning on the edge of unconsciousness.

But Barak's attention is not on Rogers, but on Korie—the first officer is sitting before the console, a strange look on his face; his eyes are intense. His hands move trancelike across the board, clearing it and setting up programs, clearing it and setting up programs, over and over and over again . . .

Twenty-nine

The only thing worse than learning the truth is not learning the truth.

SOLOMON SHORT

For seventeen hours, the *Burlingame* drifts.

Her inherent velocity is negligible. She exists without motion, without direction.

Her decks are dark, her corridors are dim. Mr. Korie has ordered the ship on power-down standby; but he has not let the crew stand down from the alert. The ship is silent and moody. The men stand at their stations like sullen zombies. Time is frozen here.

The men wait.

All but one. Chief Engineer Leen.

He is agitated, and he comes searching for Barak, the astrogator. Leen finds him coming out the door of the medical section. The two men look at each other, wordlessly studying.

"Was it there or not?" asks Barak.

"I don't know," says Leen. "It could have been. It could have been a wobbly. I'm a one-eyed man trying for depth perception. Nobody's yet figured out how to make a single set of grids act like two stress-field eyes. Theoretically, it's not impossible—but—" He spreads his hands helplessly, then drops them again. "Can we go home now?"

"If it were up to me, Chief, we'd have been on our way home two weeks ago, but the only way we're going to get that order is if you can prove that bogie was never there, was only a wobbly the whole time."

"You know as well as I, there's no way to trace that."

"Then make me another one, this time deliberately."

Leen looks glum. "Sorry, Al. I can't even give you that kind of certainty. I wouldn't know where to begin."

"Then that's it, then—"

"What—? We're going to stay out here forever?"

"Find me that wobbly and we'll go home! What do you want from me, Chief? I'm only the astrogator. I don't have the authority to order this ship about. Not while there are still two officers above me." He turns away from Leen and starts heading forward.

"Wait a minute—"

Barak shakes his head and keeps on going.

"We can't just stay here—"

Barak stops, turns, looks. "Don't ask me, Chief! I don't know what else to tell you."

"But the crew—they're starting to talk—"

"Screw the crew!" The bellow echoes down the corridor.

Leen steps rapidly after the big man, catching him by one shoulder and spinning him back against the bulkhead. "Damn you—" he starts, then catches himself and forces his voice down to an intense whisper. "You're the one officer left that this crew trusts. You're the only one who can hold this ship together."

Barak's eyes are shaded. "Then that shows how poorly put together it is. Listen to me, Leen—and listen up good. Don't come looking to unload your worries on me. I don't want them, they're not my responsibility. All I have to do is plot points in space and draw lines between them. That's all I want to do. And to be very honest, that's all I really know how to do. You—and every other man on this ship, it seems—have demanded that I be a strong man, a hero. Well, I'm no hero. I don't know how to be. And in my one attempt to be heroic, I destroyed a thirteen-year good conduct record. I was insubordinate. I refused to follow an order from my captain—*and* equally, I refused to follow the orders of my first officer. One way or the other, I'm through. I don't know if there was a real bogie out there or not, but in the heat of the moment, I undercut the authority on this ship, because you—and a lot of other men—encouraged me to do just that. But I'm the guy who has to pay the price— where are the rest of you? And now you're complaining that there's no authority left. Brandt's locked himself in his cabin again, God only knows what he's doing in there, and Korie refuses to give the order to go home, too. He's still convinced that there's something out there.

"If you want to go home, ask *them* to give the order. I can't, I won't, I don't have the authority, and I'm probably facing a court-martial." He steps forward, looming over Leen like a bear. "I'll tell you this, Chief. When Korie was running this ship, it ran. And it ran well. Complaints or no. You wanted to be free of Korie? Well, now you are. Now you have the chaos you deserve, and you're complaining again. All of you. And I'm tired of listening to it. I'm tired of being asked to do something about it."

Leen's eyes are moist. There is a hint of redness around the edges. His face looks haggard. When Barak finally runs down, he says quietly, "But it's your life too, Al; your ship too. Don't you care any more?"

Barak hesitates a half-beat before answering. "I don't know. I'm tired. I don't think so. I just want to be left alone."

He turns and goes up the corridor toward the bridge. He will sit down in the Command and Control chair and he will pretend to be in charge. But he will only be waiting, just like the rest of them.

Leen watches his departing back sadly.

He doesn't fully understand it. He knows that Brandt and Korie and Barak adjourned to the captain's cabin immediately after the unwarp fiasco. They stayed in there a long time. Their voices were raised, the shouts could be heard in the corridor, only dimly muffled by the insulating walls. When Korie and Barak finally emerged again, they weren't speaking. Korie's face was grim. Barak's countenance was ashen, haggard. Exactly what had occurred in there was unknown, and neither Korie nor Barak would comment.

Periodically, the captain's bell would ring and an aide would bring him a covered tray from the galley. That was the only evidence there was still a captain aboard this ship. Otherwise, Korie was still in charge.

Except Korie had not been back to the bridge since unwarp. Nor had he issued any order more significant than "Clean up that mess, Crewman."

The crew remains on alert.

Because the order to stand down has not been given.

And will not be given.

The shifts change. But the men stay at their stations.

And the *Burlingame* drifts.

Thirty

A little ignorance can go a long way.
SOLOMON SHORT

Korie is sitting in the galley, alone. There is no one else in the room.

On the table in front of him is a chessboard, sixteen squares to a side. There are two pieces on the board, a white flagship and a black one. Korie is studying them with a slight frown on his face. He looks tired. His eyes are hollow circles. His skin seems drawn and tight. He doesn't look up when the chief engineer enters.

"It's the problem of the two flagships," he says to no one in particular.

"Eh?" says Leen. "Are you talking to me?"

"Huh?" Korie looks up, confused, blinking. "Oh, Chief. I didn't see you come in. Get some coffee, sit down. I want to go over something with you. Do you know the problem of the two flagships?"

Leen shakes his head. "I—uh, I don't play chess that much."

"Never mind. Sit down. I want to show you something. You see here? The flagship is the most powerful piece in the game. It can move horizontally, vertically, diagonally, and hyper. What makes it so powerful is that you can't move into position to attack it without being vulnerable yourself. If you and your enemy each have a flagship only, then neither can attack the other, right?"

"If you say so, sir." Leen is puzzled, not really following what Korie is trying to tell him.

"No, no—look here. There's no other ships on the board to provide support. If I move onto the enemy's diagonal to attack him, I lose. If he moves into position to attack me, he loses for the same reason. The target gets one move in which to strike first. So it's a draw, with neither side able to move except to avoid the other." Korie adds quietly, "He's out there, Chief. He's playing a very calculated game with us."

"Sir—? You still believe there's something there?"

Korie looks up at him. "*Believe?* I'm more convinced than ever. We're each hiding from each other, waiting for that one moment of vulnerability. The question, Chief, is why didn't he attack us when we were unwarping, because that's when we were most vulnerable.

"I have to game it out from the beginning. I can't figure out the appropriate countermove until I understand his strategy. The question is this: Why did he run from us in the first place?"

"Sir—" Leen tries again to interrupt, but Korie won't stop.

"No, no, hear me out. Please."

The word startles the chief engineer. *Please?* From Korie?!! He looks at the man's face. There is desperation there. Korie needs someone to believe with him. And for a moment, Leen feels pity.

"Thank you, Chief. Thank you. Now, think—"

"Mr. Korie—" Leen blurts suddenly, "—there's nothing out there. Let's go home."

"What—?" Korie is momentarily startled to alertness. "What did you say?"

"I said, 'There's nothing out there. Let's go home.' "

"We can't go home. That would be . . . It would be quitting. It would be defeat. It's what he wants us to do."

"But there's nothing there, sir!" Leen says it a little too loudly and a little too quickly.

"No, that's what he wants us to believe. He's clever, that one. You see it, Chief, don't you? He's pretending that he's not there in the hope that we'll believe it too."

Leen is staring now. The scuttlebutt was true. Korie *had* tossed a field.

"Just listen, Chief. Just listen for a little bit. As long

as we drift here like this, we're safe. The minute we start to move, he'll see us. By our course, he'll know what we're thinking. If we turn around and go home, it'll be obvious we're breaking off. If we do anything else, then he knows we're still searching, and he'll know he has to continue to pretend not to be there. But as long as we drift, he can't know what we're doing or what we're thinking. Now we're the enigma to him. Because we're not doing anything. And as long as we're powered-down like this, he can't know for sure where we are. Or even if we're here at all, because our stress-field ripple is practically nonexistent when we're adrift. This is what he must have been doing. Floating just like this. It's eerie, isn't it? How the roles are reversed. He saw us come in, he couldn't have missed us. Now he can't start up his engines either without giving himself away. If he really wants us to believe that he's not there, then he doesn't dare move while we're here. So we have him trapped, Leen. He can't move either. We've got him in a siege of logic. And we have the advantage, I think. Because we're not trying to pretend that we're not chasing him. Our problem is to figure out how we can make the most of that advantage before he realizes that there's no further point to the game, that we're trying to outwait him. I figure we have two weeks at least. In a powered-down state, a ship can drift for months on station. I've ordered half rations, you know. And have you noticed how dim the lights are, and how dark and still the ship is—oh, yes, that's right. I gave those orders to you, didn't I? I'm sorry, Chief. I already—I mean—uh, what was I talking about? Uh, the other ship. The bogie. We uh, we don't really know for sure how much cruising range he has left, but we can reasonably assume that we have more than him. After all, he was heading for home when we picked up his trace, and that implies the end of a run and the exhaustion of his resources. We, on the other hand, had just been resupplied from a tender, so I figure we can outwait him, and I—I uh, also figure that it'll take at least two weeks because that's how long we had to chase him before we lost him—well, not quite. It was, uh, twelve days, wasn't it? Anyway, if he has the perseverance to run for twelve days, I think he also has the perseverance to hide for that long too. It's worth a try—"

Leen says softly, "This is what you told the captain and Barak, isn't it? And they bought it, didn't they? The captain anyway." Leen isn't trying to hide his bitterness. "Damn you! Damn all of you!"

Korie's gaze is calm. He betrays not the slightest hint of emotion. His voice is flat. "The strain is getting to all of us, Chief. Don't crack now. I need your strength." For a moment, it was the old Korie speaking and for a moment, Leen was startled—uncertain.

The chief engineer rubs at his nose and looks down at the table top and then looks back up to Korie and rubs his nose again and blinks and when he finishes all of that, he says, "Sir, I'm sorry for—getting loud like that—but you have to give yourself a different perspective on all of this and—"

Korie takes a sip from his mug, then makes a face. "Ugh. The stuff went cold." He exhales loudly, and the old Korie is gone again. This one is tired—and vulnerable. "Yes, I know what it looks like, Chief. I've tossed a bloody field. Strobed out. Tight-focused. I know the terms. I know more than that, I know what they mean and how to use them accurately. You didn't know I studied psychonomy, did you? That's what I wanted to do before the war. Psychonometrics. I guess I'm not very good at it. I thought I was. I thought I was a mover of men, that I could structure a dynamic for a desired result. I knew how to use a brutal tactic where soft ones wouldn't work. Brutal tactics are good for a lot of things. They're fast, they stamp the lesson in hard, they work because they overpower the system's ability to assimilate change. But the lessons don't take unless the system eventually perceives the love behind the brutality, the will for mutual gain that motivates it. Do you follow this? It doesn't matter, but it would be nice if you did. I thought I was pretty good at manipulating people." He looks up, straight at Leen, eyes clear and wet and hurting. "I like solving problems. That's why psychonomy fascinated me—it was a way to understand the most interesting problems of all, human beings. Or maybe I learned my part too well. I shouldn't have struck Rogers, he's just a kid, but suddenly it seemed like it was in character. Except that by then I didn't have to be in character any more, I'd already accomplished the task of turning this into a fighting vessel. So I didn't need the character. And now I may have lost the trust of my crew just when I need it the most. Oh, that bogie's out there, the captain knows it, Barak knows it. But that's not the issue any more. The issue is what's happening on the *Burlingame*. I guess I owe them an apology, Chief. The crew, I mean. I—I didn't have time to try to whip them into shape with . . . love."

Leen looks a little panicked around the edges. "Sir— why are you telling me? I don't know how to deal with this. I don't even know if I can believe you or not."

Korie holds up a hand. "Easy, Chief. I'm telling you this because *this* is what I told the captain and Al. You have a right to know too. Why do you think the captain has stayed in his cabin for so long? He can't run the ship—he knows it. The crew—well, you were here before. The morale was nonexistent. The captain and I, we used to sit and talk for long hours about the ship's problems. He would drink and ramble and drink, and I would drink and listen and drink. He was unhappy because he didn't want this assignment, and I was unhappy because I did— and we both recognized it, and accepted it. I know you find this hard to believe, Chief, but officers are very human, really. Sometimes. But maybe only with other officers. They're the only ones we can trust. So there we were, stuck on this boat together, wishing we could trade places—I guess I shouldn't tell this in the clear like this, but—what the hell—I suddenly realized that all that psychonometric charting of group dynamics I had learned was meant to be practiced. The captain and I structured a desperation plan—he would retire to his . . . ah, Olympus—and be Zeus, a God, enigmatic, distant, mostly benevolent, but occasionally dangerous. That was the perception of him we built up in the crew's minds. The more he kept away from them, the more benevolent he became, because the less direct action on their lives he exerted. I, on the other hand, would become a martinet, an unpopular, swaggering, manipulating—well, you know. I wasn't a very nice person, right? That was the character. The dynamic is a dangerous one to set up and even more difficult to control, but the situation required drastic steps. We're losing the war, I think. I don't know—but you know what happens when one side gets desperate. They do desperate things in the hope of a miracle. We—this ship—we're one of those desperate actions. If we're to survive, we have to be desperate ourselves. I'm terrified of being on this ship, Leen. I don't want to die. But there's not an enemy ship we can destroy in actual combat. We're old and slow and clumsy, and the enemy certainly isn't going to send ships weaker than us on missions into territory as well-patrolled—or so they're supposed to believe—as the one we're patrolling. I've lost track of the separate ploys. But the enemy is supposed to think that area is heavily protected, too well-defended to be vulnerable. But there's a flaw in that reasoning, Chief. If the enemy decides to test those defenses, even in a feint, they're not going to send a *weak* ship. They're going to test that area with something . . . unusual. Something powerful. Something certainly strong enough to destroy us." He takes breath, then continues in a strangely darker tone of voice, "And I wanted—*still want*—to survive this war. And the only way to do it was brutalize the crew into unifying, then focusing that unity into a pride of accomplishment. I told Barak this and he understood. That's what we told Barak in the captain's cabin, the captain and I. He did something very dangerous. He almost destroyed a major psychonomic matrix—that's our real problem. The fragility of the gamma-unity matrix."

"But—the captain was arguing with you, sir—"

"He has doubts, of course. Everybody has doubts, Chief. I have doubts. But I was right. And I could have won, Chief, I could have. If Barak hadn't interfered, we would have—we would have—" Korie stops, confused. He blinks uncertainly. His eyes remain unfocused. "But we did unwarp, didn't we—and the enemy wasn't there, was he? But then, the enemy couldn't know about the psychonomy of this ship, could he? I've got to—wait—let me figure a moment—anyway, yes, the captain does have his doubts about the—the, ah, wisdom of psychonometric manipulations applied—but, uh—"

"Sir, does the captain know about this—this psychonomy?"

"Yes, of course, he—"

"I mean, does he know that you're applying it. Have you discussed this with him, in language like you're using now?"

"Why, uh—yes, of course—I mean, not in exactly these terms—we've, yes, we've discussed the ah, problems and the possible ah, solutions—but you have to remember, Chief, that there's a certain courtesy involved, uh, respect for his rank. Sometimes, you speak in euphemisms, you speak around the subject, that's another psychonomic level of operation—uh, I'm sorry, Chief—" Korie is momentarily flustered. "I—I guess I should explain what's happening here. You need to understand it all, don't you? I'm dumping. The contents of my brain. I need time to assimilate the mix of problems I have to solve. I'm dumping it out like a computer, the better to—and I need someone to dump it all out on. I'm sorry it's you, you probably can't deal with it, I know, but you've got to try—I guess I should explain it all to you—I'm an alpha-matrix personality. I think I can trust you with that information, Chief. It's supposed to be classified information, but sometimes it's necessary to release that knowledge—with, uh, discretion, of course. I'm relying on your confidentiality here, of course. You know, you understand, don't you? Anyway, I'm an alpha-matrix, and alphas have large faults, but we're forgiven our large faults because we have large virtues, and one of the—one of the faults is we dump, but that's the penalty we pay for having an overprocessing mind. If you want to operate like a meta-processor, you have to operate like a meta-processor. I'm sure that doesn't make sense to you, Chief, but what it means to be an alpha-matrix is that all of your twenty-seven separate and distinct ego states are functioning harmoniously, all in tune with one another, all of them liking each other and communicating with each other, constantly, and all of them operating like a meta-processor simulator—you know how that works, don't you?—with a single processing unit switching from one state to the next so rapidly that it appears that all of the states are functioning simultaneously. Do you know what this means, Leen? Do you know people who you can't seem to figure out? People who confuse you because their repertoire of response has contradictions in it. It's because you're seeing different ego states operative in the same body, except you don't know to identify them; but it wouldn't be a mystery to a psychonomist. Most psychonomists are alphas anyway, they have to be. Anyone who seems to be confusing, who's switching from state to state rapidly, is obviously a functioning high-level matrix, whether they know it or not. The human mind can't function as a meta-processor, Leen, but it can function as a meta-process *simulator,* and that's me. I've been trained to have this ability, I should use it—I see I'm losing you, Leen, perhaps already lost you, I'm sorry, look, maybe I shouldn't have told you all of this, but you need to understand. And I know how this looks—that I'm mad. And there's probably no way to convince you I'm not. Lord, God, how do you prove to someone you're sane? Don't you think I've pondered that question too? The more you try to prove your sanity the more you have reason to suspect it. Sometimes I find myself talking to myself, and I start listening to see what I'm saying. I monitor my own mind, Leen—is that scary to you? Sometimes it's scary to me. Will I recognize it if I go mad, or, if I go mad, will the ability to recognize it be the first thing to go? It terrifies me. If I were mad, I'd truly be dangerous, wouldn't I?"

Korie drinks from his mug, neglects to make a face this time. He needs liquid to continue talking more than he needs to feign a gesture of camaraderie.

"But the point is this, Chief. That bogie *is* out there. And he did not attack us when we were vulnerable, when we were unwarping. So what does that suggest? It says to me that he *can't* attack us. I don't believe any more that he stopped because he had engine trouble. No, he stopped because it was part of a larger plan. Because he didn't think he could destroy us. And that's because *my* plan worked. If I made this ship look and act aggressive enough, the enemy would assume we really were a K-class vessel, and stay away from us. And the tactic worked, the enemy ship believed it, and he ran. And he had to convince us that he really wasn't there because he couldn't confront a K-class ship head on. He believed us when we acted like a K-class ship. Now, the question is, are we going to believe him when he acts like he isn't a ship at all? Crazy, isn't it? We're both a couple of goddamned liars, aren't we? But that's how war is fought. With lies, with pretense. With calculations and manipulations, and that's why captains don't have to be captains, but good psychonomists—not to work their skills on their crew, but the enemy—only, if you have such a tool at your disposal, why shouldn't you use it on your own crew too? After all, that's part of making them battle-ready, isn't it?—and if the alternative is killing them—hell, the navy isn't in the business of teaching men how to make nice anyway. That's the secret of a fighting force. You have to give them energy to power their emotions. You have to have someone to hate, and if you can't hate an unseen enemy, you hate your old man, and you hate him with a passion, and if he's a sharp old man, then at the right moment, there'll be a—a relationship of grudging respect for each other, and then all that angry energy will be channeled into destroying the enemy. It's a beautiful relationship, a commander and his crew, Leen—like riding a stallion, naked in the wind, it's almost an act of love—yes, I know what that sounds like too, that's another part of the price of being an alpha-matrix. You know where all of your pieces are, and you recognize them. So what? I got the job done, didn't I? The other ship ran from us, didn't he? The question—the question is this: Why is he pretending to be our wobbly? Oh, yes, I suspected *that* from the very beginning, I know this ship's patterns, Chief. I know your engine room as well as you do, and I know about flux-wobblies and all the other kinds. I suspected that it was our wobbly, except that I know what our wobbly looks like—and his was too goddamned *good*. His simulation was *too* perfect. It didn't have the jagged beta-flux edge-ripple that occurs once every thirty-three megacycles, and that was the giveaway, Chief. I looked at that wobbly long and hard, I stared at that screen. You saw me. *Something* was wrong with that wobbly, I sensed it somehow, but didn't know how I knew, or what it was I was sensing but there was something about it that just didn't look right. I had to trust my hunch, so I kept looking for the thing that my subconscious mind had recognized, but my conscious mind hadn't yet focused on and identified; I didn't even know it was a simulated echo, Chief. I just knew there was something very peculiar about a wobbly that clean, that perfect, that familiar ... so I started examining each separate function of it. Privately, because I didn't want anyone else to know what I was doing or what I suspected. But it was when I looked for the beta-flux edge-ripple that I knew. Because the ninth-order harmonics produced by that ripple are very distinctive second-level modifiers. And when I looked, Chief, I couldn't find the ripple. It wasn't there."

Leen's voice is a whisper. Very calm, very scared. "Sir? When we replaced the system, sir—when we rebuilt and jury-rigged and cannibalized, that's when it disappeared, sir." Leen is almost afraid to say it aloud. "I know that edge-ripple, sir. Believe me, I know that ripple. It always looked to me like the skyline of Tamarinth, and I know when we juried and patched those phase adapters, I had to retune, and I looked for that ripple—it was almost an old friend by then, sir—but it was gone. So I knew then that it had been sourcing in one of the units we crabbed. I used to use that ripple for fine-tuning because it was so steady, so I know when it disappeared, sir."

Korie looks haggard for a moment. "I know that," he says quickly. "I know that. I double-checked our own signal, I compared a simulated wobbly projection against the simulated echo the bogie was putting out, and when I realized that the beta-flux ripple was gone, and that our harmonic structure would be altered because of that, it was the clue I needed. Don't you see, Chief? I realized that there were certain key harmonics that he would never be able to duplicate, because he couldn't perceive them at his distance, and therefore he wouldn't be able to simulate them accurately. And I looked for them in the wobbly, and they weren't there. Now do you believe me? Check the memory if you don't." Korie sags back in his chair, gasping for breath. The intensity of this argument has almost exhausted him.

Leen's expression is that of a man who has been bludgeoned.

Korie looks across at Leen, waiting. His mind is racing, examining everything he has just said, wondering if he left anything out; he holds the moment up to the light and looks for secret messages. He looks into Leen's face and gradually it comes to him that the man across the table is almost in a state of shock.

(The question is,) Korie thinks, (is he in shock because he can't assimilate what I've told him about the psychonomy of this ship, or is he in shock because of the ninth-order harmonic gap? It's so obvious. In retrospect, it's inevitable. You must follow the logic to the end. But does Leen see it too? But what *does* Leen think—? Or does it seem to him that such a tiny fact, such an insignificant one, is not enough to justify my actions? Or is he trying to determine another explanation for the harmonic gap? I'll bet he thinks up a good one. It's amazing what leaps of rationalization the human mind will make to avoid seeing the obvious. But he's not an alpha-matrix, and perhaps it's not obvious to him. The real question, my dear Mr. Korie, remains ... why didn't the bogie attack us?

(All right, we've established that we've convinced the other guy we're a K-class ogre. Just as I've convinced my crew *I'm* a K-class ogre—damn me, but I thought it might work. I thought I cold turn that into eventual grudging loyalty. That was miscalculation. Wasn't it? Anyway, if we're convincing him that we're too big to fight, then maybe his best game *is* to convince us he's not there— because if we're really as big a ship as we're pretending to be, then the only time we're vulnerable is when we *don't believe* that he's there—

(Of course!

(That's the game! The boy who cried wolf. That captain—that other captain—he's very smart.

(Oh, yes—I see what he's done now. He's made his

ship a part of the environment of this psychonomy. Lordy, but that's clever! The bastard! He's trying to drive me mad. He's given me just enough of a hint to convince me that he's real, but not enough to convince the crew. He knows that the men won't be sharp enough to see what I see, and because their perceptions won't jibe with what I'm telling them, they'll get twitchy. Oh, yes, it's so obvious what he's doing, so subtle. . . . When two of your information sources contradict each other, you get anxious, nervous—upset. Sooner or later, one of the sources has to be devalued. That captain knows it. He's playing this game to turn my crew against me. That's been part of his plan all along. And it's working. He's made my crew and me into enemies. Oh, God, if only I could make them see what he's done to us. But that's the beauty of his plan. If they had the ability to perceive the relationships, the game wouldn't work. So he knows how vulnerable we are to this . . . this gambit. Lord, I want to write this one up. It is deliciously, calculatedly clever. A trap, a beautiful trap, and we've fallen into it. We *are* vulnerable now, and I'm scared as hell.)

Korie lowers his head into his hands, not knowing, not caring whether Leen is still there or not. There is pale stubble on his cheeks and it scruffs against his palms.

(There has to be a way out of this, I know it, there has to be—Damn that clever bastard! What a poker player he must be! All right—let me see—first, I must put aside my panic and think. What's his next move? What're my options? I think—we have three. We stay, we search, or we go home. He must have figured that if his plan worked, we would be startled by his not being there, and we would of course drift for a while, while a new hypothesis—and a new order of relationships—sorted itself out. Whatever we do when we stop drifting, he'll know how we sorted. If we search, that demonstrates that the gambit didn't work. Or hasn't worked yet. No, he's not going to rabbit, not yet. He's got to have thought this out—he's got to know exactly what he's doing. If his plan *was* to drive a psychonomic wedge between myself and my crew, then he can't be puzzled by our drifting. That's proof that it worked. So, he's got to have something more in store. . . . We still have our three options, but we have to remember that he has had seventeen hours of information about this ship's mental condition. If we search, he knows that all he has to do is stay low, and we'll destroy ourselves, and he can just move in for the kill. I wonder if he knows about the drills? But how could he? Our stress-field ripple? Would our drills have an effect on that? If he did know, then that would be one more reason to lay low. Because if we start running new drills now, and he can sense them, then he has two choices: One, attack us during a drill, which is when we're most likely to be confused about what is happening. We wouldn't be able to tell which is a real ship and which is the drill—so no more drills, none at all, we're too vulnerable. So now we've limited him to the other option—he attacks us, and we don't believe he's real any more. In that case, he's won before he ever attacks. He's got us. He wins. In fact, he's already there. That's got to be his goal—but if it is, then *when* does he attack us? We're already vulnerable now. What is he waiting for? If I could game it out, I could drill—no, no I couldn't. Any more drills and the crew would be certain I've phased out. But we can't stop having drills, can we? We have to rehearse every possible encounter as the situation keeps changing. That's part of being a good captain. And all of this is predicated on the possibility that the enemy *actually* has put into the field a generator-mask that allows one ship to simulate the echo of another.) Korie wipes his forehead. (I mean, if this is a field test of a new tactic, it could paralyze our fleet— *we've got to know the answer here*. It all depends on me. Dammit, the behavior of that wobbly fits *all* the projections of how a ship equipped with a generator mask might behave, and its behavior-set matches the psychonometric predictions too. And it's up to me to figure out the answer. Lord, God—why is this responsibility dumped on me? There isn't anyone I can turn to for advice. Or strength—Damn it, it's hard being superman. That's the joke, or course, but it's *so* true, so frustratingly true. I probably look like a madman, and I am. The super-ape is always a misfit in the company of lesser apes. These are not my people. Damn, I hope the alpha-matrix

development program pans out, I'm so goddamned
lonely—)

"What should I do?" he asks aloud. But there is no
one here to answer him. The burden is his and his alone,
and he is suddenly, terribly, and even almost wonderfully,
thrillingly afraid.

(I think we go home. Yes, we go home. We let him
think he's convinced us. Except, we stay on alert all the
way home, always looking for that moment when the
wobbly appears again. And when it does, naturally we ignore it. And then it closes on us. Right, and we ignore it.
We have to. Because if we chase it, it isn't going to be
there. It'll *never* be there if we chase it. That's the plan. So
we can't chase it. We pay no attention to it. And—and—
and then what—? It follows us right back to base, and
then he unwarps when we do. And we don't look for him
because we don't believe he's there. And that's when he
strikes.)

Korie stops a moment, stunned. "Of course! Of
course! Yes, of course! That's it! That has to be it! If you
have an advantage, you play it—"

He is breathing heavily now. The realization has hit
him like an explosion, and it's still hitting him—wave after physical wave, cold chills of realization, sweep
through his body. The terror of the moment is
exquisite—a bizarre mix of admiration, anger, and frustration. The moment when checkmate is obvious . . . and
inevitable.

(It's flawless. Such a perfect plan. Elegant. Stylish. I
wish I'd thought of it. And we're doomed, because it'll
work. I'll never be able to convince the crew to go on
alert at unwarp. They won't buy it. They won't believe it.
My God, what a psychological coup for those bastards.
Blowing up a K-class cruiser—or what they *believe* to be
a K-class cruiser—in front of a billion witnesses! The
navy won't be able to cover it up. In fact, K-class or not,
the navy will have to publicly admit that we *were* a
K-class ship because to do otherwise would clue the enemy in to the fact that the area *isn't* as heavily defended
as we're pretending it is. It's a good trap, a tight one. Almost inescapable.

(Eh? What was that? *Almost*—?

(I wonder—maybe our only hope *is* to go on as if his plan has worked and the crew really does distrust me. All the way home. And then—and then—what? How do I convince the crew to buy this plan—*any* plan—without also convincing them that I've looped off?)

Korie puts his head back into his hands and sighs. There are two flagships on the chessboard in front of him.

Korie stops. Finally. He stops completely and just exhales. The sound is like that of a man dying. But not quite. Abstractedly, he picks up his cup and finishes the coffee in it, never even noticing the taste or temperature.

Then he places both hands on the table edge and slowly pushes himself back. He rises like an old man. His back hurts. He walks slowly to the door and proceeds down the dark corridor to the auxiliary bridge. It is here that he has spent most of the last seventeen hours. Monitoring. Studying. Running simulations on the computer. Testing. Planning. Thinking. Trying to assimilate. Trying to synthesize. Listening, both inside and out.

But now—finally, *now,* for the first time, he is beginning to understand the larger pattern.

If it isn't already too late—

Thirty-one

History is written by the survivors.

SOLOMON SHORT

The captain's door opens with a tired sound. Brand
steps out into the corridor, blinking uncertainly. He
looks old. He looks unsteady. He pulls at his tunic
as if to straighten it, as if to stretch his own wrinkles into
invisibility. He turns and heads forward to the control
room.

The Command and Control chair is empty. The bridge
is unnecessarily dark. The captain sags into his seat and
gestures vaguely. "Someone bring the lights up, please."

He glances around as the room brightens, then rubs
his eyes with his thumb and forefinger. He sniffs once,
then returns his attention to the screens that line the upper circle of the room.

"What're we doing here?" he asks. "Does anyone
know? Where's Barak?"

Jonesy looks up from the astrogation console. "Uh, I
think he's in his cabin. I'll buzz him, sir."

"Yes, do that. Why are we still powered-down? Bring
the uh—bring all systems up to standard operating levels.
And—uh, secure from general quarters." He squints at
the assistant astrogator. "You—Jones, isn't it? Can you
plot a course back to base?"

"We've already got it, sir. Whenever you're ready."

The bridge crew is looking now, surreptitiously
sneaking glances—Brandt in command? Has something
happened?

"All right, set it up on the boards. And give it to the engine room too."

"Aye aye, sir!" There is a noticeable snap to Jonesy's voice. Brandt ignores it. He stifles the urge to yawn.

Goldberg leans over and whispers to another crewman. "In about ten seconds, Korie is gonna come screaming through that door."

Goldberg is wrong. Korie doesn't appear until a full minute and a half has elapsed. And when he does enter, his manner is strangely calm, almost relaxed.

He looks to Brandt. "We're going home?"

Brandt doesn't return the glance, he merely nods.

"I concur," says Korie. "I don't think there's anything more we can do out here."

Behind him, Jonesy drops his clipboard in startlement. Other members of the bridge crew also turn to look. Their expressions range from "Huh?" to "Hah!!"

Brandt almost smiles. "Giving up the ghost, huh?"

Korie shakes his head slightly, a noncommittal gesture of acknowledgment, nothing more. After a moment, Korie says, "I don't think further explanations are necessary. If you hadn't already ordered it, I was prepared to recommend just this course of action, sir."

"Well," says Brandt. "Well. That is something. Isn't it?" Brandt adds, *sotto voce*, "I should have done this before. It's time I reassumed command of my own ship."

Equally soft, Korie replies, "As you say, sir. But whether or not that bogie really is out there, whether or not I still believe he is, there's no way I'm going to convince anyone else on this ship that there's something out there tracking us, hiding from us. The most I could do would be convince you that I'm mad. I don't think I am, sir—but never mind—I agree with you that we should go home—but not because I've given up. Not for the reasons you're thinking."

"Your plan didn't work, Mr. Korie."

Korie shrugs. "I don't exactly see it that way, sir. My plan was the correct one for the circumstance as we understood it at the time. Circumstances are different now. We need a new plan."

"Ah, yes. I can agree with that. But this time, I'll make the plan, if you don't mind."

"Whatever you say, sir." He looks calmly at Brandt. "With your permission, sir, I'd like to leave the bridge."

"Certainly. May I ask why?"

"Well. There seems to be a certain . . . uh, feeling that the bogie was only a flux-wobbly. I would like to go down to the engine room and see if I can find a source. So it doesn't happen again."

Brandt's voice is cool. "You expect the wobbly to reappear, then?"

"Yes sir. I do."

"If it does reappear, you understand, Mr. Korie, then that's pretty definite proof we've been chasing nothing more than an echo."

"Yes, sir. I understand the implication. But I'm sure you can understand that I need to know *for certain*."

Brandt lifts one hand from the arm of the chair. "Permission granted. Amuse yourself. But keep out of the way, Korie. The crew is tired. I'm tired."

"We're *all* tired, sir."

"Umf," says Brandt.

Korie makes a quiet exit. His face is unreadable, almost hardened. He moves like a man playing a part.

He stops at the radec room. Rogers is alone at the console. "Rogers?"

Rogers looks up quickly, sees who it is and looks back to his board just as quickly. "Sir?" He bites off the word.

"How are you feeling?"

Rogers won't meet his gaze. His voice is sullen. "I'm all right, sir."

"Good. Will you do something for me?"

Rogers doesn't answer.

"Will you plot me some . . . ah, simulations?"

"What kind of simulations, sir?"

"Well—" Korie levers himself down into the empty seat beside Rogers. "I've been thinking about the . . . ah, behavior of that wobbly. Now, this is in the strictest confidence, you understand—but I'm not fully convinced that it was just a wobbly. I mean, think about it. What if— what if there were an enemy ship out there actually pretending to be a wobbly. We wouldn't be able to tell, would we? And at the point at which we stop believing it's a ship, that's when we're most vulnerable, isn't it?"

Rogers doesn't speak. He stares at his console. His hands are still.

"So—" Korie continues, "I was just . . . uh, wondering how such a ship might behave. And I thought that you might . . . ah, work up some simulations for me. Radec simulations."

"You want to use them for a drill, don't you?"

"Who said anything about a drill?"

"Sir—you always ask for a menu of simulations when you start planning a drill." Rogers swivels and stares hard at Korie. "You want to know something? You want to know how the crew finally started getting our scores moving toward optimum? We tapped into your files. I did it. You didn't know that, did you? That's how we finally got you off our necks with the drills. We knew what you were going to do before you did it."

Korie's face is blank. Unaffected. "That's very interesting. May I ask . . . how?"

"Easy. I tapped your console in the auxiliary bridge. I put a wire in, and made a duplicate file of everything you accessed."

"Clever. Why are you telling me this now?"

"Because there's nothing you can do about it. There's nothing you can do to any of us, any more. When we get home, you're probably going to be relieved, so why should I bother—"

Korie nods in modest agreement. "I really can't argue with your assessment of the situation, crewman. But I should give you one piece of advice. I am still the first officer of this ship. And I still outrank you. And until such time as I *am* relieved of command, I expect you to behave accordingly. Do you understand?"

"Yes, sir."

Korie rises. "Don't bother about those simulations, Rogers. I'll do them myself."

"Yes, sir. You do that, sir."

Korie steps out of the radec room. And permits himself the briefest of smiles. So far, so good. Maybe—

Thirty-two

The difference between psychonomy and chemistry is that raw chemicals are smart enough not to run experiments on themselves.

SOLOMON SHORT

Rogers thumbs his mike to life, "Jonesy? Rogers. Listen, he still believes there's something out there."

Jonesy tells Goldberg.

Goldberg tells Ehrlich.

Ehrlich tells Cookie.

Cookie tells Panyovsky.

And so on. Within fifteen minutes, every man on the ship knows that Korie still believes there's something out there. The story is repeated in whispers; at first with incredulity, then with anger, and finally with snorts and snickers of contempt. The remarks are shockingly candid.

But—listening privately in his own cabin—Korie is not shocked. He expected it, so the flicker of anger is a small one. It's a tightly focused anger, directed not at the remarks as hostility, but as noise. It interferes with the rationality of the speaker, and consequently, the coherency of the information being relayed is affected. But as the story is told and retold, a semblance of rationality begins to manifest itself. The situation is observed from the perspectives of every member of the crew, and individual deviations are averaged out.

But the process takes so damned long. And it is frustrating to listen to a conversation go astray and not be able to steer it back toward the desired consensus. Not if you want to get there.

"—Naw, he can't have any more drills. The captain wouldn't stand for it!"

"I only know what I heard, y'can ask Rogers—"

"Yah, yah—but it doesn't make sense—"

"He asked for simulations. You know what that means—"

"Maybe he just wants simulations!"

"—and Ehrlich talked to Leen—"

"Say again?"

"Ehrlich told Leen what was up and Leen said Korie's looped out. He wouldn't say how he knew, in fact he didn't want to talk about it at all. The most that Ehrlich could get out of him was that Leen ran into Korie in the galley last night and Korie was babbling about being a supermind or something, and that the captain of that other ship is trying to drive him crazy—"

Listening, Korie raises one eyebrow. (No, he sure didn't get much out of him, did he?)

"There isn't any other ship."

"Yah, you know it, I know it; everybody knows it but Korie. You know what I think?"

"What?"

"He can't stop believing for even one second that there's another ship out there—because if he does, then he'll realize how crazy he is—except when you get someone that crazy, they *can't* realize how crazy they are—"

A spasm of rage flashes on Korie's face. He forces himself to take a breath, then looks at the speaker and grins. "If I'd been holding a pencil, I'd have snapped it." He leans over and switches off the monitor. (Either they don't care any more, or they don't think I'm bothering to listen. Hardly matters. The psychonomy is working. It's really working. They're finally starting to function like a unit. I did it. I actually did it. Lordy, this is amazing. A class-A mega-response from a class-F stimulus. The dynamic is finally self-operative . . . and I know where all its buttons are.)

And then his own voice, the quiet one in the back of his skull, says, "Eh? Did you hear what he said?"

(Hear what?)

"—what that crewman said: 'He can't stop believing for even one second . . . because if he does, then he'll realize how crazy he is . . . except when you get someone that crazy, they never realize how crazy they are—' "

(So? That doesn't apply to me.)

"*Stop*," his voice tells him. "Just stop for one moment, Jon Korie, and consider: Is there even the slightest chance you could be wrong?"

(No.)

"You're not considering."

(How *you* know what I'm thinking.)

"Don't be silly. I stood on a chair and peeked over the partition."

Korie is stopped, staring at the opposite wall. His eyes seem focused on something inside of himself. (No, I couldn't be mistaken—could I?)

"It's something you have to consider. It *is* a possibility."

(No. I'm a pro. I don't . . . listen to the advice of . . . amateurs. What do they know about it?)

"The perceptions of amateurs are often surprisingly valid, you know that. You just have to know how to interpret them."

(But they don't have the information I do—)

But the thought won't go away. And Korie can't shake this sudden inner dread. (I've done all right. I—I've taken care of Leen, for instance. Leen was a big problem. And his big mouth. Unloading on him like that was the right thing to do. I gave him far more than he can handle. He'll be paralyzed, terrified because he doesn't understand—*can't* understand what I'm doing—he'll cooperate now with the first semblance of rational authority that manifests itself. I'm counting on it. I didn't expect him to talk—at least not quite that vividly, but—but that's a useful bonus. I've got them all terrified of me now. So that part's working. It's *all* working. Have I got any other crew problems that I haven't fixed? Rogers? No—) Korie allows himself a smile, puts his hands behind his head and leans back in his bunk. (That was a real challenge—integrating the little bastard into the crew.

He's sure a spoiled brat, isn't he? Always looking for a Daddy. Well, now he's got the whole crew to protect him from me. That was a hard one, a tricky one. If I'd shown even the slightest interest in protecting him, they would have resented him even more. This way is better. As soon as they thought I was abusing him, or perhaps using him as a weapon against them, they closed ranks around him . . . yes, that was the move—Lord, I don't like doing this—but I have to use every tool at my disposal, if it'll work, don't I? And it worked. Didn't it? Rogers is finally functioning *for* me instead of against me. I knew I'd done it when he finally tapped into my console. But it sure took him long enough to do it. I was starting to think they'd never figure out why I was asking for those simulations. Now there—that was one of my ideas that worked perfectly. I knew they were going to hate the drills. I had to give them a way to cheat—a way to "get even" with me. But all the time they thought they were doing it to me, I was doing it to them. The amount of time they spent in figuring how to outwit my simulations was more time than they would have spent preparing for a drill. They didn't improve their ratings by cheating; not with those exercises. They didn't improve their ratings by cheating; not with those exercises. They did it by learning how to outthink an enemy. But, Lord, what a price. I had to be the enemy.

(Do I dare question myself?) Puzzlement knits his brow. (I—I have to—it's part of the process. But I've gone over the logic of every level a thousand times. I couldn't have missed anything. Could I?)

Korie feels a sudden moment of fear, an icy sinking feeling—(*What if the wobbly doesn't reappear?!!* That would prove that it was a ship—and that I'm right. But—what if it doesn't reappear, then where is it? Good Lord—could his plan be even more complex than—? No, it couldn't possibly be—nobody could possibly juggle that many levels—unless he's trying to drive *all* of us mad—

(All of us—

(Me. He's working on me. Remember that. Trying to drive *me* mad.

(Maybe it's really working. Is this what madness feels

like? My brain hurts. A lot. And what if he does reappear, then what? What if it really is a *wobbly*? Then maybe I really am scatter-beamed. Oh, God—this is part of his plan too. The self-doubt. He really is trying to drive me crazy. And it's working. I'm the only man on this ship who believes I'm sane, and even *I'm* having doubts.

(But it doesn't matter any more, does it? Because there's nothing more that I can do. It's all been done. The last piece is in place. But, oh, it's such a fragile structure. Will it hold together for the twelve days it'll take us to get home? Or will it fracture when the bogie reappears? Or tighten? So much depends on how I react. How *will* I react?

(I have to game this out. They'll be looking for signs of madness, so I daren't obsess about that bogie—but I still have to give them *some* kind of cue—because they're going to be looking to me for a handle on how to react—and I need them to see that bogie as an enigma, not sure whether it really is there or not. They have to doubt it too—even if only a little. And as long as they see that I still believe in it, they'll doubt. Just a little.

(Hm. I'll have to keep a low profile, then, won't I? Yes, the engine room is the right course. Who knows? If they're right, and I *am* wrong, and it really is a wobbly, maybe I can source it. Hmp, that would be funny; the only person on the ship able to find the wobbly is the officer that it drove mad—because he's the only one obsessive enough to look.)

But somehow, Korie is not amused.

(I can do a little to keep the structure maintained—but there are no major steps that I can take now without destroying the balance. Either it's going to work, or it's not . . . I wonder, though—if I had foreseen this possibility from the beginning, is there anything I could have done differently? Better?—) He thinks a moment, rehearsing his recent decisions one more time. (No, I did what I had to. There wasn't any better way.)

He rubs his forehead tiredly. The hardest part is going to be the waiting.

Thirty-three

If you build a better mousetrap, you'll catch a better mouse.

SOLOMON SHORT

And then the bogie reappears.

Quietly. Almost insignificantly. A faintly detected shimmer at the edges of probability.

Rogers spots the anomaly on his screens.

He frowns, he punches up double-check programs, then checks the accuracy of them. He orders up a system analysis for the entire sensory set.

The possibility remains. There is a . . . discrepancy.

Where the field should be blank, there is a matrix of eighty-one pixels that flickers with random points of light. Possibilities. The individual points are meaningless as data. It is the fact that they are occurring within a defined matrix that gives Rogers such concern.

He clenches his hands together, leans elbows on the console, leans his chin onto his hands and bites one knuckle pensively.

Should he tell them? And who? Korie? The captain? Barak? Leen? Maybe he should ask Jonesy—?

No. He has to figure this out for himself.

What if it isn't there?

"I mean—they'll think I'm as twitchy as Korie."

But the screen before him continues to flicker.

He leans back in his chair uncomfortably—then, resolutely, leans forward again and completely repeats every scan and double-check he had previously performed. Unable to make a decision, he postpones for the moment the need to. He rationalizes, he tells himself he just wants to be certain.

Although he is certain enough already.

And he is not surprised when the results are the same as before. The instruments say that something is out there.

Except . . . maybe—

There's one other thing to check. He orders up a simulation of the *Burlingame*'s stress-field ripple, then begins altering it, trying to see if he can make it match the pattern of the bogie.

He can, but—he doesn't feel good about the match. It's too *contrived*.

"Maybe it's a wobbly—and maybe it isn't." There. It's said. "Maybe it's a real bogie."

But, *dammit!* That sounds like something Mr. Korie would say!

(I have to figure this out now—by myself. There isn't anyone else I can check with first.)

Rogers is upset, frustrated. His nervousness shows; his hands are twitching. He feels almost close to tears. It isn't fair! "We're right back where we started."

(What do they want me to do? No—that's not the question. What *should* I do?) (I should tell the Captain.) (I should tell Korie too.) (Why?) (Because—uh—what if—?)

The wobbly could be a stress-field echo. The phase adapters could be magnifying the vibrations of the inherent velocity, or it could be another starcraft of roughly comparable size. *But what class?* The classification of a ship isn't dependent on its size, but on its armament—

"That bastard!" Rogers says in frustration. "He's got me thinking like him!" (And I won't have it! I'll show him! It's only a bogie—I mean, wobbly! It isn't there! Never has been!) He stabs the communicator button. "Jonesy? Rogers. Moby Dick off the port bow."

"Eh?"

"Uh—" He hadn't thought this far ahead. "Uh—it's back. The bogie."

"Huh? Are you certain?"

"Yes, of course. I checked it three times."

"Have you told the captain yet?"

"Not yet. I thought we ought to put it on the grapevine first."

"Yah, sure. Thanks." Jonesy switches out.

Rogers touches another button. "Captain? This is Rogers. In the radec room. Uh—that bogie's back."

The captain's reply is unintelligible.

"Beg pardon, sir?"

"Tell Mr. Leen. In the engine room. Tell him to check his Hilsen units. That's probably all it is."

"Yes, sir." Rogers disconnects and contacts Leen. "Sir—Captain wants you to check your Hilsen units. It's back." And so on.

By the fifth call, the response is, "Yah, I already heard."

So he stops calling. The news is spreading. The ripple is moving faster than the object that caused it.

There's only one person who won't have heard.

(Somebody's got to tell him.)

"But I *won't*"— Rogers considers it. "No, *I* won't do it." And then he thinks. (But it sure would bug Korie, wouldn't it? To be told that his bogie was only a wobbly. Had been all along. And now there's proof. Incontrovertible evidence!) "Like hell *I* won't!" Punch, flick. "Mr. Korie? The wobbly is back. Huh? Oh, Rogers, sir. Yes, I checked. Yes, sir. You're welcome."

(But is the evidence *really* incontrovertible? After all, Korie isn't *that* stupid. If he suspects something is out there, maybe he has good reason to—) (No, don't be silly.)

He puts his elbows back on the console, folds his hands together, and leans his chin on them. Absentmindedly he begins chewing his knuckle again.

An eighty-one-pixel matrix of probability is flickering in front of him. Maybe there is something there, and maybe there isn't. But there is no way he can tell from this board.

Thirty-four

A man is known by the enemies he keeps.
SOLOMON SHORT

Korie enters the engine room quietly. He ignores the sudden startled glances and moves politely, almost timidly, to the auxiliary monitor console and taps the man sitting there out of the seat. "It's all right. There's something a little more important than that." Then, ignoring the man—and the rest of the engine room crew as well—he drops into the seat. He slips on a pair of earphones and clears the board.

On the other side of the engine room, Leen and his first assistant are standing, staring amazed at Korie. Leen starts to take a step forward, then stops himself. His eyes are troubled.

"Chief?" asks Beagle. "Aren't you going to say something to—him?"

"No. I don't think so. The captain told me he might be coming down here. He's—going to look for that wobbly. I guess we'd better let him."

"I don't think the guys are going to like it."

"I don't think they have much choice. Tell them to keep out of his way."

"Yes, sir."

Korie has an intense preoccupied expression on his face. His fingers move nimbly across the console. He is oblivious of the ship around him.

(There's just one last calculation. He's got to get close to us in time for unwarp. He'll have to be right on top of us. So he'll have to increase his speed for the next twelve, maybe thirteen days—until his echo fills our 'sky.' If he comes in too close too fast, we'll stop, afraid to continue without checking the engines.

(Hmm.

(He could attack us then. We'd be just as vulnerable.

(But it's to his advantage to kill us as close to our base as possible—except that then he has to turn around and run all the way home—with the possibility that some of our boys will be hot on his tail. So in that case, if he wanted to be cautious, he would want us to unwarp far from base, and would try to force us to stop. He could close with us *before* we're within range of home.

(And that would do it, all right. Whenever he wants us to stop, he need only move in close. As long as we're convinced he's a wobbly—as long as he can mask his true nature—it'll work.

(Do we have a countermove? Yes, but it's the same countermove as if we go all the way home. Either way. I wonder if I should arm my weapon now—

(No, I can't. I can't risk it going off prematurely. I'll just have to watch the size of the bogie.

(I think he's going to take us all the way. That's his ... style. Yes. But, then again—if his plan is calculated against an alpha-matrix, then he's got to know I won't go completely mad without also figuring that the paranoid possibility just might be true. After all, paranoids often have *real* enemies too. In that case, he might very well assume that I might figure his plan out even down to a sense of his style. And in that case, it would very well behoove him to *change* his style at some point. To catch me unawares. Is that possible?

(He's got to have figured that I would be in exactly this position—surrounded by a hostile crew and trying to outthink him and them simultaneously. I have to do something that he can't predict. But, of course, the beauty of his plan is that he's already limited my options. I *can't* really do anything because I have no control over the crew any more.

(Of course, he thinks the alpha-matrix on this ship is the captain. He doesn't realize that we have a captain

who is still very much in charge and that the alpha he devalued was only the first officer. And that's a variable in
the psychonomic equation that's in my favor. He has to
gauge the state of this ship by its external behavior. He
must think that the captain was replaced by a nervous
crew. And now we have a nervous first officer beating a
hasty retreat for home, neither he nor his crew certain
whether or not they've just committed mutiny. Yes, of
course, that's what it must look like. So maybe the actu-
ality of that situation is in our favor. We still have a captain, and the crew isn't so demoralized—

(Or is it? Just what kind of situation *are* we in?)
Korie considers it glumly. (We're not that far from where
he wants us to be, after all. What little error his misper-
ception might cause, it's not enough to be decisive in our
favor. We're still in very big trouble.

(But he can't possibly know how I plan to fight
him—because he doesn't know the internal psychonomy
here, only the external one, so—

(Except, he's got to be an alpha-matrix himself. Only
another alpha could have structured this plan. Only an alpha could perceive it.

(But do they have alphas on the other side?

(And if they don't, then who—or *what?*—am I fighting?

And then Korie stops suddenly, completely. Almost
paralyzed. His hands grip the console.

(*This isn't just a test of a new weapon, is it?* It's a test
of minds. Mine against his. This war is going to be won
by the side with the best psychonometrics. He's never
been after this ship at all—that's *never really* been the
goal. They need to find out how to neutralize an alpha!
That's his real object!)

"Sir—? Are you all right?"

Korie looks up. A nameless crewman is looking
down at him, a worried expression on his face. "Can I get
you something?"

"Uh—no, it's all right. Uh, thank you for asking.
You—you're uh, Fowles, aren't you?"

"Yes, sir."

"Well." Korie doesn't know what else to say. He

ooks bemused for a moment. Then, offering an explana-
ion. "I was uh—just thinking—about the uh, wobbly.
You know."

"Yes, sir. I hope you find the source."

"Yes. That would certainly answer a lot of questions,
wouldn't it?" Korie even allows himself a small, gentle
smile.

"Yes, sir." Fowles nods quickly, encouraging this—
the *good* side of Korie—that he sees. "I'll leave you now,
sir."

"I'll be fine here—oh, uh, Fowles. On second
thought, if you do get anywhere near the galley, or even
a sidebar, I could use a cup of coffee. But there isn't any
rush."

"Yes, Mr. Korie. I'll take care of it." And he's gone.

(Now what the hell did that mean?) Korie rests his
chin on one hand for a moment and stares off into space.
I'll bet he's trying to humor me. Hah! Primitive
psychonometrics! Still, it's a good sign. It's a forerunner
of sympathy, and sympathy is the first step toward empa-
thy. Maybe, just maybe—)

Korie starts setting up problems on the console in
front of him. After a while, he slips casually into a self-
monitoring analysis program, which—in the course of
running itself—notes by the phrasing of a certain key sentence that there is no tap on this console. At least, not
yet. Korie nods to himself, satisfied. (Thank heaven for
small favors.) But just to be on the safe side, he sets up a
dummy set of simulations anyway, and lets them run con-
tinuously. Just in case. Then he punches up Beethoven's
Pathétique piano sonata and leans back contentedly in his
chair, eyes fixed firmly on the screen. (This is going
to be the best performance of my life. And all I have to
do is sit here and look serious. And I do admit, it's going
to be hard to keep from showing a big satisfied smile—)

High above him, on the monkey cage, two crewmen
look at each other.

"How long do you think he's going to stay there?"
one asks the other.

"The way I hear it, he's going to stay as long as

there's a wobbly on the screens—and that means all the
way home."

"Twelve days!"

"As long as it takes."

"Ugh. What's he got against us anyway?"

"Nothing. He's never had anything against us. It's all
been completely impersonal. Korie's like all officers—
asshole for the pure fun of it. Ignore him—he won't go
away, but what else can you do?"

"As long as he leaves us alone . . . I guess it's all
right—I just don't like having him near me."

"Who does?"

The cage turns beneath them then, and they scramble
to their new positions, swearing softly.

On the opposite side of the engine room, Lee
watches them worriedly. Twelve days of this? He shudders.

Thirty-five

Remember, today could just as easily be the last
day of the rest of your life.

SOLOMON SHORT

On the second day, someone reprograms the music channel to play at odd intervals, and with full chorus and orchestration: "On the second day of Christmas, my true love gave to me—two phase adapters .. and a partridge in a pear tree."

The thought pleases Korie. He had expected tension. But he doesn't need them tense, not yet—and he's pleased that individual members of the crew are already finding ways to ease the pressure. Not discard it, just lower its importance. So Korie is satisfied.

It's a start.

His problem is that it's difficult for him to monitor the state of the crew objectively. Their mere knowledge of his presence indisputably alters their behavior. Korie thinks of something he read once in a quotebook. "Heisenberg was not only right, he was *absolutely* right." That is nowhere so true as in psychonometrics.

Korie is in the engine room again. Today, he is listening to Brell's *Fantasy on a Theme of Mozart*. Perhaps that's dangerous—to listen to something that cheerful—but what the hell, there are times when one must stop analyzing and start experiencing. Otherwise one has nothing to analyze except one's own analyses. And that way lies madness. Besides, he rationalizes to himself, once in a

while it's necessary to detach yourself completely from th
problem.

—Except that he knows that try as he might, he can
not and will not detach himself from this problem
Thoughts keep percolating upward from his subconsciou
mind.

For instance, the possibility that the bogie will *no*
track them all the way back to base keeps returning t
gnaw at the base of his brain.

(After all, he has twelve days in which to act. H
doesn't dare give us time to game out *all* the possibilities
He has to catch us by surprise. So he'll have to wait a few
days, at least—to give us time to stop thinking of him a
a bogie and get used to him as an ever-present and harm
less wobbly. But he can't give us too long or we'll start t
wonder too much about that wobbly.

(I guess the key variable in the equation is our dis
tance from base. If we're too far from base, then he ha
no choice but to force the issue. But how far is too far
Twelve days? Fourteen? Twenty? He can force the issu
any time he wants, merely by closing with us.

Idly, Korie clears his console and accesses the ship'
library. There is a file on paradoxes, and there's one i
particular that he wants to consider. The paradox of th
unexpected event.

The screen displays rule one: "An unexpected even
will occur during a given time-frame."

The lines scroll up, and rule two appears: "The even
will be unexpected in that those affected by it will not b
able to predict from previous information at what mo
ment it will occur."

Korie notes to himself, (And that rules out the da
we return to base. Because on that day, we know whe
and where we are going to unwarp, and therefore, th
event of his attack will not be unexpected—at least not t
me. Therefore, rules one and two eliminate the last day o
running—but all of the days before then are still prim
candidates for the unexpected event. Therefore, there i
no paradox involved. At least not until we add self
awareness.)

He taps a button, and the lines scroll up to revea

rule three: "The event will occur in such a way that it will not be possible to deduce from rules one and two when it will occur."

(And that changes the problem entirely. We still know that the unexpected event will not occur on the last day. But now we know that it will not occur on the next-to-last day either. Because if there were only two days left, and if we knew that the event could not occur on the last day and still be "unexpected" then it has to occur on the next to the last day—but then it wouldn't be "unexpected" any more. So the unexpected event cannot occur on the next to last day either. So . . . the unexpected event—*if it is actually to occur*—must occur on or before day ten.

(But—the paradox of the situation is that it is infinitely self-regressing. Now that we know that the unexpected event cannot occur on day eleven or day twelve and still be unexpected, then it follows that it cannot occur on day ten either and be unexpected. Because if it has not happened by day nine, then it must happen on day ten, because it can't happen on day eleven or day twelve and still be unexpected. And can't happen on day eleven or twelve and be unexpected. And if I know that it must happen on day ten, then it isn't unexpected on day ten either. And the same argument can be applied to day nine and day eight and day seven, all the way back to today. Lovely.

(And yet, knowing that the event cannot occur on any single one of those days and still be unexpected—when it does occur it will be breaking the rules of its own paradox, and therefore it *will* be unexpected. I cannot predict when it will occur. At least, not without considering all of the other factors involved. But that won't give me an answer either. The whole point of the unexpected event is that it *is* unexpected and you cannot predict it. The paradox is that you expect an unexpected event to occur.)

Korie is frowning now, hardly listening to the music in his earphones. (So far that bastard has been one move ahead of me all the way down the line. No matter how hard I try, I can't find the edge I need, that little advan-

tage that will allow me to—to predict what he's going to
do next. That's the key to his plan—to do the opposite of
the obvious. Every time we reach a point where I think I
should be able to predict his behavior, I find another reason to be uncertain.) Korie considers that thought for a
while. (You can drive a person mad this way. When you
can no longer predict the consequences of an action, you
can't interact with your environment safely any more.
The only thing to do is retreat into catatonia. Except—
that couldn't possibly be his goal.

(Or could it?

(Could they be so unwilling to join in combat that
they've reduced their battle entirely to feinting and maneuvering for psychonomic effects?

(I should consider that, shouldn't I? It's a possibility.
Except—that bastard is going to do the opposite of what
I expect him to—

(So, therefore, I don't dare *expect* him to do
anything—because the mere act of expecting—and preparing for that possibility—is almost a guarantee that
he'll do the opposite.

(The question is—how accurate are his predictions of
my behavior? But then—I can't know what he's predicting
any more than he can know what I'm preparing—

(And the event will be unexpected because I *cannot*
predict it.)

Abruptly Korie reaches forward and switches off the
music. It has become distracting. Thoughtfully, but resolutely, he takes the earphones off and lays them down on
the console. He pushes himself to his feet. (I think, perhaps, it's time I armed my weapon—)

Thirty-six

Learn to be sincere. Even if you have to fake it.
SOLOMON SHORT

The shower room smells of disinfectant. It's a little too crisp to be natural. Korie pauses just inside the doorway and thinks for a moment as he surveys the room. Then he steps to a wall panel and quickly reprograms the environment. He raises the temperature to ninety-two degrees. (Or is that a little too obvious?) He backs it off to eighty-eight. He switches off the air circulation, and the air cleaners too. He punches for a flowery smell that is also reminiscent of stale urine. He increases the light level almost to the threshold of pain. (I want the room bright. I want him squinting, so he won't see me clearly, and so his face will automatically be pinched into an expression of hate.) He reverses the polarity of the ion generator. The positive ions will make the room feel stuffy, cramped. (What else?) He increases the sound-pressure level of the music channel— particularly certain key frequencies—and then orders up the most annoying and discordant piece of music he can think of, Lennon's *Ode to Chaos*. The room fills with jangly noise. Korie listens a moment, evaluating. (Maybe a little old-fashioned country-western instead? No, this will do. This sounds more like it's trying to be *real* music. Besides, I *like* this. The composer was demonstrating that true art dances on the borderline of discordancy—disturbing the listener with its hints of new truth—it must continually test and stretch those borders. Yes, this piece will disconcert anyone who needs rigorous structure to feel secure—)

Korie peels off his uniform and deliberately drops it on the floor in the middle of the room, taking care to make certain that his briefs are casually obvious. The effect of that particular reminder of the *physicality* of his presence is most important. He will be dealing with the animal levels here, and he needs to stimulate the animal level of response to an operative level. (But this should do it—)

He programs the shower to cycle slowly between lukewarm and steaming. Before stepping into it, he dampens several towels and throws them casually around the room. Then he steps into the jets of water and begins silently scrubbing.

He bathes slowly, allowing himself to enjoy the luxuriousness of the sensation. He allows himself to relax—that is, as much as it is possible to relax in an environment tuned specifically to jangle. But Korie's awareness of the deliberateness of the stimuli grants him a certain immunity from their effects. He retains his control.

"Shit!" cries a distant voice. "What a mess!"

Without breaking from his reverie, Korie leans around the edge of the partition. "Yah? Who's there?"

A startled Rogers. "Uh—oh, sorry, sir. I didn't know you were in here—I'll uh—" But Korie has disappeared back into the steaming shower. Rogers leaves quickly—without using the urinal at all. He'll go to the aft head rather than risk being alone with Korie again.

Korie resists the urge to whistle. He forces himself into an exercise mantra, a combination of mental and physical routines that are designed to tune the body into a more harmonious gestalt. He begins to feel almost—cheerful.

Each time a new person enters the room, Korie peers around the edge of the partition. Nope. Still not the one he's waiting for.

He holds his face under the water, rubbing at his eyes to make them swollen and red. (I hope I don't have to wait too much longer. If I'm in here too long, the whole ship will know and then he'll never come in.)

But even as he thinks that, the door whooshes open and Korie peers around the wall to see Wolfe coming in. Korie pulls back quickly, rubbing his eyes hard. He takes a deep breath, then as he lets it out, he seems to sag. He lets himself slump like a tired bag of bones. He pulls his shoulders in, as if he's become a coward, flinching against even the slightest threat. He turns off the shower and moves toward the door with timid steps. (Oh, God, I hope I'm not overdoing this. If this doesn't ring true—)

He steps cautiously out to where he can see Wolfe, and immediately, as he does so, cups one hand protectively over his groin. (Ah, nice touch that.) He turns quickly and grabs his towel, holding it lengthwise in front of himself as he blots at himself. He never takes his eyes off Wolfe, and he keeps a slightly worried expression on his face. Wolfe is standing at the urinal with his back to Korie—but he is aware of his presence. His quick sideways glance and unnatural stiffness are the cues Korie needs.

"Uh—excuse me—" Korie says, stepping quickly past Wolfe and scooping up his clothes from the floor. He retreats back to the other end of the room, then turns away from Wolfe, deliberately concentrating on the floor as he continues to dry himself.

"You're not so big any more, are you?" Wolfe sneers.

"Uh—" Korie looks up, startled. (I could kiss him for that. It isn't often that someone walks right into it so perfectly.) "I beg your pardon, Wolfe?"

"Mr. Hot-Jets Korie—" Wolfe snorts derisively. "—now you know what it feels like to be shit, don't you?" His expression is tight and ugly.

Korie allows himself to look upset. "I only—tried to do what I thought was right. So I made a mistake—everybody does."

"Yah—you made a mistake all right, when you signed on. This used to be an easy ship. No sweat until you came along, you and your goddamn drills. Always driving, driving, driving at us—how the hell did you think we were going to react to that? With kisses? You're such an asshole, you did it to yourself. We were just waiting for you to screw up—but you surpassed even our wildest dreams—"

"Look," begs Korie. "Take it easy, will you? Don't you think I have some feelings too? Don't you think I'm feeling bad enough? Why do you have to rub it in?"

"Because that's what you did to me!" Wolfe snarls. "And how much pity did I get out of you? Nothing. *Nada.* Zero. Zilch. So why should I give you any courtesy now? I want to see you hurting, asshole. I've wanted to see it from the first day you came aboard this ship. I've waited a long time for this." Wolfe even takes a bold step forward. He is standing very tall and very firm now.

Korie wonders, (Now? Or should I wait a moment longer?...) He decides to stretch the moment out. "I—am still an officer, Wolfe. I suggest that you ... remember that."

"Hah! You're still an officer only by the courtesy of the old man!"

"—Uh, I don't think—that you have all the facts, Wolfe—" Korie lifts his eyes slowly to meet the other man's. His expression is deliberately calculating, and for an instant, Wolfe is panicked, wondering if he has said too much.

But the momentum of the moment carries him forward. "I know what I *want* to know. And I hope they sell tickets to your court-martial, *sir*! Because I want a front-row seat."

(Good! That's the cue!) Korie steps deliberately forward, grabbing Wolfe's tunic at the throat and shoving the man back against the wall. Wolfe's eyes go suddenly wide with terror. Korie steps in very close to him, pressing his wet and naked flesh firmly against Wolfe's, even to the extent of spreading the man's legs with his knee. It's a neat trick to pretend to dry off while still leaving yourself wet enough to be uncomfortably clammy to the touch. Wolfe tries to shrink away from Korie's grasp, but there is a wall behind him. Korie is saying, "You listen to *me* now—I may be going down the tubes, but I'm not going alone. I'm taking you with me. I told you I would nail you, Wolfe—you should have believed me. Whatever

made you think Rogers—or anyone else—would stick up
for *you*? You and your shipmates are the most disloyal,
backbiting, scummiest collection of maggot-brained bim-
bos I've ever had the displeasure to serve with. And I'm
going to make damned sure that each and every one of
you suffers for it—starting with you, pea-brain! It's going
to be a very messy hearing, count on that! You better
start worrying now, Wolfe—" Korie is breathing hard,
right into Wolfe's face. He has deliberately not brushed
his teeth in three days. "—because you know as well as I
do that they never nail an officer as hard as they do a
crewman—especially not an officer who was only trying
to do the job. At least I have a defense, asshole. But
you're going to be up on assault charges. What're you going to use for an excuse when they ask you why you
broke Rogers' collarbone?"

"You can't prove that!"

Korie steps back, looking deliberately smug. "You
think so? You just keep on thinking that." He releases
Wolfe then, and grins at him maliciously; his tone of
voice is quiet, calm—the *old* Korie. "I've got all I need to
nail you, Wolfe—" He lowers his voice to conspiratorial
whisper. "—so now, you tell me. Who's the asshole?"

"You're just trying to con me. Rogers didn't say anything!"

Korie shrugs noncommittally, still grinning. "Why
don't you ask him and find out?"

"I don't believe you—" Wolfe's voice cracks.

"So, don't—" Korie picks up his towel again. He is
strangely calm now.

Wolfe is shaken. His face is white. "You *are* crazy,
aren't you? You know, that's what they're saying about
you—"

"So? Who wouldn't be a little crazy—trapped on the
same ship with a bunch of dildoes like you?" He looks
Wolfe up and down with a deliberately disparaging expression. "Why don't you put your cock back in your
pants now and get out of here." He is still grinning
smugly.

He watches Wolfe like a parent as the man fumbles
with himself, then scrambles for the door—

(Oh, Lord—I wonder if that last touch was too much. I don't want to demoralize him—only trigger him.)

Korie stands where he is for a moment, reviewing the scene he just played. (No, it should work out all right. Wolfe has too limited a set of responses. Sooner or later— he'll follow through. I only hope it's sooner.)

He steps to the wall and reprograms the environment of the shower room. Then he pads back to the shower and a cold spray of water. Incongruously, Korie starts humming to himself as he lathers up.

Thirty-seven

Every artist should have a large burly assistant standing behind him with a mallet—to stop him with it when the job is finished.

SOLOMON SHORT

Feeling clean and refreshed, Korie returns to his cabin. He does not switch on the intercom to listen to the chatter of the crew. One of the axioms of psychonometrics is that the early returns are *always* disappointing. And listening for results too soon often encourages the psychonomist to return to the scene of the crime and apply more stimuli to the system. No, the important thing is to trust your first instincts long enough to give the situation a chance to mature. Of course, there *are* exceptions to the rule—but the proper practice of psychonomy is an art in any case.

In fact, the first axiom of the craft is that psychonomy is a science of *process*. One can manipulate individual rounds, but the process was probably in progress before you started working, and will certainly continue after you stop. It is wise to take this into account before practicing any manipulation.

The most successful psychonomists view their craft as a series of applied nudges to keep a system moving in a desired direction, but the system provides its own energy for that motion.

Eventually the point is reached where it is necessary to just *stop*—and wait to see what will happen next. And Jon Korie is at that point.

He lies down on his bunk, puts his hands behind his head, and allows himself to relax, completely relax, for the first time since he came aboard this vessel. For the next few hours, he can let go of each and every one of the thousand little controls he has been maintaining as a constant operating system for Jon Korie, first officer of the U.S.S. *Roger Burlingame*.

He begins by telling the various parts of his body to let loose of their myriad little tightness. His legs, his arms, his neck, his back, his spine—especially his spine. He slows his heartbeat, he depresses the level of his metabolism, and even his breathing becomes shallower. He can hear the sound of the air circulating in his ears, a soft-roaring rustle. He can feel his pulse, sweeping in waves outward from his heart to his extremities and then rushing back again in almost the same instant. He feels like a single-celled throbbing organism.

His mind drifts, and uncoordinated visions suggest themselves to him.

The people of a world he has never seen live in four-meter-deep trenches on a world covered with a jungle of hallucinogenic ivy. Their forebrain functions are permanently dulled and they wander in their ruts forever. Huge globular fruits hang from the vines; the milk is sweet and the meat is savory. No one wants. They wander naked, some in clusters, some alone. There are not many children here. The urge to mate is almost nonexistent. There are no mates. There are no families—just . . . they would be called tribes, except they have not even that much structure. Occasionally the fruit ferments and triggers an orgy of clumsy couplings. Occasionally children are born. Often, by the time they are old enough to walk and pick their own fruits, they are forgotten by their mothers.

Here, on this world that Korie has never seen, the human race has reverted to a lesser breed. The climate is warm, the days are pleasant, and there are tuneless songs as the wanderers hum their way up and down the channels. Korie dreams of this place. How peaceful it would be to be just a member of the herd somewhere. How peaceful to not have any worries at all.

The planet's name is Eden.

Korie falls asleep dreaming about it.

Asleep, he looks just like a little boy. He rolls over onto his side and pulls his arms close to his chest and his knees upward. Occasionally, he shivers, but not because his cabin is cold.

Very long ago and very far away, a little boy once asked, "Paw-paw, will you hold me?"

And his paw-paw held him warm and close all night. That secret core that lies at the center of Jon Korie is hiding in that memory again.

He smiles once, faintly, and is still.

Thirty-eight

I'd feel a lot better about doctors if it weren't called practice.

SOLOMON SHORT

Three hours later, looking deliberately haggard, Korie steps into the sick bay of the cruiser.

Panyovsky's aide is just cleaning off the operating table. He drops the last piece of soiled gauze into a bucket on the floor, then turns to wipe the blood off the operating table. There are drops of blood on the floor too. His gown is splotched.

Korie raises one eyebrow. "What happened?"

Mike looks up at him, concerned, but before he can open his mouth to answer, Panyovsky enters the room, still wiping his hands with a small towel. "I should be asking you that, Korie. What did you do?"

"Huh—?"

The doctor studies him curiously. "You don't know?"

"I've been trying to get some sleep for the past four hours."

"Something wrong with your buzz-box?"

"No, I just need something a little stronger, I guess."

"You really *are* out of tune, aren't you?" Panyovsky looks at him thoughtfully. "Mike—leave that for now. It'll wait. Go get yourself some coffee. And don't talk to anyone. Let me make my report to the captain first."

Mike nods professionally and shrugs out of his gown. He is quickly out the door.

Korie looks to Panyovsky, "What *happened*?"

"You really haven't heard? Wolfe took another shot at Rogers. This time, he cracked three ribs and ruptured his spleen. Also broke his nose. He's in pretty bad shape. Looks like hell."

Korie doesn't respond immediately. He doesn't look at Panyovsky. He says, as much to himself as anyone, "That poor kid—he sure takes a lot of abuse—"

"You certainly haven't helped him any, Jon."

"What do you mean by that?"

"Oh—nothing. I guess I'm just feeling a little touchy. The worst part of medicine is repairing acts of cruel violence. And it hurts even more if you *like* your patients."

"Yah, I guess so."

"You want a drink?"

"No. You go ahead without me."

"I don't like to drink alone."

"All right, I'll keep you company, but make it a small one for me."

As Panyovsky fusses with the glasses, he says, "I guess I should have expected you'd be having trouble sleeping—it's a hard thing for a man to confront himself, isn't it?"

Korie doesn't answer that.

The doctor slides a glass over to Korie. Korie doesn't pick it up. Panyovsky studies the first officer shrewdly, "Tell me something, Jon. Are you running some kind of scam?"

"Huh—?"

"Jon. This is Pan you're talking to. Pan, who has access to medical files that even you and the captain can't see unless I decide to show them to you. Not only medical files, but psychiatric files too. I know you're an alpha-matrix, Jon. I've known it since the day you came aboard. I guess Brandt knows it too. But even if it weren't in your file, I'd have figured it out by now. You're up to something. I can't tell you how I know, but I know—I sense it. Something feels askew—pressured. And then Rogers comes in here, looking like something Cookie couldn't hide under gravy, and insisting the whole time that he didn't tell you anything. He was very insistent about that.

It was very important to that kid that somebody believe him that he didn't tell you anything about Wolfe kicking the shit out of him—not that it matters any more. This time there are lots of witnesses. Barak and the captain, to name two. But, for what it's worth, Jon, I believe him. He didn't tell you anything, did he?"

"Nope. And I stopped asking at least a week ago."

"Then why would Rogers be so insistent? And why would Wolfe attack him if he didn't believe that Rogers had said something? Somehow Wolfe was given that idea—and I know enough about psychonomy, Jon, to know that nothing happens in a monitored system without there being a cause for it. This cause looks a little too suspicious. Your name was mentioned too many times."

Jon looks directly into the doctor's eyes, and speaks in a voice that no one on this ship has ever heard before—complete adult candor—"Even if I *were* working something, Pan, I couldn't discuss it. Heisenberg, you know."

"I was afraid you were going to say that." Pan looks at him professionally. "Are you absolutely sure you know what you're doing, Jon?"

"I really—don't think—we should discuss this, Doctor."

"Jon, you're the only man on this ship who has no one to confide in. I had been hoping to function as a—a confessor for you, if you needed one. I tried to be always available for you. I figured you were probably the loneliest person on this ship—after all, there's no one else aboard who even comes close to being your intellectual equal—I kind of thought, and maybe it was a foolish conceit, that maybe you needed me."

"I—do appreciate what you're saying, Pan—"

"But—?"

"But, I really can't—discuss some things—"

"You told something to Chief Leen." Pan says it without emotion.

Korie looks up sharply.

"Uh huh. That's one of the rumors. You told something to Leen and he figured out that you weren't all you were supposed to be. Except that Leen can't figure out

anything without help." Panyovsky stops himself and
looks mock-shocked. "Oh, did that come out of *my*
mouth? How hostile."

"But true," Korie notes.

Pan shrugs. "The point is, Jon—an alpha doesn't
reveal himself unless there's a need for it. And now this
business with Rogers. So you can't blame me for wondering what's going on."

"I guess not."

"Are you going to tell me?"

"No."

"I have to ask you this, Jon. Do you still believe
there's a real bogie out there tracking us?"

Jon returns the doctor's gaze impassively. He doesn't
speak.

"I assume that means yes."

"I'm not going to cooperate with a guessing game,
Doctor. I only came down here for a sleeping pill."

"If you're really an alpha, Jon, you not only don't
need a pill; you wouldn't take one if you did. Alphas
don't like surrendering controls to drugs. For what it's
worth, I'm a zeta-class empath—"

"I know that."

"—and I'm trying to be helpful."

"I know that too."

"Jon—" Pan leans toward him and lays a kindly
hand on Korie's arm. "Jon—have you considered the possibility that—how can I phrase this so it's non-
judgmental?—have you considered that maybe, just
maybe, you could be wrong about that bogie? Is it possible that you've tight-focused on it to the point that it's an
obsession?"

Korie phrases his reply carefully. "Yes. I've considered the possibility."

"And—?"

"And, I've considered the possibility."

"That doesn't completely answer the question."

"It answers the question you asked."

Pan looks frustrated.

Korie says quietly, "It doesn't matter *what* I think
any more. I no longer have the authority to give any or-

ders. Oh, that's not an official position, but you know as well as I that everything I say and do is being double-checked with the captain. So I'm not saying anything that would contradict our present course of action. So it doesn't matter what I feel, does it?"

"It matters to you. It's important to your own mental well-being."

Korie nods, then he allows himself a gently chiding smile. "But if I really *am* an alpha, then I shouldn't have any trouble dealing with my internal psychonomy, should I?"

Pan looks dour. "You always have an answer for everything, don't you?"

"Not always," Korie admits. "But I try."

"—but it's not always the answer we want to hear. Jon, if there's something going on, let me help you." Panyovsky is suddenly intense.

"I'm sorry, Pan, I really am; I wish I could tell you something that would put you at ease; but there is nothing—absolutely *nothing*—that either you *or I* can do now that would make one bit of difference."

Pan's eyes are shaded. He is trying to decipher the subtext of that statement. "I don't know what you're doing, Korie—but it's finished, isn't it? In fact, you want me to stay clear, totally clear of it, don't you?"

Korie allows himself a very slight nod of the head. "That would probably be . . . a good idea."

Pan considers that statement too. "There's just one more thing, Jon." He looks directly into Korie's heart. "Was it necessary for Rogers to be so badly beaten?"

Korie is silent for a very long time. "Would it make you feel better if I said yes?"

"Probably not. It would probably make me feel— even more uneasy."

"Then put yourself in my place. If I had—somehow— been responsible for that beating he took—how do you think I would feel about it?"

Pan sips at his drink. "I'm sorry. I withdraw the question. Whatever it was, it must have been *very* necessary."

The two men sit in silence, sipping quietly at their

drinks. After a while, Korie says, "Sometimes, I don't like myself very much."

Panyovsky nods. "I can understand that."

They sit quietly a while longer.

Panyovsky is just pouring them each a refill when Mike sticks his head back in the door. "You want the scuttlebutt now? Or are you still in conference?"

"Come on in. Talk to us. What's up?"

"Well—" begins Mike, perching himself on a stool. "Everybody wants to know how Rogers is doing. They're genuinely concerned. It's amazing how protective of him they are. I told them he was still in recovery, and probably out of danger, I had to tell them that much."

A flicker of annoyance crosses Panyovsky's face. *Mike, the gossip.* He sighs. "That's all right. I just didn't want the details discussed."

"Oh no—anyway, captain's got Wolfe in the brig. For his own protection."

"Eh?"

"Oh, yeah—Rogers is the crew's little pet now—uh—there's a thing he did—" Mike breaks off, looking meaningfully at Korie.

Korie lifts one hand to wave it away. "It's all right, I know about it."

"About what?" Panyovsky asks.

"The tap into the console."

Mike looks surprised. "You knew?"

"Rogers told me." Korie explains to Panyovsky, "He accessed the set-ups for the drill simulations for the crew."

"They cheated—?"

Korie shrugs. "I guess so."

Pan looks speculatively at Korie for a half second, then dismisses the thought and turns back to Mike. "Go on, Mike. What else?"

"Oh, not too much more. I'd say their mood is pretty ugly. They were beginning to like Rogers—so now they're mad as hell. At everybody. At Wolfe. At the captain. Barak. Even Jonesy got bawled out, I'm not sure why. Funny—it's the first time in a week I've heard language like that without Mr. Korie's name in the same sentence—uh, sorry, sir. No offense intended, but—well, you know what I mean—"

Korie smiles easily. "It's all right."

"Anyway—they're pretty wrought up. I guess the best way to describe it is that they're looking for somebody to kill."

Panyovsky digests that for half a beat, then turns abruptly to look at Korie. Korie is remarkably impassive. Panyovsky stops himself from giving voice to the thought in his head. *Mike, the gossip.* "Uh—yah, Mike, thanks. That's about what I figured they would feel—uh—" He turns to Korie. "You still want that sleeping pill?"

Korie nods.

"Mike—will you get me a couple Valex? Now, listen Jon, you've just had a drink, so do your doctor a favor and don't take this pill for at least an hour. All right?"

Korie says, "I'm no dummy."

"You probably haven't had enough to make a difference, but different systems react differently, and I'd prefer to operate on the safe side." He takes the capsules from Mike and passes them to Korie. "Let me know if you need anything else, Jon. I'll be here." He locks eyes with Korie. There is a moment of understanding. And then the moment is past, and Korie turns away with a mumbled thanks. Panyovsky looks after the departing officer with a troubled gaze.

Korie returns to his cabin and puts the two Valex in the disposal.

Then he lays down on his bunk again, wearing a thoughtful expression.

(Whatever is going to happen next,) he tells himself, (it is very important that I be nowhere near the bridge when it starts.)

He thinks about the status of the three psychonomies he has been juggling—the relationship with the other ship, the group dynamic of the crew of this ship, and his own internal psychonomy. He has done all he can for each of them.

There is nothing more to do.

Except . . . play it out to the end.

After a while, he dozes.

Thirty-nine

Nature abhors a hero.

SOLOMON SHORT

K orie is roused by the alarm. His body is out of bed and racing toward the bridge even before his mind is fully awake. The raucous sound of the klaxon scrapes him into awareness.

It's happening!

The bridge is panic and confusion—Brandt is standing before the Command and Control Seat demanding to know what is going on. Before him, on the big red screen, the wobbly has swollen to enormous proportions. At the astrogation console, Barak is screaming into a mike—"I don't care what your instruments show—the damn thing just blew up like a—"

And Leen's voice is a confused blur from a speaker: "—but the monitors are as steady as—"

Korie doesn't stop for amenities. He crosses to Brandt, pushing him roughly sideways. "Goldberg! Initiate emergency unwarp procedure!"

"Aye, aye, sir!" Goldberg snaps back, not even looking up.

Korie doesn't have time to notice Brandt's startled expression. "Barak, belay that noise! Jonesy, cross-vector and set up a non-standard evasion pattern. Don't wait for recalibration after unwarp."

"Huh—? Uh, yes, sir!"

Korie unclips his hand-mike from his belt. "Radec! We're under attack. Set up a probability locus and initialize the proximity fuses. Set for automatic activation thirty seconds after release."

An unfamiliar voice responds, "Huh—?" And, "Who is this?"

"It's Captain Ahab, asshole! Now load that goddamn harpoon or I'll nail your fucking hide to the mast!"

Startled looks flash his way—but suddenly the bridge is too busy for reaction—

"Kill that klaxon!" Korie whirls about. (My God! Willis! I completely forgot—) "You—!! Willis! Log this with everything you've got. And don't screw it up!"

"Uh—uh, yes, sir!"

(—and hope for the best!)

"Korie! What are you doing—?"

"Sorry, Captain—there's no time to explain. Al, if you're not going to help, then get out of the way! That's no fucking wobbly!"

The astrogator flinches, then bends to his board.

Korie studies the screen for a full second. Good. Just as he thought. He starts snapping new orders. "Reverse all field polarities on my mark, stand by."

"Standing by."

"Minus three—two—one—*mark*!"

The ship shudders momentarily—

And Leen is screaming through the communicator, "What the hell is going on up there!"

"Leen—this is Korie, and I'm in command, and you're going to do exactly as you're told, or I personally will come down there and separate every single one of your bones from every other one. Prepare for unwarp."

"Uh—prepare for unwarp."

He checks the bogie again—it still hasn't changed course. (Probably—maybe!—we've moved faster than they can react!)

Brandt grabs Korie by the shoulder. "Is this another one of your drills—?"

Korie shakes loose, ignoring him. To the mike, "All right—don't worry about the details—emergency unwarp—*now!*"

Another shudder and—

"Answer me, dammit! This is another one of your mind-games, isn't it—"

"Drop the eggs!" Korie orders. "Three spreads of three."

The *ka-chunka-chunka-chunk* of three missiles breaking free from the launch bay shudders through the ship. Brandt's face goes white—

"Two!" Korie cries. *Ka-chunka-chunka-chunk!*

Barak turns to stare. Jonesy too, astonished.

"Get back to your boards! Prepare to rewarp! Leen, have you got that?" He doesn't wait for Leen's "Aye, sir." A quick glance back up to the screen and "Drop three!"

And as soon as he feels the solid *ka-chunka-chunka-chunk,* he calls, "Rewarp, *now!*" He strides forward to the helm and looks at the board over the helmsman's shoulder. "Cover all sensors. Null polarity on those grids." To the mike, "Radec, leave one eye open on the stress field! All radiation shields at full power!"

The screens are blank now.

The ship shudders once and a voice calls, "We're back in warp—"

"Stand by," Korie says.

And takes a breath. And then another one. And another.

Brandt is staring at him. Barak too. Slowly, other heads turn to look.

"What's. Going. On. Mr. Korie?" Brandt is absolutely rigid.

Korie lifts up one hand, as if to signal time out. "Just stand by. Watch the screen—"

"There's nothing there—not even the wobbly—"

"It's all right. We didn't have time to recalibrate. Just watch—"

"Counting," says the helmsman. "Fifteen seconds."

Barak is standing now, "What was that maneuver, Korie?"

"All right," Korie says. "He was coming in at us—I knew our only chance would be to dogleg just before we unwarp, so he couldn't accurately fix a probability radius. But he had to be well into his own unwarp procedure already, so we at least could get a *rough* fix on him—"

"Thirty seconds—"

There is a flicker of light on the screen, then a second, then a third. "First three missiles into warp."

To the mike, "Radec, is our warp coded?"

"Yes, sir—and scrambled. Those missiles won't come home."

"Thank you."

Three more flickers of light appear on the screen, the second spread.

"But there's no ship—"

"He has to be still unwarped. He would have dropped out just about the same time we did. Either way—"

All the men are staring at Korie now. *What is he talking about?*

The last spread of missiles climbs into warp. The missiles have only enough power for a short-range run in warp. But if they're close enough—

"Our only chance," says Korie, "was to drop our spread and be climbing back into warp before he could realize what we were doing. He might have been able to see us dogleg and unwarp—but I'm betting that he couldn't react fast enough to—"

Barak is incredulous. "Is that what this is all about? You still believe there's a bogie—!"

"If I'm wrong, Al—we've lost nothing—except three spreads of missiles. But if I'm right—I just saved our lives!"

"It was only a wobbly—one of your goddamn Hilsen units probably threw a circuit—"

"We'll know in a minute—look, the missiles are hunting—"

"That's not an accurate scan—"

"It's close enough for me." Korie drops into the Command and Control Seat, staring intensely at the screen. Barak and Brandt exchange glances—*is the man mad?* Or what—?

"Five minutes—" says Korie. "He's got to be within five minutes of us. How long have those missiles been out?"

"Two minutes, fifteen seconds."

"No sweat yet—"

Brandt opens his mouth to speak, then closes it. He turns resolutely and stares at the screen. He isn't sure what to believe any more. Barak wants to say something, but—he throws himself back into his seat instead.

"Two minutes, thirty seconds. Still running."

And then—there's a new flicker on the screen. "That's him—he's climbing back into warp!"

There is a stunned moment, an instant of time frozen, as if sealed in amber, as one by one, the men on the bridge of the starship *Burlingame* turn to stare at the single new point of light on the screen.

"No," says Barak. "It's just our wobbly come back." But even he isn't sure.

From Brandt comes the question, "Did he drop his missiles?"

"Probably," says Korie. "I don't think we scared him *that* much that he'd forget." Then, to the mike, "Stand by to change warp-codes. Just let them get a fix on the old ones first."

"We won't see them till they go into warp—"

"Stand by with scramble evasion warp."

"Standing by."

"Three minutes."

Barak is staring with a near-wild expression. There has to be some better explanation! "There's no missiles, yet, Korie—" he says. "That's no bogie. It's just our wobbly come home again."

"Sure, Al—that's right. Be sensible." Korie swivels to look at Barak. "But I don't have to be sensible. I'm already mad. So I might as well go for the big one. I don't have anything else to lose!"

Barak stares back at him. Almost regretfully, he says, "I never expected this of you, Jon."

"Don't teach your grandma how to suck eggs, Al," Korie slaps the chair arm impatiently. "I haven't got time for that one, now. Another couple minutes and we'll *all* know the truth." He swivels forward again.

The warp on the screen is steady—the *Burlingame*'s missiles are moving toward it, but uncertainly.

Someone says, "They're having trouble tracking."

"Not a good sign, Korie."

"Shut up, Al—he's probably doing evasions. But if we dropped them fast enough, they'll find him before they power-out. They're too close not to."

"If he's there."

"There was a time when you wanted him *too,* Al— *unh!*" That last was in response to a sudden burst of twenty-seven new points of light on the screen.

"Oh, shit! He dropped his whole load."

"*Recode and go!*" To the hand-mike, "Leen! Give me everything you've got—I need fifteen minutes flat-out!"

"Aye, sir! You've got.it!"

Barak is still staring at the screen. "*He really was there!*"

"What do you think I've been trying to tell you? That he wanted to blow kisses at us and play tag! We're not out of the woods yet."

"Look—"

On the screen—the enemy missiles are veering toward their own—

"Oh, shit!"

"Shut up—" Korie thumbs his hand-mike and prepares to give an order. Then stops. Closes his eyes and counts. Then, "How many missiles have we got left?"

"Twenty, sir."

"Damn. Barely enough."

"Enough for what?"

"Enough to drop another spread."

"You're out of your mind. We don't dare unwarp—"

There are three flashes of nonexistence. "First spread destroyed. They homed on the warps."

"We don't have any choice—if we don't stop his missiles with *something,* one of them is sure to stop *us.* It's dangerous—but have you ever heard of the Valsalva maneuver?"

"The experimental—?"

"Not even experimental. Theoretical. Won't be experimental until they find a ship captain stupid enough to try it. Here we go—"

Another three flashes of nonexistence and the second

spread of missiles is destroyed. "If he gets our last three, he's still got eighteen left to hunt with."

"Right." Korie thumbs the mike. "Arm those harpoons, me swabbies! All of them. Set for hunt and code them to activate all on the same signal."

"Huh—?"

"Just do it! Don't question it." He switches off in time to see the third spread of missiles disappear from the screens. "Eighteen left. Here we go. How long till they close?"

"Three minutes."

"All right, men—this is where we find out if those drills did any good. On my commands now—missile bay, start dropping your torpedoes *now!*"

"Huh—?"

"*Who is this?!!*" Korie roars.

"Dropping missiles, sir!!"

"Leen—?"

"Sir!"

"Stand for emergency unwarp—and then rewarp ten seconds later."

"I don't know if the generators can handle that—"

"There's only one way to find out—"

They are interrupted by the sudden thundering vibration of missiles breaking free—*KA-CHUNKA-CHUNKA-CHUNKA-CHUNKA* . . . The sound goes on and on and on.

"Dropping missiles while still in warp?!!"

"By the time they get to the edge of the field, the field won't be there—" Korie is counting silently.

"Last missile away—"

"*Unwarp!*"

A violent shudder of discontinuity and—

"We have unwarp—"

Korie cries—"Activate missiles!"

"Signal sent!" A beat. "Acknowledgment. Sixteen, seventeen, eighteen, nineteen—and twenty! All gone!"

"Thank you, General Missile Corporation! *Rewarp!*"

And another shudder of discontinuity and—

Korie thumbs the mike again, "Mr. Leen! Get us out of here. Let's run like hell!"

"Aye, aye, sir!"

"Field polarities?" asks the helmsman.

"It hardly matters. Any direction at all. Al, give him an evasion scramble."

Korie stops then, and sinks back into the chair. He can't remember when he stood up. He is gasping for breath, but he never takes his eyes off the screen. "Total elapsed time out of warp?"

"Seventeen seconds, sir."

"We may have a chance. We may just have a chance."

"I can't believe it," Barak is saying. "How could you know—?"

Korie turns to his astrogator and gives him his biggest possible cat-who-ate-the-canary smile.

The helmsman calls, "Missiles up and running. His eighteen to our twenty."

"I'd sure like to see the look on that bastard's face right now," says Korie. "When he realizes what we've done—"

The helmsman starts counting off missile collisions. "Two down. The score is sixteen to eighteen. One more, and another. "Fourteen to sixteen. We're still two up."

"I hope those two will be enough. That was our last shot—"

Brandt has not said anything through the entire battle. Now he turns and looks at Korie. He steps close and lowers his voice. "If you *knew* this was going to happen, Mr. Korie—why didn't you tell me?"

Korie returns his accusing look with steady eyes. "I don't think you would have believed me, sir. I'm sorry. There are a lot of things I did that I wish I hadn't had to."

The helmsman: "Four and six—oops. Three and five. No, make that three and four. One of his birds took out two of ours."

"If he can do that once more, we're dead," says Barak grimly.

"Not dead, just stalemated again. Except now we know for sure that he's out there."

"One and two . . . and there they go. One left! And it's ours! And closing!"

"Go, baby, go!"

"Mr. Leen—you can unwarp whenever you're ready. Shut your engines down and recalibrate for long-range scanning, please—"

Before Korie can finish the sentence, the helmsman reports, "We've lost our scan—to a sudden field-overload!"

Korie, Brandt and Barak exchange glances. "It could have been the missiles," says the captain.

"But not very likely," responds Korie. "A missile warp is much too small. You have to be right on top of its collapse for it to blow your scan."

"It could have been a cumulative effect."

"Do you believe that?"

"Uh—"

"Neither do I." Korie grins. "I think maybe—" He looks to Barak. "Al?"

"We *were* closing on him—" His eyes are bright.

"Anyone else?" Korie looks around the room. He is surrounded by hopeful expressions.

"I think—" He hesitates, then shouts out loud, "I think—*we got him!*"

And then everybody is shouting, cheering, yelling, whistling, stamping, roaring, laughing, slapping each other's backs and butts, hugging each other and jumping up and down and—

"Hey! Hey! Hey!—Hold it!" That's Barak hollering. "Wait a minute! Wait a minute! It hasn't been confirmed yet! We have to confirm it!"

The shouting dies away. Confused glances ricochet back and forth.

Korie looks to Barak. "You're right." And then he grins. "But I think *I'm* the one who should be demanding the proof now." For once, the laughter on the bridge is almost good-natured.

Korie remembers something. He turns and looks at Brandt, standing glumly alone and thoughtful in the center of the bridge. He hands the microphone to his captain. "Sir? Do you want to direct the search for debris?"

Brandt looks at the proffered mike, then at Korie—

There is only the tiniest discontinuity as the *Burlingame* unwarps.

—then at the mike again. "You've done a fine job, so far, Mr. Korie. You may continue."

"You *are* the captain, sir. I believe this is your privilege. To confirm the kill."

"It was *your* kill, Mr. Korie."

"Sir? I'd be honored to have you confirm it." He meets Brandt's gaze with his own. "Please?"

Brandt takes the mike reluctantly. "I know why you're doing this, Korie. I'm beginning to figure you out."

"Yes, sir—if you say so."

The communicator beeps. "Well? Did we get him? Come on, what's the story?"

"Stand by, Cookie," says Brandt. "We're going in for a look with broom and dustpan."

"I just want to know if I should break out the champagne?"

"Stand by." The captain switches off with a gentle smile. Brandt looks to his first officer. He moves to take his proper position in the Command and Control Seat. "Mr. Korie, we'll schedule a full debriefing at eleven hundred hours tomorrow morning. But there's really only one thing I want to know." He looks at Korie shrewdly. "We have one man in the brig, another in sick bay with multiple injuries, and a body in the morgue. Was it worth it?"

"Sir." Korie straightens almost to attention. "It hardly matters whether it was worth it or not. That was the price. And we never had any choice."

"That's hardly a satisfactory answer."

"I'm sorry, sir—would you prefer I say something more to the effect of 'Next time, suckers, maybe you'll believe me'?"

"To be quite honest—I'd be afraid to disagree with you again."

"Except—" Korie says, and there is not the slightest hint of a twinkle in his eye. He says it straight-faced, "Next time, I *might be wrong.*" (And I'm glad you don't know the errors I made *this* time.)

Brandt nods thoughtfully. "As soon as we confirm the kill, Mr. Korie, there's one thing I want you to do."

"Sir?"

"*You* give the order to go home."

"Aye, aye, Captain."

Forty

Violence is the last word of the illiterate. Also the first.

SOLOMON SHORT

ABOUT THE AUTHOR

David Gerrold made his television writing debut with the now classic "The Trouble With Tribbles" episode of the original *Star Trek*® series. Since 1967 he has story-edited three TV series, edited five anthologies, and written two nonfiction books about television production (both of which have been used as textbooks) and over a dozen novels, three of which have been nominated for the prestigious Hugo awards.

His television credits include multiple episodes of *Star Trek, Tales From the Darkside, The Twilight Zone, The Real Ghostbusters, Logan's Run,* and *Land of the Lost.*

His novels include *When H.A.R.L.I.E. Was One: Release 2.0, The Man Who Folded Himself,* and *Voyage of the Star Wolf,* as well as his popular *War Against the Chtorr* books—*A Matter for Men, A Day for Damnation, A Rage for Revenge,* and *A Season for Slaughter.* His short stories have appeared in most of the major science fiction magazines, including *Galaxy, If, Amazing,* and *Twilight Zone.*

Gerrold also writes a regular column for *PC Techniques,* a computer magazine. He averages over two dozen lecture appearances a year and regularly teaches screenwriting at Pepperdine University.

David Gerrold is currently working on the new Chtorr novel, *A Method for Madness.*

BANTAM SPECTRA

CELEBRATES ITS TENTH ANNIVERSARY IN 1995!

With more Hugo and Nebula Award winners
than any other science fiction and fantasy publisher

With more classic and cutting- edge fiction
coming every month

Bantam Spectra is proud to be the leading publisher
in fantasy and science fiction.